THORNS IN THE DARK

CASSANDRA BRIARWICK

Contents

Chapter 1

Once upon a time, Princess Briar Rose sneaked out of her castle to meet the witch in the woods. As the castle faded into the distance, and with no sign of pursuing guards, she pushed the hood back from her face, allowing the gentle breeze to caress her skin. It had been months since she had left the castle, and it almost felt like a lifetime to her. She missed the forest, the trees, the vibrant flowers, and the open sky. She yearned for the songs of the birds and the company of the animals. She missed her friend, witch Lavonna, and her magic cottage. Most of all, she missed being free and running around wherever pleased.

It was horrible to live under a watch all the time as if she was a prisoner.

As Briar stepped into the forest, her anticipation quickly turned into disappointment. A feeling of unease enveloped her as she surveyed her surroundings. The vibrant flowers that once adorned the forest floor had lost their brilliance, their petals withered and grey. The leaves of the trees had transformed into a deep, ominous shade of black. The air, devoid of the sweet fragrance of wildflowers, felt heavy and stagnant. The joyful melodies of the birds were replaced by an eerie silence as if the forest had been stripped of its life and replaced with a foreboding stillness.

And the trees were covered in something sharp.

"Thorns?" Briar gasped, stepping closer to examine one of the trees more carefully. The branches and even the leaves were covered in small, sharp thorns. How could trees grow thorns all of a sudden? Was it some kind of natural adaptation? Was it even possible?

She slowly raised her hand to touch the thorns.

"STOP!" a voice shouted,

Shocked, Briar pulled her hand back and turned around. Prince Leon was running toward her. His deep blue tunic shimmered with golden embroidery, complemented by pristine white trousers. A red cape cascaded from his shoulder, while a magnificent gold crown, decorated with sparkling diamonds, graced his head. He was holding a large sword that gleamed in the sun.

"Leon?" Briar gasped.

"Don't touch the tree," the prince pulled Briar away from the tree.

"What are you doing here?" Briar asked.

"Making sure you don't get in trouble," he answered.

Briar glared at him. "Are you stalking me?"

Without any hesitation, the prince replied, "Yes."

"Why?" Briar asked.

His expression turned solemn as he responded, "I've already told you. It's my duty to ensure your safety. I am your true love."

With a flourish, he brandished his sword and struck a heroic pose. "Protecting you is my purpose."

Briar sighed. Here they go again.

On Briar's christening, her parents organized a lavish party. They invited everyone, even the fairies. But forgot to invite one fairy, who was evil. And the Wicked Fairy wasn't pleased. She showed up and cursed Briar that on her fourteenth birthday, she would prick her finger on the spindle of a spinning wheel and die. However, the good fairies altered the curse, transforming it into a deep slumber instead. They prophesied that Briar and her kingdom would remain hidden from the world, sleeping for one hundred years. Then, a prince, destined to be Briar's true love, would discover her kingdom, awaken her with a kiss, and break the curse of eternal sleep.

On her fourteenth birthday, Briar accidentally pricked her finger on a spindle, causing her and her entire kingdom to fall into a deep slumber. True to the fairies' prophecy, Prince Leon eventually discovered Briar, kissed her, and broke the curse, awakening both the princess and her kingdom. From that moment on, Prince Leon became an instant hero, adored by the entire kingdom. Briar's parents, filled with gratitude and concern for their daughter's well-being, confided in Prince Leon and pleaded with him to remain in their kingdom.

Prince Leon took the responsibility of protecting Briar too seriously. Following her around to the point that it was irritating.

"You don't have to worry about me," Briar said.

"The outside world is dangerous for you," he argued.

Briar rolled her eyes. "I've heard that countless times."

"Because it is true."

Briar folded her arms across her chest. "Then tell me, what is so dangerous out here? What will harm me?"

"There is..." Leon hesitated. "There is danger."

"Yes, that's what I want to know," Briar insisted. "What kind of danger?"

"There is so much you don't understand, Briar," Leon said desperately.

"I don't want to understand anything," she said, turning her back on him and beginning to walk away. A second later, Leon caught up to her.

"At least listen to your mother," he said. "She is worried about you. All she wants is for you to be safe"

"The curse has been broken," Briar said. Couldn't she have a normal life just because she was cursed? It happened a hundred years ago. Why did mother make such a fuss about it? "Mother needs to realize that confining me to my chamber won't keep me safe. It is not fair," Briar said. "I understand that the curse has left her frightened, but she has to overcome it."

Once the curse was broken, everything went back to normal. Briar got the freedom that she longed for so long. She was allowed to visit the town and the forest. But then one day her mother showed up in her chamber early in the morning and declared that Briar would no longer visit the outside world. Briar had asked for the reason a thousand times, but no one explained it to her. Because no one thought the princess deserved an explanation. You could just lock her up and she wouldn't complain.

"Anyway, where are you going?" Leon asked, changing the subject as Briar's mood was getting darker.

"To see the witch," Briar replied.

"The witch? Why?" Leon questioned, his eyebrows knitting together in concern. He quickened his pace to catch up with her.

"This morning, I received a message from Lavonna," Briar explained, her tone hushed as if the surrounding trees were eavesdropping. "She's been trying to get in touch with me for a while now. I couldn't leave the castle until today. I need to know what she wants. It must be important."

Leon's eyes widened in surprise. "The witch has been asking to meet you? What could she possibly want?" he said. "This witch... she's dangerous. You know that."

"I can handle it," Briar assured him. "You don't need to—"

Suddenly, something rustled behind the trees. Leon's head jerked toward the sound, his grip tightening on his sword.

"It's probably a rabbit," Briar said.

The rustling grew louder, more insistent, and then a figure emerged from the shadows of the trees. It wasn't a rabbit. It was something Briar had never seen before. The creature's form resembled a human, but there was nothing remotely human about it. Its body was a sickly shade of green, covered in thorns. Red and purple veins bulged out of its skin, snaking across its body. Its eyes were pits of darkness, devoid of any spark of life.

"What... what is this?" Briar said, as she instinctively backed away from the creature.

"The reason you shouldn't come to the forest," Leon said, brandishing his sword at the creature.

The green monster let out a roar, a sound so filled with rage and pain that it sent shivers down Briar's spine. The forest around them seemed to shudder in response.

And suddenly the creature leaped at Briar.

Screaming, the princess rolled to the ground with the creature on top of her. A putrid stench, reminiscent of decaying animals emitting from the creature, filled the air, suffocating Briar and leaving her gasping for breath. Each time she tried to push the creature away, its thorns pierced her skin, causing blood to trickle down her arm.

"Get off of me," Briar cried out.

"Briar," Leon yelled. He grasped the creature by the shoulder, pried it off of her, and flung it aside.

The creature lay on the ground, hissing.

"You, okay?" Leon asked, helping Briar to her feet.

Briar was too stunned to speak, her breath coming in ragged gasps. She could only manage a shaky nod.

Leon pointed his sword at the creature. "Go!" he shouted, his voice ringing through the forest. "Go away!"

Slowly, the green monster climbed to its feet, its thorny body trembling with a low, rumbling growl. Saliva dripped from its mouth, a thick, viscous fluid that left a dark stain on the forest floor.

"Go away!" Leon yelled again, his eyes never leaving the creature. He kept his sword aimed at its chest. "I have no intention of causing you harm."

The creature seemed to hesitate, its dark, empty eyes locked onto Leon's. For a moment, it appeared frozen, as if under some sort of spell. Then, to Briar's surprise, it turned and dashed away, disappearing into the dense forest.

"What... what was that?" Briar asked. She watched the direction in which the creature had fled, her heart still pounding in her chest.

"A thorn monster," he said, his tone grim.

"A what?" Briar asked.

"A thorn monster," Leon repeated, his eyes scanning the forest as if expecting the creature to return.

The name sent a chill down Briar's spine. "I've never heard of this creature. Where has it come from?"

"I can't explain it right now," Leon said. He turned to face her, his eyes filled with worry. "Please, Briar, you need to go back to the castle. It's not safe here."

"And where are you going?" Briar asked, her eyes narrowing with suspicion. She knew Leon too well. His adventurous nature was bound to get him into trouble. "You're not planning to go after it, are you?"

"No," Leon said, shaking his head. "I need to inform your brother about this creature. He's the one dealing with them."

Briar's voice trembled as she exclaimed, "Wait... there are others?" The thought of more creatures like the one she had encountered froze her with fear.

"Yes," Leon said. "Now please, go back to the castle." He gave her a gentle push toward the path, his eyes pleading with her to listen.

Briar's eyes widened in realization. "Is...is the creature has something to do with why I'm being locked down in my chamber."

"I'll tell you everything later," Leon promised.

"No," Briar said, her voice firm. "I'm coming with you. I need to know what's going on."

"It's not the time to argue," Leon said impatiently.

"Then don't argue with me," Briar insisted. "Just take me along. I have a right to know what's happening."

"I can't," he said, shaking his head. "It's too dangerous. Your parents would never forgive me if something happened to you."

"And I'll never forgive myself if I don't find out the truth," Briar said, her eyes blazing with determination. "Please, Leon, take me with you."

"No Briar," he said and turned to leave.

"What if the creature returns and attacks me?" Briar said, her voice trembling with a feigned note of fear. She cast a pleading look at Leon. "Don't you think it's unsafe for me to go alone? You have to protect me."

Now the prince couldn't deny taking her with him.

"Fine," Leon sighed. "Come with me." He gave her a stern look. "And I hope what you see gives you nightmares and inspires you to stay in your chamber."

CHAPTER 2

A s Briar entered the town, an unsettling sense of unease washed over her like a dark, invisible mist. It clung to her skin, prickling her senses and whispering that something was deeply amiss. She couldn't quite place it, but the very air seemed charged with a heavy tension, thick enough to cut with a knife.

The townspeople caught her attention. Their faces were etched with lines of fear and worry, eyes darting nervously at every small noise. They spoke in hushed, hurried whispers, casting glances over their shoulders as if expecting something dreadful to appear at any moment. The usual bustling energy of the marketplace was replaced with a grave silence. Even the children, who normally played and laughed in the streets, wore grim expressions.

What had happened to this once-vibrant town? Briar's heart ached with confusion and sorrow. She remembered the cheerful laughter of children tossing coins into the fountain in the town square. The man selling talking toys, and the wise old lady who predicted futures with a touch of mystery and a twinkle in her eye. Now, the fountain stood still and silent, its water reflecting a sky that seemed too gray, too heavy. The market stalls were empty, their colorful wares replaced by shuttered doors and windows. The town, once filled with life and joy, now seemed like a ghostly shadow of its former self.

And the other thing she noticed was the armed soldiers patrolling around the town. They marched in pairs, their faces stern and unyielding, weapons at the ready. The clink of their armor and the rhythmic thud of their boots were the only sounds breaking the eerie silence.

Briar's heart sank as a disturbing realization struck her. Was her kingdom in danger? Was there a war going on? But they had a good relationship with all the neighboring kingdoms. In fact, there wasn't any war among the kingdoms in years. They all believed in peace and friendship.

Just to be sure, Briar asked the prince, "Is there a war going on?"

"Something much worse than war," Leon replied, his tone low and filled with a tension that sent a chill down Briar's spine.

Frustration and fear bubbled up inside Briar, threatening to overflow. "Then what is this?" she demanded. "I feel like I'm dying with all these mysteries. Why won't anyone tell me what's happening?"

"I can't tell you now?" Leon said, glancing around anxiously. "I have to find your brother. He'll know what to do."

"Leon, please," Briar pleaded, her voice breaking. "I need to understand. Why are the people so afraid? Why are there soldiers everywhere?"

Leon gripped Briar's hand tightly as they made their way through the bustling town square, weaving through anxious townsfolk and watchful soldiers.

Henry, her towering brother, was easy to spot. His stature was imposing, and his broad shoulders were draped in a heavy suit of armor. He stood at the center of a circle of soldiers, his voice low but commanding as he handed out small bottles filled with a smoky liquid.

"Use it only when you need it," Henry advised his tone grave. "We only have two bottles left."

The soldiers nodded and departed, leaving Henry standing alone for a moment, a look of deep concern etched on his rugged face. He turned, and his eyes widened in surprise as he spotted Briar and Leon approaching.

"Briar... why are you here?" he asked. He then directed a stern gaze at Leon. "Prince Leon, why did you bring Briar to this place? You know the danger, especially with things getting worse today."

"We are just leaving," Leon said. "I just want to inform you that one monster is running wild in the forest. It even attacked us."

Henry, who usually appeared tough, seemed on the brink of a breakdown. "I know. I've sent soldiers after that one. The monsters are getting more aggressive. It's been chaotic since this morning."

"Can someone please explain what is happening? I deserve to know!" Briar demanded.

Henry's eyes softened for a moment, but his tone remained firm. "Briar, this is the last place you should be. It's dangerous. Please, return to the castle where it's safe."

"I'm not leaving until you explain everything to me!" Briar said, planting her feet firmly on the ground and crossing her arms defiantly.

Before Henry could respond, a bone-chilling roar echoed through the town, reverberating off the stone walls and sending a shiver down Briar's spine. She spun around to see a thorn monster barreling through the town, pursued by a group of soldiers. The hideous creature ran around like a mad animal, kicking and destroying everything in its path.

Screams filled the air as townspeople fled in panic. Shopkeepers hastily closed their shutters, and mothers clutched their children tightly, running for safety.

The thorn monster let out another blood-curdling roar, swinging its massive arms and sending wooden crates and market stalls flying. Its claws, sharp and jagged like the thorns that covered its body, slashed through anything that came too close. Briar could feel the ground trembling beneath her feet with each heavy step the creature took.

Henry cursed. "It got away once more." He uncorked the bottle filled with a swirling, smoky liquid and quickly dipped the tips of his arrows into it.

"What is this?" Briar asked.

"It's a potion," Henry replied, securing the bottle and stowing it back into his pocket. "It's designed to weaken the monster, making it easier to capture." His gaze shifted to Leon. "Leon, take Briar somewhere safe."

"Do you want my help?" Leon asked.

Henry shook his head, his armor clinking slightly with the movement. "I've got the soldiers to assist me. Your priority is Briar. Ensure her safety and then head back to the castle. Now hurry!" he commanded, turning on his heel and charging toward the direction where the monster had vanished, his bow and freshly coated arrows ready.

"Be careful," Briar shouted after him. The sight of him charging towards the monstrous creature sent shivers down her spine.

"Come on," Leon urged, grabbing her hand. He led her down the cobblestone street, weaving through the frightened townspeople. They ducked into a nearby bakery, where a small group of people had taken refuge. The smell of fresh bread, normally comforting, was now tainted with the acrid scent of fear.

Briar pulled her hood low over her face, trying to blend in with the frightened group. Her eyes scanned the room, taking in the mixture of fear and despair etched on each face.

"Look at the monster," said a lanky man with a long ponytail, his voice trembling. "It's furious."

A terrified old man beside him wrung his hands. "When will this nightmare end?" he asked.

"When all of us turn into monsters, that's when." Snapped a plump, middle-aged woman. A terrified little boy clung to her. The little boy muttered softly as if reciting a prayer.

"I thought they had found a way to control it," said a man wearing an apron, his face pale and his hands shaking as he clutched a spatula like a weapon.

Briar peeked out from under her hood, her eyes darting from one anxious face to another, trying to piece together what they were discussing.

"They're lying," the plump woman's voice cut through the air sharply, filled with bitterness. "They always do."

The man with the ponytail shook his head. "Oh, lord. Tuesday, when one escaped... the soldier... it ended horribly."

"No," the man with the apron let out a distressed cry, pointing a shaky finger toward the chaos outside.

Everyone in the bakery gasped in unison, eyes wide with terror, as the thorn monster seized a man by the neck. The man's face turned a ghastly shade of white, his mouth open in a silent scream before the panic erupted, and he began thrashing wildly in the monster's grip.

Briar felt a wave of nausea wash over her. She clutched the edge of a wooden counter for support, her knuckles white. "I s...is the monster going to eat him?" she whispered, her voice barely audible over the cacophony of panicked murmurs.

Leon stood beside her, his jaw clenched. "No," he muttered, his eyes never leaving the horrifying scene outside the bakery.

Just as the monster's thorny fingers tightened around the man's throat, a group of soldiers surged forward, forming a tight circle around the creature. They unleashed a barrage of potion-dipped arrows. The arrow pierced the monster's back, chest, hand, and thigh. Each strike emitted a faint hiss as the potion sizzled upon contact with the monster's flesh.

The monster howled in agony. It released it grip on the man, who fell to the ground gasping for air. Freed from the monster's clutches, he scrambled to his feet and ran, his eyes wide with terror, disappearing into the chaos of the fleeing crowd.

The monster, now weakened, collapsed to its knees. Seizing the opportunity, the soldiers quickly moved in, binding the monster with thick iron chains.

The monster struggled against the chains, its roars echoing through the streets. With a sudden, violent jerk, it stood up, its muscles bulging with raw, untamed power. The iron chains snapped with a deafening clang, scattering pieces across the cobblestones.

A collective gasp rose from the crowd.

The woman clutched her terrified child tighter. "Oh lord," she whispered.

"No, no, no!" the man with the ponytail shrieked, his eyes squeezing shut.

Henry fired three arrows in rapid succession. The arrows embedded themselves deep into the monster's chest, right above its heart.

With a final, anguished roar, the monster's eyes rolled back, and it crumpled to the ground. Its body shuddered one last time before falling limp. The soldiers wasted no time, pouncing on the creature and wrapping it in chains. The monster groaned a low, guttural sound that resonated with pain, but its struggles were weak and futile.

The soldiers shoved the monster into a large, iron-barred cage, locking the door tightly. One soldier closed the curtains in front of the cage, concealing the monster from sight. Henry and a small group of soldiers clambered onto the wagon attached to the cage and sped away from the town.

"Will they kill him?" Briar whispered. Although the creature had been a monster, the thought of it being killed troubled her deeply. Perhaps it had something to do with the way the monster was growling when they locked him up—it didn't sound angry, but miserable. Did it know it was going to die?

"Absolutely not!" Leon shook his head. "The monsters are being transported to a fortress constructed by the fairies. They intend to keep them locked until a cure is discovered."

Briar's eyes widened with a glimmer of hope. "A cure?" she asked eagerly. "Is it possible to cure them?"

"Cure?" spat out the woman, still staring at the street where the wagon had gone. "There is no cure for this. The king is deceiving us. He is doing nothing. The fairies are not helping us."

"Pauline, control your tongue," warned a man who had been standing silently in the corner, his face lined with worry.

"Listen to your husband, Pauline," advised an old man with a long, gray beard. "You'll attract trouble for speaking against the royals."

"Why should I stop?" Pauline retorted, her face twisted with anger. "I have no fear. I'll shout in the king's face that the royals are responsible for all of this chaos."

"I understand we are going through a terrible period, but you cannot blame the royals," said the man with the ponytail.

"Right, I shouldn't blame them," Pauline said, panting as if she had just run a great distance. "I should blame the princess. I wish she was dead."

Briar's breath caught in her throat, and her mind raced with shock and disbelief. She could hardly process the woman's words.

"We should leave now," Leon said urgently, grabbing Briar's hand and pulling her toward the door.

"Prince Leon?" the man with the ponytail said. Everyone bowed at the prince, seeming to notice his presence for the first time.

"The princess?" Briar asked and pushed her hood away, revealing her face.

The crowd gasped in shock when they saw Briar. They bowed even deeper, averting their gazes from her as if looking at her might bring misfortune.

Pauline's gaze remained fixed on Briar, her eyes burning with an intense hatred.

"What about the princess?" Briar asked, her voice cracking. "What have I done?"

"You?" Pauline's voice was filled with venom as she locked eyes with Briar. "Princess Briar Rose is the reason all of this is happening. You are cursed," she shouted, her voice rising with each word. "The kingdom is cursed. We are cursed."

Cursed!

The words sent a painful jolt through Briar's head, as though her skull had been slammed against a wall. She could barely process the torrent of emotions rushing through her.

"Pauline, stop." The man, presumably Pauline's husband, abruptly tugged her aside.

The man with the ponytail rushed forward. "Forgive us, princess," he said. "Pauline knows nothing."

"A curse? But the curse was broken." Briar muttered.

Pauline laughed bitterly. "Your good luck, princess. You got cursed again," she said, her words dripping with sarcasm and resentment. "And we are getting punished for this. People are turning into monsters. They are losing their souls. If this continues, the kingdom will be brought to ruin."

Briar's head spun as she tried to comprehend Pauline's words. "Wait, what do you mean by people turning into monsters?" she asked.

"The monster we just saw wasn't a monster yesterday. He was the only child of an old parent," Pauline said. "But today..." She took a deep breath, her eyes glistening with unshed tears. "Today, he is a creature who can't recognize his parents, not even himself. And soon he'll lose his soul. And do you know who did this to him?" She pointed an accusing finger at Briar, her eyes blazing with fury. "You."

Briar couldn't listen to the woman anymore.

Every word Pauline spoke felt like a sharp knife piercing her heart, making it difficult for her to breathe. She stumbled out of the shop, the word "curse" echoing relentlessly in her mind like a dark, foreboding chant.

All she wanted to do was run away from the town. It wasn't her town. They weren't her people. Her town was happy, and the people loved the king, the queen, and the princess. They loved her. They would never wish she was dead.

"Briar," Leon said softly. "Don't listen to them."

"Everyone hates me." Briar's voice trembled, barely holding back her tears.

"I warned you," Leon said.

"I don't understand it," Briar said, her tears streaming down her face, leaving wet trails on her cheeks. "How is this possible? When did I get cursed again? And if I am cursed, why did another man become a monster?"

"Briar, I don't know how to explain all this," Leon said.

"You don't have to," Briar said, wiping her tears with the back of her hand. She turned towards the path that led to the forest.

"Where are you going?" Leon asked, chasing after her.

"I'm going to see the witch," Briar said firmly, her eyes blazing with determination. "She's the only one who can help me."

"Are you out of your mind? Look at the time!" Leon caught her arm, stopping her from running into the forest. "The sun will set soon. Your mother will notice that you are not in your chamber."

Briar's gaze shifted towards the sky, where the sun was fading behind the mountains. But she didn't care. She didn't care if the sun never came up again. Her entire world had been enveloped in darkness.

"Fairies are helping us. And they are searching for a solution. They helped build the fortress to keep the monsters and try to calm them," Leon explained quickly. "They will help us."

"Fairies are helping us. What will they do? Five hundred years of sleep this time," Briar shouted, wrenching her arm from Leon's grasp. "I don't trust the fairies."

"Your father is in the fortress, Briar," Leon said, his tone softening as he tried to reassure her. "He is handling the matter."

Briar stared at the prince, her eyes flashing with anger. "So that is where my father has been for the last few months. He is not visiting a friend." Suddenly, her frustration boiled over. "Everyone lied to me again and again."

"The point is, he is taking care of it," Leon insisted, reaching out to grab her arm again. "Don't you believe in your parents?"

"I don't know who to believe anymore," Briar said. "Everyone hides the curse from me."

"Only to protect you," he said.

Briar had reached the breaking point. "PROTECT ME!" she yelled, her voice echoing through the still evening air. "NO ONE CAN PROTECT ME FROM MY FATE."

"Please calm down," Leon said.

Briar turned away from him and began to stride away, her steps heavy with anger.

"We can come tomorrow," Leon pleaded. "I'll help you sneak out of the castle. You shouldn't meet the witch in the evening. Witches are evil."

"Based on my experiences, fairies are evil," Briar said, her voice laced with bitterness. "I haven't met a witch who cursed me."

Leon didn't argue anymore, and they walked in silence. Soon, the witch's cottage emerged into sight.

Positioned amidst two towering oak trees, the cottage boasted a vibrant red oval door, complemented by two expansive glass windows and four chimneys. It looked the same since Briar last visited the witch. As if it was the only part of her world that hadn't changed.

Leon looked at the cottage with a scowl.

"You can either wait for me or leave," Briar told him. "I'm going inside."

"I can't let you enter a witch's cottage in my presence. It is too dangerous," Leon protested.

"I'm used to this danger," she said.

"I'm coming with you," Leon insisted.

Briar didn't say anything and made her way toward the door. Suddenly, a dark and furry creature leaped right in front of her. Briar let out a yelp and stopped, her heart pounding in her chest. As her racing heart gradually calmed down, she glared at the large black cat.

"Rico," Briar said disapprovingly. "You scared me."

She took a cautious step forward, and the cat hissed, its fur bristling with unease.

"What is wrong with you?" she said, attempting to soothe the agitated feline. "Don't act like you don't know me?"

"Maybe we should go back," Leon suggested.

"No," Briar answered and looked at the cat. "Let me go, Rico."

The cat narrowed his yellow eyes at Briar, his gaze piercing and intense, and then his attention shifted to her sword.

"Oh!" Briar exclaimed, a sense of realization washing over her as she noticed the cat's focus on her weapon. For a moment, she was scared the witch didn't want to see her. "I almost forgot to drop my weapon."

Briar carefully placed her sword in front of the cat.

"The cat wants my sword." Leon looked surprised. "Great idea. Enter a witch's house unprotected."

"You don't have to come," Briar said again.

"I'm coming," He looked at his sword sadly and then placed it in front of the cat. "Careful, cat, it's a legendary sword."

The cat stepped aside, allowing them to proceed towards the door.

Briar knocked, and in an instant, the oval door swung open, and they entered the witch's cottage.

Chapter 3

"Am I really inside a witch's house? I can't believe it." Leon walked around, his eyes wide with curiosity as he examined the array of potions, herbs, and mysterious objects that filled the room. "I thought it would be full of horrible child-killing equipment."

"I told you, the witch is nice," Briar said, her voice calm as she followed him, her gaze sweeping over the familiar surroundings.

"Why is this room full of smoke?" he asked. "Is something burning?"

"It's not smoke, it's sage. It's meant to purify the energy," Briar explained. The soothing scent of the herb wafted through the room, wrapping them in a comforting embrace.

"What is this?" Leon approached a table where a large crystal ball rested, its surface shimmering with an otherworldly glow. He leaned in and peered into the depths of the mystical sphere. "Is it where the witch sees the future?"

"Don't touch anything," Briar warned him as he tapped the crystal ball with his fingers.

Everything was fascinating in the witch's house. However, Briar dared not to go near any of them in the absence of the witch because some objects were dangerous. For instance, the small flower that looked beautiful but would burst into flames in your hand as soon as you touched it. Then there were the knives, capable of stabbing if provoked, and the haunting flute that emitted a dreadful note, persisting until deafness consumed its listener.

"Is the mirror magical?" Leon's gaze shifted to a large oval-shaped mirror framed by intricately carved wood. "Or does the witch just want to see her ugly face?"

"You are so rude!" a ghostly voice reverberated from within the mirror.

Leon jumped away from the mirror. "It can speak!"

"Of course, it is magical," Briar said, stepping forward to stand before the enchanted mirror. The mirror was one of the most powerful magical objects that the witch possessed. It possessed the knowledge of spells, potions, and hidden realms beyond the mortal world. Unlike the other objects in the witch's house, the mirror was safe. It was friendly and very talkative.

"Sorry Mirror. He was only joking," Briar said.

"Oh, princess, look at you," the mirror responded, its voice tinged with concern. "Your aura is so weak today. It is so hard for me to focus on it."

The mirror showed Briar her reflection. The princess looked like someone whose aura had died. Her cheeks flushed with a feverish hue, her once radiant golden locks now tangled and unkempt, and her emerald eyes dulled by the weight of sorrow.

"What happened to you?" the mirror inquired.

"Bad day," Briar replied.

"I can give you a spell that will make you happy when you chant it three times," the mirror offered eagerly.

"Thank you, Mirror," Briar said. "But I don't think any happy spell can make me happy anymore."

"Who is the rude boy? Did he make you unhappy?" asked the mirror.

"He is Prince Leon," Briar answered.

"So, he is Prince Charming, your true love," said the mirror. "I thought he would be nice, but he is very rude."

"Stop using the word rude," Leon exclaimed, joining Briar at the mirror's side. "That is not the word you used to describe me. I'm a hero."

"You are rude," the mirror repeated, unimpressed by Leon's protests.

"Mirror," Briar said. "Where is the witch?"

"She is making a potion." the mirror sounded sad. "She's very busy lately and does not ask me for spells anymore. All day I'm just standing here with no one to talk to. I'm very lonely."

Briar smiled sadly. "I understand."

"Why don't you spend some time with me," the mirror said cheerfully.

"Sorry Mirror," Briar said, "but I have to see the witch urgently."

"Oh," the mirror said sadly.

"Well," Briar suggested. "You can talk to Leon."

"Even though he's rude," the mirror replied, "I'll still talk to him."

"What?" Leon said, his mouth hanging open. "I'm not familiar with how to talk to a talking mirror. I'll come with you."

"You stay here," Briar ordered. "The witch doesn't like it if you disturb her while she is making potions. She might transform you into something, like a frog."

The mirror chuckled playfully.

"Fine," Leon said. "Try to return quickly."

"Sure." Briar nodded.

With caution, she navigated through the magical objects, making her way to the potion room. In the center of the room, a fire crackled warmly beneath a large cauldron, the flames licking the sides and casting flickering shadows on the walls.

Lavonna, sat beside the fire, her slender fingers moving deftly as she added ingredients to the bubbling brew. The cauldron hissed and spat with each addition, flames occasionally bursting forth in colorful eruptions of light. Surrounding her were an assortment of items like dried leaves, various stones, and bottles filled with liquids of all shades. The entire room felt like a living thing, vibrant and pulsating with magical energy.

Lavonna herself was a striking figure. Her skin was pale, almost luminescent, and her hair, usually a deep black, had been transformed into a mesmerizing mix of red and silver that cascaded down her back in soft waves. Her eyes, usually stormy gray, now had a hint of amber, a color that shifted subtly as she worked, as if reflecting the magic, she was conjuring.

"Hello, Lavonna," Briar said as she approached.

Lavonna glanced up, her gaze warm. She paused in her stirring, a small smile playing on her lips. "Briar," she greeted in a voice as calming as a gentle breeze. "You've come."

"Yes," Briar replied, trying to peer into the cauldron without getting too close to the unpredictable flames. "What kind of potion are you brewing?" she asked. "Mirror said you've been very busy."

Lavonna's smile widened slightly. "The full moon is just a week away," she explained, resuming her stirring. "I'm preparing a potion for Vesper. He needs to be in perfect health before the transformation. This will help ease the pain that comes with it."

Briar's gaze drifted to the corner of the room where Vesper loomed, half-hidden in the shadows. The sight of him sent a shiver down her spine. Even in his human form, he was an imposing figure, his frame tall and muscular, his features sharp and predatory. His eyes, a piercing yellow that seemed to glow with an inner fire, followed her every movement, a sly smile revealing the tips of his unnervingly sharp teeth.

Vesper was the witch's boyfriend. He was a werewolf. Briar couldn't understand why the witch loved him. He was a monster. On the other hand, Lavonna was a kind-hearted and naturally beautiful woman. She could have easily married a prince. But again, like once Lavonna said, it was love, and Briar was too young to see beyond the curtain of the physical realm and saw the true soul of someone.

"Good evening, Vesper," Briar said, her voice faltering slightly as she tried to sound polite. "It's... good to see you."

Vesper's smile widened. "Princess, it's always a pleasure," he replied. His voice, a low, velvety growl that sent another shiver through her. "But you should be careful coming here so close to the full moon. It's not exactly safe."

"Stop teasing the princess," said the witch. "Your potion is almost ready."

"Well," Briar said, turning her attention back to Lavonna, "what is it that you wanted to talk about?"

Lavonna set the ladle aside and rose gracefully from her seat, moving with an almost ethereal fluidity that made Briar wonder if she was walking or gliding. She gestured for Briar to follow, leading her to a long, weathered table tucked away in the corner of the room. The table was cluttered with an assortment of magical items—crystals that seemed to pulse with an inner light, bundles of dried herbs, and various alchemical tools.

"Would you like some herbal tea?" Lavonna asked as she began to prepare a fresh pot. "I've discovered a new blend that I think you'll like."

"Sure," Briar agreed, watching as Lavonna's face lit up with a delighted smile. The witch added a mix of herbs and tea leaves to the boiling water, the fragrant steam filling the air with a calming aroma.

As Lavonna worked, Briar couldn't shake the feeling of unease that gnawed at her insides. "I think I know what you want to talk about," she said.

"You do?" Lavonna asked as she poured the steaming tea into two delicate cups.

"Before I came here, I visited the town," Briar said, taking the cup Lavonna offered her, the warmth seeping into her cold hands.

Lavonna took a deep breath and waited for Briar to speak.

"Am I cursed?" Briar asked, her voice trembling. "Am I the reason people are turning into monsters?"

The question hung in the air. Lavonna's face grew pale, her expression becoming a mask of sorrow. The room fell into a tense silence, broken only by the crackling of the fire and the distant, mournful howl of the wind outside.

"Yes, princess," Lavonna finally admitted, her voice cracking as she spoke. "It's true." Her eyes filled with tears, and she slammed her hand on the table in a sudden outburst. "And it's about the curse that I wanted to talk to you."

Briar felt as though the ground had been ripped from beneath her, her heart plummeting into a chasm of despair. She had clung to the hope that Lavonna would deny the existence of the curse, to reassure her that it was all just a horrible misunderstanding. But now, faced with the witch's confession, the weight of the truth pressed down on her like a crushing burden.

"I will become a monster as well," Lavonna continued, her voice shaking. "I'm dying of worry over what will become of my magic, my home, and Vesper once I'm gone."

Vesper stepped forward and gently wrapped his massive arm around Lavonna's shoulders. "I'll still love you, even after you become a monster," he murmured.

Lavonna looked up at him, her eyes brimming with sorrow. "I know, darling," she said, wiping away her tears with a trembling hand. "But I cannot bear the thought of losing my soul."

Lavonna picked up one of the cups of herbal tea and handed it to Briar, her hands shaking. "Drink this," she urged softly. "It will bring you some comfort."

Briar held the cup in her trembling hands, staring down into the swirling tea leaves as if they could reveal the secrets of her past and future. "When did this happen?" she asked.

Lavonna's breath hitched as she began to sob quietly. "After the sleeping curse was broken," she started. "The kingdom awoke from its long slumber, and we celebrated your fourteenth birthday. Everything was wonderful as if time had stood still and then resumed with joy. Everyone picked up their lives where they had left off. The kingdom was happy once more." She paused, her eyes clouding with pain and regret. "Then, out of nowhere, the Wicked Fairy arrived and cursed our kingdom with the deadly Curse of Thorns. The curse is so powerful that even the good fairies could do nothing to help us."

"What is the Curse of Thorns?" Briar asked, her voice trembling.

Lavonna took a deep, shuddering breath, her hands gripping the edge of the table as if to steady herself. "According to the curse, each day at sunset, some people in the kingdom will transform into thorn monsters," she explained. "And on your next birthday..."

Briar's anxiety tightened its grip around her heart. "What will happen on my birthday?" she asked.

"Every single human in this kingdom will be turned into a thorn monster," she said, her words dropping like a hammer blow. "Forever."

The cup slipped from Briar's grasp, shattering on the ground in a cascade of porcelain shards and dark tea. "WHAT?" she cried out.

Vesper let out a dark chuckle. "You should never celebrate your birthday," he said. "It's jinxed."

A chilling realization struck Briar. "My birthday..." she whispered, "it's only a week from now."

The room seemed to close in around her, the air thick with an intense sense of dread. Lavonna remained silent, her hands shaking as she watched the pieces of the shattered cup on the floor.

"Why?" Briar cried out. "Why did the Wicked Fairy curse me?"

"The reason is unknown," Lavonna said. "Perhaps the Wicked Fairy was angry that the sleeping curse was broken. Perhaps she couldn't bear to see the happiness of the kingdom. She is wicked, after all."

"Can't you break this curse?" Briar pleaded. "You know magic. You must be able to do something."

"My magic is not strong enough," Lavonna said. "If there were anything I could do, I would have done it a long time ago. There is nothing I can do."

"There has to be a solution," Briar insisted. "There is always a way to break a curse."

"There is a solution, but it's not an easy one," Lavonna said.

Briar's heart was pounding with a mixture of hope and fear. "I'm ready to do whatever it takes," she said. "Please, tell me what to do."

Lavonna took a deep breath, her gaze locking onto Briar's. "I had a vision. A prophecy about the curse," she began. "And you know very well that my psychic abilities are strong. All my predictions about your birth, the sleeping curse, and even the Curse of Thorns have come true."

Briar reached out and grasped the witch's hands, her grip tight with urgency. "Lavonna, I believe your predictions. What does your vision say?"

Lavonna hesitated for a moment, glancing nervously over her shoulder as if afraid someone might overhear. Then, she spoke in a hushed tone, "You have to go on a quest to break the curse," she said.

Briar nodded at the witch.

"But if the king and queen discover I've shared this with you, they will kill me," she said, her voice trembling slightly. "They made it clear that the prophecy should remain a secret."

Briar gasped, a cold dread settling in her stomach. "My parents know about the prophecy?"

"Yes," Lavonna confirmed. "They were the first to know. But they chose not to believe it. I understand them. They're your parents, Briar. They're worried about you, and they think the fairies will find a solution."

"Your parents are selfish," Vesper said. "They are willing to destroy the kingdom to save you. Isn't the kingdom their first responsibility? They vowed to prioritize the kingdom's safety above all else, including their own children."

"Vesper!" Lavonna snapped, casting him a reproachful look.

"It's okay, Lavonna. He's right," Briar said, her voice firm despite the turmoil in her heart. "Tell me what I have to do. What is the quest?"

Lavonna took a deep, steadying breath. "Princess, there is a book called the Book of Curse. It was written by the fairies thousands of years ago. It contains rituals to break every kind of curse that has ever existed."

Briar's eyes lit up with a flicker of hope. "That means the book also contains a ritual to break the Curse of Thorns."

"Yes," Lavonna confirmed. "If the curse is broken, all the monsters will regain their souls and transform back into humans."

Briar's brow furrowed with confusion. "So, if the fairies have a ritual to break the curse, then why aren't they helping us?"

Lavonna sighed, her shoulders sagging. "The fairies of Fairyland don't have the book. But the forest fairies do," she explained. "Their leader, Viatrix, owns a magical library that contains thousands of books about magic, including the Book of Curse. But the fairies of Fairyland and the forest fairies are enemies. The forest fairies will never help humans, and the fairy queen can't forcefully take the book."

"Your quest is clear," Vesper said, his voice a deep rumble that filled the room. "Get the book from the forest fairies, find the ritual to break the Curse of Thorns, perform the ritual, and save the kingdom."

Briar took a deep breath. "Then I accept the quest," she declared confidently. "I'll break the curse."

Lavonna's face clouded with concern. "Briar, don't rush into any decisions," she said. "The quest is full of danger. Have you any idea where the forest fairies reside?"

"In the forest," she replied.

"Not just any forest," Vesper said, his eyes narrowing. "The Midnight Forest."

The name sent a chill down Briar's spine, but she tried to hide her fear. "So," she said, attempting to sound unfazed, "it's an enchanted forest. What of it?"

Vesper chuckled darkly. "So, it's an enchanted forest that will try to eat you alive."

"You're just trying to scare me," Briar retorted, though she couldn't keep the tremor from her voice.

"He's speaking the truth," Lavonna said. "Briar, I don't want to throw you into danger, but..."

"But, Lavonna, we know it is the only way," Briar said.

"Briar, I'm filled with dread. Part of me wants you to break the curse, but another part is terrified for your safety," Lavonna said.

Briar reached out, squeezing Lavonna's hand. "If fate wants me to go on this quest, then it will also give me the strength to complete it. I'd rather die trying than sit here waiting to become a monster."

"You seem eager to die," Vesper teased, though there was a grudging respect in his voice.

"If you've set your mind to this, I won't stop you," Lavonna said. "But remember, this might end horribly."

"I know," Briar said. "Can you help me find the forest fairies?"

Lavonna walked over to a small cabinet. She carefully selected a parchment from the neatly rolled maps and made her way back to Briar. "This map," she said, unfurling the parchment with care, "was made with the help of Mirror. It will guide you to the forest fairies' village."

Briar unrolled the map, her eyes tracing the detailed lines that depicted the sprawling Midnight Forest stretching across the northern expanse of the kingdom. "Thank you, Lavonna," she whispered.

Lavonna pointed at a spot on the map. "This is the Enchanted Garden," she said, her finger following a meandering brown line that cut through the garden. "Follow this path," she instructed, "and it will lead you to the forest fairies."

Briar nodded, carefully rolling up the map and tucking it into the pocket of her cloak.

"And," Lavonna added, placing a delicate hourglass on the table, "this will help you track time." The sands in the hourglass were already beginning to trickle.

"And lastly this," Lavonna whispered, holding a tiny vial containing a crimson liquid, "is your secret weapon. Only use it when you have no other choice. It has the power to temporarily immobilize your enemy, giving you a chance to flee." Gently, she entrusted the vial into Briar's open palm.

"Remember, the forest is infested with packs of werewolves," said Vesper.

"Don't frighten her." Lavonna scolded him.

"I'm not scared," Briar said.

"Briar, be careful," The witch warned. "And do not go near anything that seems too enticing. The forest is full of traps."

"I will be careful," she promised, giving Lavonna a reassuring smile. "Thank you for everything."

Lavonna's eyes shone with unshed tears. "I wish you good luck, Princess," she said. "I hope you break the curse and save us all."

"Well then," Briar said, forcing a smile, "I'll see you after I break the curse." She gave Lavonna a final nod and left the room.

Leon stood before the mirror, listening to its incessant chatter.

"What took you so long?" Leon asked, his voice tinged with impatience. "What did the witch say?"

"Everything I needed to know," Briar replied, her hand resting protectively over the map tucked inside her pocket.

"Now, can we leave?" Leon almost pleaded, casting a wary glance at the mirror.

"So soon?" the mirror said, its reflective surface rippling slightly. "I haven't even told you everything yet."

"I don't want to know any more spells that involve blood and eyeballs," Leon said, making a face of exaggerated disgust.

Briar assumed the mirror was telling the prince about the horrible ingredients on purpose.

"See you later, Mirror," she said, turning towards the door. "Come on, Leon."

They left the witch's cottage, the door creaking shut behind them. The evening air was crisp and cool, a stark contrast to the warmth of the potion room. They retrieved their swords from the cat and began the long walk back towards the castle.

CHAPTER 4

When Briar and Leon arrived at the castle, they found Charles and Charlotte waiting by the old door, the same one Briar had used to sneak out that morning. The twins looked worried.

Charles and Charlotte were the head cook's children. The twins had round, innocent eyes, a face full of freckles, and curly blonde hair that made them look adorable. They spent a lot of time with Briar, asking her endless questions and following her everywhere. Briar didn't mind at all. Without them, she would have been terribly lonely. The twins supported all her mischievous plans. They had even shown her the abandoned servant's room and helped open the sealed door so she could sneak out of the castle.

"Why aren't you in my chamber?" Briar asked them.

The twins were supposed to be in her chamber, pretending to play with her so no one would notice she was gone.

"Thank God you are back," Charles said. The fear on his face wasn't a good sign. He didn't get scared easily. He was brave for ten years.

"Princess," Charlotte said nervously. Tears welled up in her eyes, threatening to spill over.

Briar gently grasped the young girl's hand. "What's the matter, Charlotte?"

The girl only sobbed in return.

"Did Charles break your toys?" Leon asked.

"No..." the girl sobbed. "The... queen."

"Mother?" Briar asked in confusion.

"Princess..." Charles hesitated, "the queen is aware that you are not in your room."

Briar's eyes widened. She couldn't blame Charlotte for crying—she felt like crying herself.

Charles lowered his eyes. "We tried to lie, but the queen already knew you weren't in the castle."

"How?" Briar asked.

"A maid saw you leaving," Charles said.

Briar wanted to punch herself. Couldn't she have been more careful? She glanced at Leon, hoping for some support, but he merely shrugged. It was as if he was enjoying her misery.

"You're on your own," he said, turning to leave.

"I'll remember this when you need my help," Briar shouted after him.

"The queen is waiting for you in your chamber," Charles said. "She is furious."

"Fine," Briar said, her voice trembling. "I'll see what happens."

Briar hurried towards her chamber. Her mind was buzzing with the newly acquired knowledge about the curse that she had no time to think about the possibility of getting caught by her mother.

As she reached her chamber door, she paused, trying to steady her racing heart. "It's not like she will turn me into a moth," she told herself, attempting to muster a bit of courage.

Slowly, Briar opened the door and entered her chamber. Her eyes scanned the room, landing on her mother, who stood by the window, gazing outside. The queen's golden hair flowed gently in the soft evening breeze, her red lips set in a thin line of disappointment, and her crystal blue eyes fixed on something in the distance. The setting sun bathed her in a warm, soft glow, making her look like a beautiful yet intimidating sculpture. Briar put on a cheerful smile as she approached, stopping at a safe distance in case the situation turned drastic.

"How was your visit mother?" Briar asked, trying to sound casual.

"Good," her mother replied, without even glancing at her. "I see you have been taking advantage of it."

"Mother, I—"

"DON'T YOU DARE LIE TO ME!" the queen shouted. "The maid witnessed you heading towards the forest."

Briar looked at the ground.

"I have been so worried." The queen grasped Briar's shoulder and forced the princess to look her in the eyes. "If I told you the outside world is not good for you, then there must be a reason. But you think your mother is overreacting. Your mother is stupid ..."

The queen swallowed, fighting back tears.

It killed Briar to see her mother cry. She never wanted to make her mother sad. Briar took the queen's hand and said, "Mother, I'm sorry."

The queen's face softened. "I understand you feel trapped inside the castle. I never want to take away your freedom. But it is for your safety. Just a few more days, then everything will be alright."

Briar couldn't tell her mother that nothing was going to be alright. The faith they had in the fairies was futile. The fairies couldn't break the curse. It was Briar who could break the curse, but she knew her mother would never like to hear it.

"But, if you don't stop sneaking out from the castle," the queen's eyes shone fiercely. "I'll lock you in your chamber."

"I'm sorry, mother," Briar said. "I will never do that again."

"Promise me you will not leave the castle without my permission," the queen said and held up her hand.

"I promise," Briar said, taking her mother's hand. But in her heart, she knew she would break this promise soon.

The queen's anger seemed to melt away, and she broke into the warm smile that Briar loved so much. "Very well," she said. "Now go clean up. It's time for dinner." Her grin widened mischievously. "And I have a surprise for you."

Before Briar could ask any more questions, the queen left the room.

Briar shut the door behind her and made her way to her bed. She retrieved the map, the hourglass, and the vial Lavonna had given her, tucking them safely beneath her pillow. After freshening up and changing her clothes, she made her way to the dining hall. Her mother, Henry, and Leon were already seated at the table. Briar hoped Henry hadn't told her mother that Briar knew about the curse.

Briar walked over to the table and quietly sat down.

"Hello everyone," said a familiar voice.

Briar looked toward the voice to find her father approaching the table.

"Father!" Briar exclaimed, rising from her seat and running to him.

The king embraced Briar tightly, his face beaming with a wide smile.

"Do you like your surprise?" the queen asked, her eyes twinkling with joy.

"Yes, mother," Briar grinned, feeling a rush of happiness.

"Missed me?" the king asked, a wide grin spreading across his face.

"Yes," Briar said. She hugged him tightly, savoring the warmth and comfort of his presence.

The king looked around the table, his gaze settling on each family member with affection. "It's good to be home," he said. "Now, let's enjoy this meal together."

Briar carefully observed her father. He seemed to have aged years in just a few months. Dark circles surrounded his eyes. His complexion had turned pale, and he appeared to have lost a significant amount of weight. She wished she could talk to him about the curse and take his worries away, but she couldn't do it. She had to pretend like everything was good while her parents and the kingdom suffered. The weight of guilt pressed heavily upon her.

The king gestured for her to take a seat beside him. "How are you father?"

The king smiled, though it didn't reach his tired eyes. "Amazing," he replied.

"And how was your visit?" Briar asked, studying him closely.

The king and queen exchanged glances before the king replied, "Brilliant."

"Briar, it is a political thing. You'll understand when you get older," the queen said, her tone gentle but firm.

"Father, are you sick?" Briar couldn't help but ask.

The king smiled again, a touch of sadness in his eyes. "I'm not sick, just a bit weary. I'll recover in a few days," he said, touching her face gently. He looked at the queen, who seemed on the verge of tears, but pulled a strong face for her husband and nodded.

"Now, shall we eat?" her father said, trying to lighten the mood. "I missed our food. I have traveled the world, but no one prepares such delectable dishes as you do," he praised the cook.

"Thank you, Your Majesty," said the cook, placing roasted chicken, cheese balls, meatloaf, garlic bread, and grilled river fish—all of which were her father's favorites—on the table. The cook also served Briar's favorite berry tart and sweet bread spread with jam and nuts, her mother's favorite spicy vegetable soup, and Leon and Henry's favorite strawberry and chocolate cake.

Despite the situation, Briar's mouth watered, and she filled her plate with everything. The table buzzed with the sound of clinking cutlery and murmured conversations.

"So, how was your day?" asked the king, looking at Briar.

"Um..." Briar hesitated, aware of her mother's scrutinizing gaze. "I..."

Suddenly, the king began to cough uncontrollably, his face turning red.

"Father!" Briar exclaimed, handing him a glass of water.

The king gulped the water, and after a moment, stopped coughing. He took a deep breath, his eyes watering from the effort.

"Are you okay?" the queen asked, as she reached out to touch his arm.

The king nodded, still unable to speak.

"How many times have I told you to stop talking while you eat?" the queen scolded gently, her face hard but her eyes wide with concern.

"Roseanne," the king said, giving her a mischievous grin despite his ordeal. "I have lost count."

The queen rolled her eyes. They all resumed eating in silence. Briar noticed her father's hand trembling as he lifted his spoon to his mouth. Several times, she had the urge to take the spoon and feed him herself. She also caught her mother, sending worried glances toward her father.

Suddenly, the king started coughing violently again, grabbing his face with both hands. "Guards!" the king screamed, his voice filled with panic. As he pulled his hands away from his face, green saliva spilled from his mouth. "Henry, call the guards!"

"Father, what's happening?" Henry shouted, leaping to his father's side.

"Elliott!" the queen yelled, rushing closer to her husband. Her face was a mask of fear.

Briar grasped her father's arm. "Father, what..." But she couldn't finish her sentence. Horror washed over her as she saw her father's skin turning a sickly green. She exchanged a terrified glance with Henry. They both knew what was happening.

The curse was taking hold.

The king was transforming into a monster.

The queen stared at him, too shocked to utter a word.

Suddenly, the king threw his plate across the room and let out a guttural growl. The next second, he jumped to his feet and kicked the table over. The table crashed on the floor, causing everyone to scream and jump away in fear.

The king clutched his neck and howled in agony as if experiencing a burning sensation in his throat. As he tore off his clothes, thorns began to sprout from his body, piercing through his skin.

Briar stifled a scream, her hands flying to her mouth.

"Get the chains!" the king roared, his voice barely human. "I can't control it much longer!"

"Guards!" Henry shouted, pain etched on his face as he watched their father roar like a wounded animal. The desperation in his voice echoed through the chamber.

Within moments, the guards rushed in, their faces pale with fear. They surrounded the king, who didn't even struggle as they chained him. His once regal form was now grotesque, covered in thorns.

The king's eyes, now filled with a wild, uncontrollable rage, met the queen. "I love you," he managed to say before another wave of pain took over, and he howled again, the sound reverberating through the castle walls.

"Get him to the fortress!" the queen commanded, her voice shaking but firm. The guards nodded and began to lead the chained king out of the dining hall.

"Father!" Briar cried. Her mother gripped her shoulder tightly.

"Nothing will happen to him," her mother said firmly, though tears were streaming down her cheeks. "You heard me, Briar. Nothing will happen to your father."

"Where are you taking him?" Briar broke free from her mother's hold and raced toward her father.

"Briar," Henry said. "We have to take him to the fortress. It's the only place where we can keep him safe."

"No!" Briar shouted, her voice echoing through the hall. She wanted this to be a nightmare, something she could wake up from.

Ignoring everyone's warnings, Briar stepped forward and grasped her father's hand. It was still warm, and his eyes, though filled with pain, still shone with life.

The king looked up at the queen. "Roseanne..." His voice was rough and strained. "Take Briar away."

"No, Father," Briar yelled, clasping his hand even tighter. "I want to be with you."

"I'm a monster," he drawled, the anguish clear in his eyes.

"No, father, you are not a monster," Briar insisted, her voice breaking.

The queen pulled Briar away. Her father's hand slipped away from her grip.

"No! Father!" Briar screamed, tumbling to the ground as her mother's strong arms encircled her.

The guards lead the king away, his chains clinking ominously with each step. Briar watched, her vision blurred by tears, as her father was taken from her.

As they reached the doorway, the king turned his head, his eyes meeting Briar's one last time. "Be brave, my darling," he whispered, his voice barely audible.

Briar could only watch in helpless despair as the guards dragged her father through the door, his form disappearing into the darkness of the corridor beyond.

CHAPTER 5

Briar stood near the window, staring at the night sky adorned with shimmering stars and a crescent moon. The cool night air whispered against her skin, carrying the scent of blooming night flowers, but tonight their fragrance brought no comfort.

She couldn't stop thinking about her father. The way his body had twisted and changed haunted her. Was he a monster now? He was one of the bravest men she knew. Yet she couldn't forget the look on his face when he was taken away. He looked dejected as if he had lost any hope of living.

Her mother had locked herself in her chamber since the king was taken yesterday. When Briar went to see her, she didn't speak. It was as if her mother had turned into a breathing statue. She had lost her husband. The kingdom had lost its king.

And all of this was happening because of Briar.

"No one is going to suffer for me anymore," she said to herself, her voice trembling with determination.

She moved to her bed and placed the letter she had written earlier on her pillow. It was her first-ever letter to her mother, explaining that she was leaving to break the curse. The weight of guilt for leaving her vulnerable mother was overwhelming, but she couldn't see any other option.

She closed her eyes tightly, trying to push away the thoughts of how her mother would react upon reading the letter. Would she be angry? Devastated? Would she understand?

"I hope she will understand," Briar whispered to herself.

She glanced out the window. The nightfall had deepened, enveloping everything in a serene stillness. It was the perfect time to make her exit from the castle.

Briar changed into her green-colored traveling gown and a midnight blue cloak. She put the map, hourglass, and vial in the pocket of her cloak. The fabric felt heavy with the weight of her resolve. She took a deep breath and steeled herself for what lay ahead.

Earlier in the day, Briar had packed a large satchel with food, water, a traveling gown, and a few gold coins. She had never travelled before and had no clue what to take with her, but she hoped what she had packed would be enough. The satchel felt heavy with both provisions and the weight of her impending journey.

As the seconds ticked by, her heart rate quickened, pulsating with anticipation. She was venturing into a dark forest filled with evil creatures. A mixture of fear and exhilaration coursed through her veins, intertwining in a whirlwind of emotions.

Briar grabbed her sword and the satchel, took one last look at her chamber, and left quietly.

As she crept through the darkened corridors of the castle, the flickering torchlight cast eerie shadows on the walls. Every little noise made her heart race. The castle seemed to hold its breath, the silence only broken by the occasional distant clink of armour from the guards. She passed the door to her mother's chamber and paused for a moment, her hand resting on the cool wood. She could hear her mother's faint sobs from within, and it took all her strength not to burst in and comfort her. But she knew that staying would only prolong their suffering.

Just a few steps from the door to the servant's room, a sharp voice pierced the silence. "Where are you going?"

Briar stopped dead in her tracks, her heart pounding in her chest. She turned around slowly, half-expecting to see a guard ready to drag her back to her chamber. Instead, she was relieved and furious to find Prince Leon standing there, his arms crossed and a confused expression on his face.

"Will you stop spying on me?" Briar glared at him.

"Shouldn't you be sleeping right now?" he said, ignoring her question.

"I can ask you the same question," Briar snapped back, clutching the satchel tightly behind her to keep it out of his view.

Leon scrunched up his face. "But I asked first."

"I don't find it necessary to answer you," Briar retorted. "It is my castle. I can go anywhere I please."

Leon raised an eyebrow, clearly not buying her excuse. "Really?"

"I can't sleep," Briar said, trying to sound nonchalant. "So... I am going for a walk."

Leon stepped closer, his eyes narrowing suspiciously. "To the servant's room," he said, "in your traveling clothes with a satchel. Is your walk that long?"

Briar clenched her jaw. "Go away."

Leon didn't budge. Instead, he walked forward, his eyes filled with concern. "Don't do something stupid. Your parents already have enough to worry about."

"I'm not doing anything wrong," Briar insisted. She could hear the faint sound of guards patrolling the other hallway.

"I'm your true love," Leon said. "I will not let you do stupid things."

"Leave—" Briar started, but the sound of rapid footsteps interrupted her.

"Guards," Briar gasped. She snatched Leon's hand, and they bolted into the servant's room, closing the door behind them. Briar pressed her eye to the keyhole, watching as the footsteps grew closer.

Moments later, two guards arrived at the spot where Briar and Leon had been standing just seconds before. The tall guard peered around suspiciously, while the other guard seemed more relaxed.

"Who's there?" the tall guard demanded.

The other guard, creeping up behind him, leaned closer to his ear and whispered in a ghostly voice, "Ghost."

The tall guard flinched but tried to maintain his composure. "Funny," he muttered.

"Told you there is no one," the other guard chuckled, his laughter echoing softly in the hallway.

"I heard voices. It sounded like a girl," the tall guard insisted.

"Probably a banshee," the other guard said with a smirk. "She calls men at night and hunts them. So, I advise you to stay away from voices that only you can hear."

The tall guard went pale, and he stuck close to his companion as they walked away, their footsteps fading into the distance.

Relieved, Briar slowly opened the door and looked at Leon. "Now leave."

"You're going to meet the forest fairies," Leon said, crossing his arms.

Briar's mouth hung open in surprise. "You... how?"

"I heard you, the witch, and the hairy man talk about it," he said nonchalantly. "I eavesdropped, and I'm glad I did."

Briar gaped at the prince. She couldn't have a single secret when Leon was around. And the shameless boy wasn't even sorry.

"Fine," Briar said. "I'm going to meet the forest fairies."

"And why?" Leon asked.

"You know the answer?" Briar said. "I need the book to break the curse."

Leon nodded. "And I also know that they will not help you."

"They will," Briar insisted. "I'm going to make them."

"This is a bad idea," Leon said, shaking his head.

"Do you have another option?" Briar challenged. "Please tell me."

Leon sighed. "Believe the fairies," he said. "They are working to break the curse."

"The fairies can't break this curse," Briar said, frustration creeping into her voice. "And I can't wait for a fairy godmother to come and help me."

Leon was silent for a moment, then said, "I'm coming with you."

"What?!" she yelled, her eyes widening in disbelief. "No, no. You can't—"

"A quest. An adventure," he interrupted, his eyes gleaming with excitement. "How can you forbid me from coming? It is like forbidding me from breathing."

"Leon, no—"

"I'm born for adventure," he declared, clutching his chest dramatically. "It is the purpose of my life."

Briar rolled her eyes at the prince. He was being dramatic again. "Still, I forbid it. It's my journey and I can't put your life in danger," she said. "Besides, you are very irritating."

"You need me," he said desperately. "I'm your true love. With me, you will have protection. And my skill in the forest will help you."

"No—"

"Think practically," Leon urged, talking quickly. "You are going to the forest. You don't have the skills to survive there. There will be animals, even plants, that will try to eat you. At night, you need to find a safe place to sleep. Paths you need to find. Soon you'll be lost and, worse, trapped somewhere to be someone's food."

Briar thought about what Leon said. She wouldn't admit it to him, but he was right. She had no experience in the forest. But he had. He could help her. And if a monster came, she could always push him forward. After all, he was too eager to protect her.

"So, are you taking me?" Leon asked a hopeful glint in his eyes.

"Well, I—"

"If you refuse to take me, I'll scream and tell everyone that the princess is leaving."

"At least let me finish before you threaten me," Briar said. "Fine, you can come."

Leon did a small victory dance, a wide grin spreading across his face.

"But," Briar said, raising a finger. "Promise me something."

"Anything."

"You will do as I say. You will not risk your life."

"Okay," he said, nodding earnestly. "I promise."

"And," Briar continued, scrutinizing his appearance. "Change into something suitable for the forest. And wait... do you sleep with your crown?"

The crown was a gift presented to Leon by the kingdom after he broke the sleeping curse. Its symbolized love, respect, and heroism. Briar had never seen Leon without the crown, but she didn't know he didn't even remove it at night. She wouldn't be surprised if he had glued it on his head.

Leon went red and touched his crown self-consciously. "I... must have forgotten to take it off."

"Quick," she said, gesturing for him to hurry.

Leon grinned and opened the door.

Briar stopped him. "And please don't attract everyone."

"I'm great at this." He dashed out of the room.

She didn't have to wait too long. The prince returned quickly.

Dressed in a red tunic embroidered in gold, sleek black pants, a flowing blue cloak, and his crown, he appeared ready for a ball.

Briar gaped at the prince. "Can't you wear something simple?"

"What's wrong with this?" he said, looking down at his attire. "And hey, look, our cloaks match."

"And what have you packed?" she asked, pointing at the two large satchels he was carrying.

"My supplies," he said proudly.

"Have you packed the whole castle?"

"Just necessary things," he said.

"We should carry as light as possible—"

"Don't worry," Leon said confidently. "The horse will carry it."

"We are not taking the horse."

"Why?" Leon asked, looking genuinely puzzled.

"There are too many guards near the stable and the horses make too much noise," Briar said.

"I can get the horse from the stable," Leon offered excitedly.

"No, please don't," Briar pleaded, her eyes wide with anxiety. "We'll have to walk."

"Where are you going?" said a small voice from behind them.

Stunned, Briar turned around. The door was ajar, and Charles and Charlotte stood there.

"Why?" Briar cried, looking up in exasperation. "Why is everyone spying on me?"

"We followed Leon," Charlotte said, stepping into the room.

"Where are you going?" Charles asked, his gaze flicking between Briar and Leon.

"Are you running away to marry?" Charlotte giggled. "Like the prince and princess from the story."

"No!" Briar said, her frustration mounting.

"We're going to the forest," Leon said, a hint of pride in his voice. "On an adventure."

Briar shook her head. "Why don't you just announce it to the entire castle?"

"We want to come with you," Charles said, a determined look on his face. "I love adventure."

"What?" Briar shouted, forgetting to stay quiet. "I'm not going to a party."

Charles puffed out his chest, trying to look brave. "I know there are dangers," he said. "We're ready for it."

"For anything," Charlotte agreed, nodding vigorously.

Briar threw Leon an angry look and turned to the twins. "You two go to bed right now."

"We're your best friends," Charlotte said, her voice trembling as tears welled up in her eyes. "Leon is going with you because he's your true love. We want to help you, too." Her lips quivered and her cheeks turned red, a dangerous sign that she was about to wail and wake the entire castle.

"You are very helpful," Briar said, her tone softening. "But you are not coming."

"But Leon is going," Charles insisted, his voice rising in defiance.

"You can't compare yourself with me," Leon said. "I'm Briar's true love, and I can always kiss her if something bad happens to her."

"Don't make me angry," Briar sighed, pinching the bridge of her nose. "Listen, you two. This isn't a game or a storybook adventure. It's dangerous, and I don't want you getting hurt."

"We won't get hurt," Charles said, his voice firm. "We can help you."

"Return to your chamber," Briar said.

"But Leon is going," Charles repeated, glaring at the prince.

"You know what, if that's your problem," Briar said, her patience wearing thin. "Leon is not going."

"What?" Leon gasped, his face a mixture of shock and betrayal. "But you promised. I'm coming."

"So are we," Charlotte declared, clenching her fists.

Briar knew she had to use another tactic to persuade them. "The forest is full of deadly things," she whispered. "And there are ghosts. Big, fanged ghosts. They hunt humans, and children are their favorite."

Charlotte's eyes widened with fear at the mention of ghosts. "Ghosts?"

Charles didn't look quite so brave anymore, either. "Ghosts?"

"I don't want to put you in danger," Briar said gently, grasping Charlotte's shoulder. "You can still help me by taking care of my mother. This is a bigger responsibility. Can you do that?"

The twins exchanged glances and then nodded solemnly.

"Thank you," Briar smiled. "Now go to sleep."

Charlotte shook her head, her eyes still wide with fear. "No."

"Why?" Briar felt like she was about to give up.

"I'm scared," Charlotte admitted. "Take me to my chamber and tuck me into bed."

Half an hour later, Briar left Charlotte and Charles in their chamber. She sneaked back to the servant's room where Leon was waiting, pacing impatiently.

"Now let's go before anyone else comes," Briar said.

And so, Princess Briar Rose and Prince Leon slipped out of the castle, their hearts pounding with the thrill of the unknown adventure that lay ahead. They tiptoed through the shadowed corridors, each step taking them further away from the safety of the castle and closer to the dangers of the dark forest.

CHAPTER 6

"I can't walk anymore," Briar said. "Let's take a break,"

"But we are almost there," Leon said. He held up the map to show her. "We can't take a break now."

Briar sighed heavily, pushing the map aside. "I don't care how close we are, Leon. I need to rest." She settled herself beneath a large oak tree, giving her aching legs a much-needed stretch.

It had been two days since they left the castle, and they had spent most of that time walking. Every muscle in Briar's body screamed for relief. The constant trudging through the uneven forest terrain had taken its toll, and the rough, sleepless nights hadn't helped.

Night in the forest was a particular kind of torture. The forest floor was an unforgiving bed, and they were completely exposed under the open sky. The rustling of leaves and the distant, bone-chilling howls of nocturnal animals kept Briar on edge, her sleep fitful and fragmented. Each time she managed to doze off, she was abruptly awakened by a terrifying sound that seemed to come straight from one of her childhood nightmares. Only this was much scarier and all too real.

Briar was grateful to have Leon with her. He could track the water source and find a safe clearing to camp at night. The prince was good with navigation and map reading, so Briar handed him the map and the responsibility of finding the correct path in the dense forest. Although she would never admit it to him, she knew she wouldn't have made it without his help.

"My legs are killing me," Briar groaned, massaging her calves.

Leon propped himself against a nearby tree. "If only you had allowed me to get the horse, none of this would have happened," he said.

"You don't have to taunt me," Briar said, her eyes closed as she leaned back against the tree. "I didn't want to take the risk."

They sat in silence for a few minutes, the forest around them growing darker and quieter. The occasional chirp of a cricket or rustle of leaves was the only sound that broke the stillness. The air was cool and damp, and the scent of pine needles and earth filled Briar's nostrils, calming her slightly.

Leon finally broke the silence. "Do you think they will come after us?"

Briar's chest tightened. Since they were in the forest, she had been avoiding any thoughts about the castle, especially her mother. The guilt pierced her like a sharp blade. But she kept reminding herself that she had to do this. She was the reason for all the trouble in the kingdom, and she was willing to go to any lengths to break the curse, even if it meant causing pain to her mother.

And she hoped one day her mother would forgive her.

"They will not come after us," Briar answered. She didn't write about the midnight forest and forest fairies in the letter.

"I'm sure your mother will understand," Leon reassured her with a smile. "Don't be sad. You need all the courage to break the curse."

Briar sighed, her gaze drifting to the canopy above where the leaves danced in the gentle breeze. "And food," Briar said, changing the topic. "I'm starving. Do we have anything to eat?"

Leon opened his satchel and rummaged through its contents. His face fell as he pulled out a few crumbs. "Oh, no."

"What's wrong?" Briar asked, peering into the satchel.

"My cake is gone," he said. "Now all I have is this." He produced two apples from the depths of his bag, their red skin glistening in the fading light.

Briar chuckled softly and reached into her satchel. She retrieved a modest loaf of bread, slightly crushed but still intact. "We'll manage with what we have," she said, tearing off a piece and offering it to Leon. "Then we'll need to collect more food. I know a few wild berries that are safe to eat."

"If there's one thing I miss about the castle, it's the food," Leon said wistfully. He took a bite of the apple. "I'd give anything for a slice of the cook's famous pie right now."

As Briar nibbled on her bread, a wave of unease washed over her. Doubts began to creep into her mind, like shadows slithering through the underbrush. What if they got lost in this vast forest? What if they never found the forest fairies? The enormity of their quest weighed heavily on her, stealing her appetite and replacing it with a gnawing fear.

Leon finished his bread and brushed the crumbs from his hands. He discarded the empty satchel and hoisted the other one onto his shoulder. Rising to his feet, he looked at Briar with determination. "I think we'll reach the fairy village before nightfall," he said, looking at the map.

Briar looked at the map, then at the path ahead, shrouded in shadows and uncertainty. "I hope so," she murmured, more to herself than to Leon. With a deep breath, they set off.

As they ventured deeper into the heart of the woods, the landscape began to shift, morphing into a twisted labyrinth of towering trees and tangled undergrowth. The air grew heavy with the scent of earth and decay, and a sense of foreboding settled over them like a suffocating shroud. The whispering of the wind through the leaves felt like the murmuring of ghosts, warning them to turn back.

After hours of walking, the forest seemed to close in around them, the density of the foliage making it difficult to see more than a few feet ahead. The trees loomed ominously overhead, their gnarled branches intertwining to form a thick canopy that blocked out the sunlight. Even in the daytime, the forest remained cloaked in shadow, casting an eerie pall over the landscape.

The ground beneath their feet grew uneven, the roots of the ancient trees snaking across the forest floor like serpents lying in wait. Briar stumbled over a protruding root, her heart racing as she struggled to maintain her balance. The twisted roots seemed to claw at her as if the forest itself were trying to hold her back.

Leon cast a concerned glance her way. "Are you alright? You look pale," he said. His hand hovered near her, ready to catch her if she fell.

"I'm fine," Briar insisted, though her voice trembled slightly. She forced herself to keep moving, her eyes scanning the dense underbrush for any sign of danger. Each rustle of leaves, each creak of a branch, made her heart skip a beat. The oppressive atmosphere made it hard to breathe.

Suddenly, Briar froze, her breath catching in her throat as she spotted a pair of large red eyes peering at her through the foliage. The eyes glowed eerily, unblinking and cold. She let out a startled scream.

Leon glanced over and then burst into laughter. "That's just an owl," he said, pointing at the bird nestled among the branches. The owl blinked slowly, almost as if it were amused by Briar's reaction. Its feathers were mottled with brown and white, blending perfectly with the tree bark.

Briar took a shaky breath, her pulse gradually returning to normal. "It looks... unusual," she admitted, her eyes still fixed on the creature lurking in the shadows. The red eyes were unnerving, and despite Leon's reassurance, she couldn't shake the feeling of unease that had settled over her.

"Yes, the red eyes," Leon said with a playful smirk. "If you're frightened, you can hold my hand." His tone was light, but his eyes were serious.

"I'm not scared," Briar insisted. She reached out and instinctively grasped Leon's hand, the warmth of his touch providing a slight comfort in the chilling forest.

"Good," Leon said, giving her hand a reassuring squeeze. He turned and led the way forward, his steps confident. "Let's keep moving. We need to reach the fairy village before nightfall."

Briar followed Leon in silence, her footsteps slow and hesitant. She wrapped her cloak tighter around her, seeking solace in its warmth, though it offered little comfort against the chill that seemed to seep into her bones.

Why was she so afraid? It was just a forest, after all. Yes, it was dark and eerie, but there was nothing to fear. She glanced at Leon. The prince seemed completely unfazed by the sinister atmosphere. He moved with ease as if he were strolling through a beautiful garden rather than a haunted forest. His calm demeanor was a stark contrast to the anxiety gnawing at her.

"Leon, how can you be so calm?" Briar asked. "Doesn't this place scare you at all?"

Leon turned to her. "I've faced far worse than a spooky forest," he said with a wink. "Besides, I have you with me. How could I be afraid?" His words were meant to comfort, and they brought a small smile to her lips.

Suddenly, Leon came to a sudden halt, his eyes fixed on something ahead. "Look," he said, pointing toward a clearing up ahead. "A cottage."

A small cottage stood in the middle of the clearing. The cottage seemed oddly out of place, its presence a stark contrast to the untamed wilderness that surrounded it.

"A cottage?" Briar said. "But Lavonna said no humans lived here."

Leon sniffed the air, and his eyes widened with delight. "Can you smell that?" he said, taking another deep inhale. "Strawberry tart, pudding, pancakes, wafers, apple pie, chocolate, dough nuts..."

Briar paused and took a deep breath, the mouthwatering scent of freshly baked treats and desserts filling her senses. The rich aroma wrapped around her like a comforting blanket, momentarily dispelling the chill of the forest. "I smell it too," she murmured, savoring the delicious blend of sweetness and warmth. "It's incredible."

Leon inhaled again and again, his excitement growing with each breath. "It smells yummy!" he exclaimed.

"Strange," Briar said, her brow furrowing in confusion. "Who could be baking here? And out here in the middle of nowhere?"

Leon, following the intoxicating aroma, started walking towards the cottage, his steps quickening. "The smell is coming from the cottage," he said. "Oh, maybe it's a food shop for travelers. Bless them! Thank goodness I have some gold coins." He patted his pocket, where the faint clink of coins could be heard.

As they approached the cottage, Briar suddenly stopped, her eyes widening in astonishment. It wasn't just the aroma that emanated from the cottage-it was the cottage itself. The walls were made of gingerbread, with delicate icing piping creating intricate designs. The roof was a cascade of chocolates, candies, and cookies, all expertly arranged to create a mouth-watering mosaic. The windows were framed with twisted ropes of licorice, and the door was a massive slab of chocolate, adorned with a doorknob that seemed to be a giant gumdrop.

Cupcakes and pastries grew on the porch like small bushes, while a fountain stood nearby. The mouth-watering cottage was surrounded by a fence made of candy canes.

Briar's stomach growled. Suddenly she craved sweets. How did she wish to eat a cupcake and drink from the fountain?

Her legs seemed to have a mind of their own, and she almost ran to the cottage. All she wanted to do was eat, eat, and eat.

It was just like the story her mother used to read to her.

A witch with a candy house.

A witch!

Briar planted her legs firmly on the ground to stop herself from running into the cottage.

"Leon, stop!" she yelled, her voice sharp with urgency.

The prince paused near the fence, turning back to her with a puzzled expression. "What?"

"Don't go. The cottage is dangerous," she said, her voice trembling with both fear and the effort to keep it low. Her eyes darted around, scanning the dense forest for any sign of movement.

Leon chuckled. "Yeah, rotten teeth maybe," he said with a playful smirk. "But seriously, I want to eat the wall, the floor, and the whole cottage." His gaze was fixed on the chocolate, his mouth practically watering.

"Trust me, Leon," Briar whispered as loudly as she dared. Her eyes were wide with fear, darting between Leon and the cottage. "It's the witch's magic-"

Before she could finish, the door made of candy swung open with a creak, revealing a plump woman clutching a massive fruit cake. She had a square-shaped face framed by narrow, calculating eyes that gleamed with an unsettling mix of kindness and cunning. She wore a dark green gown and gray cloak.

"Welcome, dear children," the witch's voice was sweeter than her candy house. Her smile was wide and inviting, but there was a coldness in her eyes that set Briar on the edge. The witch held out the fruitcake, its rich aroma filling the air with an almost overpowering sweetness. "You seem lost and weary. Why not step inside and enjoy a delicious cake?"

"And become fat so you'll eat us," Briar muttered under her breath.

Leon beamed at the witch. "That's so nice of you," he said, stepping closer to the cottage. "Is it a shop? I must say, it's a brilliant business idea to decorate your house with all these sweets."

The witch's eyes flicked to Leon's crown, her gaze lingering on it for a moment before she looked him up and down. Her tongue flicked out to lick her lips in a gesture that was more unsettling than hungry. "Royal blood..." she murmured, her voice barely above a whisper. Then she smiled again, wide and toothy. "I mean, you look like royals."

Leon smiled back. "I'm Prince Leon, and she-"

"We're in a rush," Briar interrupted quickly. "We'll visit your shop some other day." Her eyes were wide with terror, and she gripped Leon's arm, trying to pull him away from the witch.

The witch's smile never faltered as she took a step closer, her eyes gleaming with a predatory light. "A cake bite won't hurt you," she said, her voice a sickly-sweet singsong that sent shivers down Briar's spine.

"But your bite will," Briar muttered under her breath, tightening her grip on Leon's arm. "Leon, let's go." She yanked him away, her eyes never leaving the witch's face.

"We haven't had a decent meal in days," Leon pleaded, as he looked at Briar with wide, pleading eyes. "Please, let's accept her offer. I'm starving."

Briar glanced at the witch, who was inching closer with every passing moment. She forced a smile at Leon, her heart pounding in her chest. "She is hungry too," she said, her voice laced with a tension she couldn't hide. She watched from the corner of her eye as the witch took another step toward them, her expression growing more predatory.

"Don't you remember the tale?" Briar continued, trying to keep her voice steady. "We shouldn't accept candy from strangers, especially someone living in a candy house." Her eyes flicked to the candy-laden cottage, the sight of which now filled her with dread rather than delight.

"I've read enough stories," Leon said, his smile faltering slightly as he continued to look at the witch. "Of course, about the candy house..." His eyes suddenly widened in realization, and he turned to Briar, the pieces of the puzzle finally falling into place. "Candy house..."

"Candy house," Briar echoed, relief washing over her as she saw understanding dawn in his eyes. "Witches."

Suddenly, the witch was standing right in front of them, her presence so abrupt and menacing that it felt like the shadows themselves had delivered her. "Come inside," she ordered, her voice losing its sugary sweetness, replaced by a cold, commanding tone. Her smile was gone, replaced by a hungry, sinister look that sent chills down Briar's spine.

"Never," Briar said. She took a step back, pulling Leon with her.

The witch's face twisted, her features contorting into a grotesque mask of fury. Her skin turned wrinkled and leathery. Her robe slipped from her shoulders, revealing a body covered in scars and sinewy, misshapen flesh. She threw the fruitcake to the ground with a hiss. "No one rejects my cake," she spat.

Before Briar could react, the witch seized her arm with a grip like iron, yanking her towards the cottage. Briar screamed, the sound tearing from her throat as she struggled against the witch's vice-like hold. Summoning all her strength, she delivered a swift kick to the witch's stomach. The witch staggered backward, her grip loosening just enough for Briar to wrench her arm free.

"Run!" Briar yelled, her voice hoarse with panic.

The witch moved with a speed that defied her grotesque form, leaping to block their path. Her teeth bared in a snarl, her eyes bulging with malevolent glee. "No one rejects my offer," she hissed again, as she lunged at them, her mouth wide open and ready to devour.

Briar swung her fist at the witch's face, her knuckles connecting with a sickening crunch. Leon kicked her in the knees with all his might. To Briar's horror, the witch's entire leg detached from her body, falling to the ground with a thud.

But the witch seemed unfazed. She advanced toward them on one leg, her outstretched hand grasping for them, her eyes gleaming with a nightmarish hunger. She was a vision of horror, a creature straight from the darkest of nightmares.

Leon kicked her other leg. The witch crumbled to the ground, her body collapsing in a heap of ragged cloth and twisted limbs.

"Is she dead?" Leon shouted, his voice trembling with shock and disbelief. "Did I kill a witch?"

"You feel bad for her," Briar screamed, her eyes wide with panic as she grabbed his arm and started pulling him away. "She's not dead. Let's get out of here before she...fixes her leg!"

Not wasting any more time or wanting to see the horrible sight as the witch mended her legs, Briar and Leon took off running. They had no idea where they were heading, only that they needed to put as much distance as possible between themselves and the witch's cottage. The forest seemed to stretch endlessly before them, a maze of shadows and twisted branches that threatened to engulf them.

Finally, after what felt like hours of frantic running, they slowed to a stop, their chests heaving with exertion. Briar glanced over her shoulder, half-expecting to see the witch still pursuing them. But the forest was quiet, the only sound was the distant rustle of leaves and the rapid thudding of their hearts.

Briar glared at Leon. "Honestly, I can't believe you didn't recognize the witch. The candy house should have been a dead giveaway."

Leon, still gasping for breath, ran a hand through his tousled hair, his face flushed from their frantic escape. "It was a bedtime story," he said defensively. "I forgot."

"Some stories are to teach us valuable lessons," Briar said.

"Fine, I learned my lesson," Leon muttered, rubbing his temples as if trying to erase the memory of the witch's horrifying face. "We aren't stopping anywhere near a candy house ever again." He glanced at her, a hint of a smile twitching at the corners of his lips. "But you can't blame me for wanting to eat it. The house looked delicious."

"The witch felt the same way about you," Briar said dryly, her eyes scanning their surroundings with a wary gaze. "Anyway, where are we now? We need to keep moving."

"Let me check the map," Leon replied. He pulled out the map and compass from his satchel, his brow furrowing as he carefully traced their route with a finger. After a moment of studying the map, he looked up. "Thankfully, we are on the right path. We should reach the fairy village soon."

"Good, I can't walk much further," Briar said, her shoulders slumping with exhaustion. She felt utterly drained, her legs heavy and aching from their harrowing run. She didn't even bother checking the hourglasses to see how much time was left. Three days had already been wasted.

"This is only the beginning of our adventure," Leon said cheerfully, trying to lighten the mood as they resumed their trek through the forest.

"You seem to enjoy it too much," Briar said.

"Maybe a little," Leon admitted, his eyes twinkling with excitement despite their recent ordeal. "Can you blame me? The enchanted flower garden, and forest fairies-it's our opportunity to see rare things that only a few lucky people get to see in their lives. We're living a story, Briar."

"There are also creatures like the witch," Briar added. "I didn't feel lucky to meet her."

"There are always going to be obstacles in a quest," Leon said. "But we have to overcome them if we want to reach our destiny."

Briar looked around the forest. She just wanted to reach her destiny without any more obstacles stopping her.

CHAPTER 7

As the sun began its descent toward the horizon, casting a warm golden glow over the landscape, Briar and Leon finally arrived at the enchanted flower garden. The vast expanse of the field stretched out in every direction, captivating Briar's gaze. The flowers' vibrant hues paint a mesmerizing tapestry against the backdrop of the setting sun.

Roses, with their velvety petals in shades of crimson and blush, danced alongside cheerful marigolds with their fiery orange and golden blooms. Dahlias flaunted their intricate patterns, while sunflowers proudly displayed their bold, golden faces, basking in the warm embrace of the fading daylight. Daffodils swayed gracefully, their buttery yellow trumpets nodding in the gentle breeze, while tulips stood tall and elegant, their petals unfurling like delicate works of art. Daisies dotted the landscape like clusters of delicate stars, while irises unfurled their regal blooms in shades of royal purple and deep indigo. Pansies nestled close to the ground, their cheerful faces beaming up at the sky, while orchids dangled like delicate jewels from their slender stems.

The air was filled with the heady perfume of flowers, a symphony of fragrance that enveloped Briar in a soothing embrace.

Butterflies flitted and danced among the blooms, their delicate wings shimmering in the fading light as they sipped nectar from one flower to the next. One butterfly, in particular, caught Briar's eye, its deep purple wings a striking contrast against the riot of colors around them. To her surprise, the butterfly transformed before her eyes, revealing itself to be a stunning deep purple fairy with captivating golden eyes.

"Told you this forest is not that bad," Leon grinned.

"Yes," Briar nodded in awe.

Briar's eyes widened in wonder as she nodded in agreement. Having spent most of her life within the walls of a castle, the outside world seemed like a fantastical realm that only existed in dreams. There was so much to see. Briar couldn't decide which flower to admire first. Her weariness was gone, and she was filled with joy just looking at the flowers.

As she approached a large marigold, Briar couldn't resist the urge to gently caress its delicate petals. She was afraid that her touch might somehow ruin its perfection.

This garden was like heaven. A place of joy. Flower and honey and sky. In the garden, she could watch the beautiful flowers all day, drink the nectar, and live happily ever after.

She did not need to break the curse.

The curse!

In an instant, realization struck Briar like a bolt of lightning. The curse. Briar snapped out of her daydreaming, her face dangerously close to the marigold. A shiver ran down her spine, causing her to jerk back instinctively. It was just like the candy house—a trap.

"Leon, we must go," Briar urgently pleaded, but there was no response from the prince. She turned around to see him walking towards the shimmering river that twisted through the garden and vanished into the depths of the forest.

"Leon, stop," Briar chased after him.

"Look, clean water," he said as Briar reached him, pulling the canteen from his satchel. "Now we don't have to worry about finding water for two days."

The water appeared crystal clear and completely calm, its surface glistening like diamonds in the sunlight. The lake bed was covered in smooth, colorful stones. The river possessed an unnatural beauty, but it could also be a trap.

"No," she stopped the prince before he went to fill the canteen.

Leon gave her a puzzled expression. "But we need water."

"We will find a pond or something later, but not this water," she said firmly. "This place is an enchantment."

"Oh, come on," Leon rolled his eyes.

"Don't take the water," Briar insisted.

Leon relented. "Okay, but you have to find water later." He put the canteen back into his satchel.

As Briar turned to leave, she suddenly caught sight of something peculiar. A ripple disrupted the calm surface of the water. Something was swimming toward them.

Instead of going away, Briar moved closer to the river, straining her eyes to get a better look at the thing she had noticed. To her surprise, she realized that it was her reflection staring back at her from the water's surface. However, there was something strange about her reflection.

Her appearance was completely unrecognizable. Her green eyes were now a haunting shade of red, and her skin had turned an eerie, snow-like pale. The hunger in her expression sent shivers down Briar's spine. Briar felt like she was watching a ghost vision of herself.

Filled with bewilderment, Briar shifted her gaze towards Leon's reflection, only to find that the prince's image was absent from the water's surface.

"Can you see your reflection?" Briar asked. "Does your reflection look different?"

Leon focused on the water and gasped. He reached out to touch his face, observing the water with curiosity. "Something wrong with my eyes." He rubbed his eyes and blinked.

"Something very wrong with the river," Briar said, looking at her peculiar reflection. "Let's go." Briar turned her back to the water. She couldn't look at her creepy face anymore.

"Wait," a familiar voice called out, its echo rippling through the air like a whisper on the wind.

Briar spun around, her eyes darting towards the riverbank. The voice had seemed so close.

"Come closer," the voice beckoned, its tone gentle yet strangely alluring. "Please don't leave so soon."

Briar's gaze fell upon her reflection in the shimmering surface of the water. Her reflection seemed to shimmer and dance with an otherworldly light.

"Come closer, Briar," her reflection said with a smile. "I have a lot to tell you."

"It's talking," Briar stammered, her voice barely a whisper as she struggled to comprehend what she was witnessing.

Leon's brow furrowed in confusion as he followed Briar's gaze to the river. "What's talking?"

Briar trembled, unable to tear her eyes away from her reflection. "My reflection... it's speaking to me."

Leon's eyes widened in disbelief. "That's impossible. Reflections don't speak."

"But it spoke to me, using my voice," Briar said. She knew what she had heard. The voice had been unmistakably her own.

"He doesn't understand you, Briar," the voice continued, its tone filled with concern. "We do."

"We?" Briar echoed, her voice trembling.

As if in response, a second reflection materialized beside the first one, identical in every detail, ethereal and unsettling.

"Who are you?" Briar asked.

"We are you," the first reflection spoke again, its voice a haunting echo of Briar's own.

"We know you are on a quest to break the curse," the second reflection chimed in.

"How?" Briar gasped, her mind reeling with disbelief.

"We know about the curse," the reflections said in unison, their voices blending in an eerie harmony. "We know everything."

Briar's breath caught in her throat as she struggled to comprehend their words. It creeped her out to talk to her reflections.

"You are afraid, aren't you?" the reflections said.

Briar swallowed nervously, her heart pounding in her chest.

"And burdened with guilt," added a third reflection, emerging on the surface of the water.

Briar's eyes widened in terror as the fourth reflection materialized on the surface. Then another and another and another. Suddenly, the surface of the river was full of her reflection, all looking at her with a knowing look.

"Who are you speaking to?" Leon asked, his eyes darting around in confusion.

Briar's voice trembled as she replied, "The reflections... they're talking to me."

"But I can't see anyone," Leon said, worried.

"We know the past, the present, and the future," said one reflection, its voice echoing across the water. "We hold the key to your quest's destiny."

Despite how scared Briar was, the reflection's words made her curious. "Do you know the future of this curse?"

"Yes," another said in a gentle voice.

"Want to know about the outcome," another said, beckoning Briar into the river. "Come here and we'll tell you."

Briar's breath caught in her throat as she leaned closer to the water's edge. "Tell me," she pleaded.

The reflections began to glide into the water, their ghostly forms disappearing beneath the surface, leaving Briar with a head full of questions.

Briar wanted to hear the reflections talk. She wanted to know about her quest. They knew the secrets of the curse, the fate that awaited her. She couldn't let them slip away. "Tell me!" Briar shouted.

She could hear Leon asking her something, but his voice was unclear as if he was miles away.

"We will help you," the reflections chanted. "Come with us."

"Wait," Briar reached for the reflections. "Don't go."

A reflection paused and turned to Briar. "You will die."

"What?" Briar asked. "Tell me more," she pleaded. Then without thinking, she jumped into the river.

CHAPTER 8

Clawed hands pulled Briar deeper into the bone-chilling cold water, each grasp like a vise on her skin. Underwater, it was a world of liquid mist, a thick, swirling fog that obscured her vision. Indistinct silhouettes loomed around her, shadowy figures just out of reach, their forms wavering in the murky depths.

Running out of breath, the princess opened her mouth in a desperate gasp, only to gulp down the freezing water. It was as if icy knives were slicing through her throat. She struggled to break free, but the hands were relentless, iron grips that tightened with each passing second, dragging her further into the abyss. Her legs kicked out blindly, hitting nothing but the cold water.

Briar's lungs were on fire, an unbearable ache swelling in her chest. She opened her mouth again, choking on the water that filled her mouth. Panic surged through her. Hundreds of voices whispered and hissed in her ears. They felt both near and far, echoing in the watery void around her.

"Come with us," the voices whispered.

"We know all the secrets."

"We will show you the future."

"We will not let you die!" they hissed, the word slithering like a serpent through her mind.

The pain in Briar's chest grew more intense with each passing second. She felt as if her lungs were about to burst, the pressure inside her building to an agonizing peak. Desperation clawed at her, and she tried to scream.

"Leave...me!" she shouted, her words distorted and lost in the liquid expanse.

Briar's panic grew, her thoughts spiraling into a dark whirlpool of fear. Was she dying? Was death so excruciating? The thought of never seeing her parents again, of never returning to her kingdom, tore at her heart. She could see their faces, and their smiles, and felt a surge of sorrow and rage.

They would all turn into monsters.

"NO!" Briar screamed, a fierce determination igniting within her. With every ounce of strength, she had left, she yanked her hands and feet, thrashing against the unyielding grip of the claws. For a fleeting moment, the hold on her body weakened, and she propelled herself upwards, kicking furiously through the water.

Just as she was about to break through the surface, the hands returned, stronger and more relentless. They wrapped around her, claws digging into her skin with renewed ferocity. Briar cried out in pain, the sound a muffled echo in the watery depths, as they began to pull her back down.

"We are almost there," the voices cooed, a chilling promise that sent shivers down her spine.

"Let me go!" Briar gasped as she fought against the inescapable pull.

"Trust us," the voices murmured, their tones filled with a sickly sweetness. "You belong with us."

"No," she whimpered, tears mingling with the cold water around her. "I won't let you take me."

But the hands were unyielding, their grip like iron as they dragged her deeper into the darkness. Briar's vision began to blur, her strength waning as the cold seeped into her bones. The voices grew louder, their whispers a cacophony that filled her mind.

Briar's body was giving up. Her head pounded like a drum, and her vision blurred into a swirling mess of colors and shadows. Gradually, she began to lose awareness of her surroundings, succumbing to the cold, suffocating darkness that enveloped her.

Suddenly, a force yanked her away from the grip of the reflections. She felt herself being dragged out of the river, their ghostly hands clawing and screaming to pull her back into the watery depths. The cacophony of their furious hissing filled her ears. Finally, her back collided with the solid ground.

Briar coughed violently, expelling the water from her lungs. She took huge gulps of air, savoring the sensation of oxygen flooding her system. It felt so good to breathe again.

As she opened her eyes, Leon's worried face swam into view.

"Briar!" he yelled, his voice trembling. He looked as pale as the reflections themselves. "Breathe, Briar, breathe!"

She lay there, drawing in slow, deliberate breaths. After what felt like an eternity, the burning in her lungs began to subside, and her head stopped spinning. She sat up slowly.

Leon stroked her back, his touch warm and comforting. "Are you alright?" he asked.

"Yeah," Briar replied, her voice shaky. "Drowning is...painful."

"Why did you jump into the river?" Leon demanded, the color gradually returning to his face now that Briar could speak. "What were you thinking?"

"I...I wanted to talk to them," Briar answered, shuddering as she recalled the horrible hissing and the icy grip of the reflections.

"Them?" Leon asked, his brow furrowing in confusion.

"The reflections," Briar said, her voice barely above a whisper. "My reflections. They tried to drown me."

"It doesn't make sense," Leon shook his head, disbelief etched on his face. "How can our reflections want to kill us?"

"This place is magical, and in a bad way," Briar said, her eyes scanning the eerie surroundings. "Full of traps. Lavonna warned me about this."

"Briar, I'm so sorry," Leon apologized, his voice breaking. "I nearly killed you. I should have come back when you told me to."

"It's not your fault," Briar said, placing a reassuring hand on his arm. "I jumped into the river. I wanted to hear their prediction."

"What prediction?" Leon asked.

Briar said nothing. The words of the reflections echoed inside her head. A deadly whisper. You will die. Did they truly predict her future?

She glanced toward the river, its surface as clear as glass, motionless, and deceptively beautiful. Yet, despite its serene appearance, Briar could still feel the malevolent red eyes watching her from beneath the surface.

With a shudder, she scrambled to her feet. "Let's get out of this garden."

"You sure you can walk?" Leon asked.

"Yes," Briar nodded firmly. "I don't want to be here anymore."

They picked up their satchel and made their way cautiously out of the garden, keeping a wide berth from the treacherous river. The garden, once a place of enchanting beauty, now felt like a sinister trap. They were almost out when Leon suddenly halted and spun around, his eyes filling with sorrow as he gazed at the vibrant flowers, as though bidding farewell to a dear friend.

"It's one of the most beautiful creations of our world," he said wistfully. "I wish it wasn't evil."

"Me too," Briar agreed.

Leon hesitated, looking around the garden with a longing gaze. "I want to take a memory with me," he whispered.

Briar rolled her eyes. "Fine," she sighed. "Take whatever memory you want, but make it quick."

Leon's face lit up with a grateful smile. He dashed towards a golden rose bush. The petals shimmering like spun gold under the sunlight. With careful precision, he plucked a single, perfect rose and tucked it gently into his cloak pocket.

All of a sudden, the ground beneath their feet began to tremble violently.

"An earthquake?" Leon questioned, as the garden continued to shake with each tremor.

Briar stood frozen in fear. The once serene garden now seemed alive, as if possessed by an otherworldly force. The vibrant flowers were twisting, their petals transforming into grotesque mouths that gnashed hungrily.

"What's going on?" Leon asked, his voice rising with panic.

"The garden is alive," Briar whispered, watching in horror as a flower grew to a monstrous size before her eyes. "It doesn't look good for us."

Leon shouted, "RUN!"

They tore through the garden. The flowers snapped at them like feral beasts. Roots emerged from the ground, writhing and twisting, trying to trip them up. A massive marigold lunged at Briar, its petals gnashing and snapping.

Briar swung her sword, slicing through the stem with a clean cut. The enormous flower fell to the ground, thrashing like a dying animal. Leon stomped on the fallen marigold repeatedly, a green gooey substance pouring out with each impact until it finally stopped moving.

"It's disgusting," Briar gagged, wiping the goo from her blade.

At that very moment, a thick branch swung at Briar, knocking her off her feet and causing her to fall face-first onto the ground. Instantly, thick ivy snaked around her legs, dragging her toward the gaping maw of a gigantic sunflower.

"AH!" Briar screamed, fumbling with her sword. She managed to chop through the ivy just in time, the severed vines recoiling as she scrambled away from the menacing flower.

"This way!" Leon shouted, rushing to her side and helping her to her feet. Together, the princess and prince fought their way through the treacherous garden, hacking at menacing flowers and slashing through deadly vines.

When they finally made it out of the garden, they were soaked with the foul, green sticky substance. Briar wiped it from her face with her cloak, grimacing.

"Ew! I doubt I'll ever be able to get rid of this awful smell," she complained, her nose wrinkling in disgust.

"Yeah," nodded Leon, as he tucked the golden rose dangling from his pocket.

"You woke the garden," Briar yelled.

"What?" Leon asked, his face a mask of confusion. "How?"

Briar yanked the rose from his pocket and hurled it back toward the garden. "By plucking this rose!"

"It was a memory," Leon protested.

"A horrible one," Briar retorted. "Are you here to help me or give me more trouble?"

"Hey, I didn't know the garden would try to eat us," Leon said defensively. "Why do beautiful things have to be dangerous?"

Briar sighed, her anger softening. "Forget about it," she said, shaking her head. "Let's go."

They headed away from the garden, their steps more assured now. To Briar's relief, the forest gradually became less dense. The oppressive canopy thinned out, allowing the evening light to filter through and creating a more inviting path. The tangled underbrush gave way to a clearer trail, making their journey easier without the constant hindrance of trees and bushes.

As they walked, the tension between them eased. Briar glanced at Leon, noting the way his eyes scanned their surroundings with newfound caution. "I'm sorry I snapped at you," she said. "I was scared."

"I know," Leon replied, offering her a small smile. "I was scared too. But we made it through."

Briar nodded, returning his smile. "Yeah, we did. Together."

However, they didn't reach the fairy village. As the sun vanished from the sky, darkness enveloped the forest. Leon suggested they rest for the night, and Briar, feeling the exhaustion from nearly drowning, readily agreed.

They found a small pond nestled among the trees, its water clear and cool. They washed off the foul green substance, savoring the refreshing sensation. Briar refilled their canteens while Leon gathered some wood for a small fire. The sound of the forest at night surrounded them—rustling leaves, the distant hoot of an owl, and the gentle croaking of frogs by the pond.

"If we hadn't gotten stuck in the garden, we would have reached the village today," Briar said as they sat by the fire, eating wild berries and fruits they had found near the pond. The firelight cast flickering shadows on their faces.

"We'll start early tomorrow," he said, chewing thoughtfully. "Relax tonight."

Briar tried to listen to his advice, but the nagging thought of another day wasted gnawed at her. She gazed into the fire, watching the flames dance and flicker. "I just can't shake the feeling that we're running out of time," she admitted, her voice tinged with worry.

Leon reached over and placed a comforting hand on her shoulder. "We're doing our best, Briar."

She sighed, appreciating his words, but still feeling restless. The fire crackled softly as they sat in silence. When she finally lay down to sleep, her mind was still buzzing with anxiety.

Despite her fatigue, Briar found it difficult to sleep. She tossed and turned, the events of the day replaying in her mind. When she finally drifted off, her sleep was plagued by nightmares. She dreamed of monstrous flowers with gaping mouths, of roots that ensnared her, dragging her back to the river. She could feel the cold, dark water closing over her head again, and hear the reflections whispering their deadly prophecy.

Chapter 9

The next morning, Briar and Leon woke up before sunrise. With weary, yet resolute steps, they walked for hours searching for the fairy village. As time ticked away, Briar's anxiety grew, fearing that they might lose yet another precious day.

Suddenly, Leon halted in his tracks, his gaze fixed ahead. "I think that's the village," he said, pointing towards a cluster of colorful cottages nestled among the trees.

Briar felt a wave of relief wash over her, her heart lifting with renewed hope. "Really," she said.

Leon carefully folded the map and placed it in his pocket with a triumphant smile. "See, I told you. We will find it today," he said as they headed towards the village.

The fairy village greeted them with a scene of enchanting beauty. Colorful cottages with hay roofs dotted the landscape, some built on the ground while others perched gracefully atop tree branches. Floating wooden staircases zigzagged around the trees, joining one cottage to another, forming a complex canopy of staircases overhead. The intricate architecture of the village took Briar's breath away.

Fairies flitted about the village. Their graceful movements and tinkling laughter filled the air with magic. Some were huddled together, engaged in conversation, while others danced through the sky, their delicate wings shimmering in the sunlight. Briar's heart swelled with joy at the sight of the bustling village.

The fairies resembled humans in appearance, but their ethereal beauty set them apart. Their skin had a flawless, marble-like texture, glowing with an otherworldly radiance. Their eyes came to a range of captivating colors. And each fairy had their wings neatly tucked behind their back. Some fairies sported delicate antlers, while others had majestic horns or whimsical antennas sprouting from their heads.

Briar and Leon walked up to the nearest cottage where a fairy was singing and watering the flower bushes in her small garden.

"Hello," Briar said, her voice gentle as she smiled at the fairy.

The fairy turned to them, her huge violet eyes widening in alarm. In an instant, she let out a piercing shriek, "SPIES, SPIES!"

The sound seemed to set off a chain reaction. Within seconds, the entire village gathered around Briar and Leon, their voices rising in alarm and accusation.

"Are they humans?" one voice cried out.

"How did humans find us?" another exclaimed.

"Human in our village. A terrible sign," murmured a worried fairy.

"They are the spies of the fairy queen!" accused another.

"Inform Viatrix!" shouted someone else.

"Alert the fairy army!" chimed in another voice. Panic rippled through the crowd like wildfire.

"Excuse me," Briar attempted to speak, but her words were drowned out by the clamor of the fairies as they scattered, fleeing from her as though she were a fearsome dragon about to breathe fire upon them.

Soon, what had been a peaceful village descended into chaos. Fairies darted into their homes, slamming doors shut behind them. The scene reminded Briar of her town when the thorn monster attacked.

Briar felt a mixture of confusion and frustration. Why were the fairies reacting as if she were some kind of monster? All she had done was utter a simple greeting. Briar sighed. "Seriously, all I did was say 'hello'"

"Maybe 'hello' is a triggering word here," Leon said, shaking his head.

"How dare you set your smelly feet in our land?" thundered a voice. "You filthy humans!"

Briar and Leon turned around to find a group of fairies marching toward them, their menacing dark armor gleaming in the sunlight. They were armed to the teeth with fireballs, spears, swords, bows, and arrows. At the forefront of the group strode a young fairy, clad in armor seemingly too large for his frame. In one hand, he gripped a red flag adorned with a pair of golden fairy wings, while the other held a wand, crackling with magical energy. As the army came to a halt, their leader, the teenage fairy, stepped forward. His chest puffed out with confidence.

"Everyone, go stay in your houses and lock your doors and windows," he commanded, his voice ringing out with authority.

"I, Rex, the youngest child of Viatrix, assure you that I will protect you and,"—here he shot a disdainful glance at Briar and Leon—"chase the enemy out of our land."

Briar stepped forward. "Sir, we are not spy," she said politely, her voice calm but firm.

Rex regarded Briar with a look of disgust as if her very presence offended him. "You, a mere human, will never be able to locate us," he sneered. "Especially without the help of a magical being. It seems the fairy queen has revealed our location to you."

"Not the fairy queen," Leon said as he stared down at the smaller fairy. "The witch helped us."

"Witch!" Rex exclaimed, his eyes widening in shock. He turned to his army, aghast. "Can you believe it? The fairy queen has joined forces with witches to conquer our land!"

"Witches!" echoed voices from the fairy army, filled with horror and revulsion. "They're incredibly wicked."

"Humans always support the fairy queen," cried another fairy soldier.

"The humans are under the control of the fairy queen," shouted one fairy soldier, his hands trembling as he struggled to restrain a fireball aimed at Briar and Leon.

"We won't show mercy, even if our enemies are children," declared another, brandishing his spear menacingly.

"Let's punish them!" a voice cried out from the crowd.

"Punish them!" The chant began to rise among the fairies.

"Please listen," Briar pleaded, her voice cutting through the uproar. She turned to face Rex, her eyes pleading. "We have no interest in claiming your land. We simply want to meet Viatrix."

"Viatrix!" Rex shouted, his voice trembling. "See, they plan to attack the queen."

"We have to protect our queen, Rex," declared the elder fairy, his pale face contorted with rage.

"We don't want to attack anyone," Briar yelled, her voice rising above the chaos in a desperate attempt to reason with them.

Ignoring Briar's plea, the elder fairy thrust his spear toward Rex. "Rex, now you are our only hope," he proclaimed. "Save our land."

Rex seemed to be swelling with pride as he nodded at the old fairy. Then he turned to face his army. "Attack!" he commanded, his voice echoing across the battlefield.

Briar barely had time to react before the attack began, arrows and fireballs raining down upon her with deadly precision.

"HEY!" Briar screamed, dodging the arrows.

"YOU CAN NEVER TOUCH OUR LAND!" Rex's voice rang out. A fierce determination burned in his eyes as he launched a massive fireball toward Briar.

Leon pulled Briar out of the way as the fireball missed her and hit a tree, exploding it into pieces.

"We don't mean any harm!" Briar shouted, her arms raised defensively in a gesture of surrender. "We surrender!"

"Are we surrendering to a bunch of idiots with wings?" Leon asked, surprised.

"We need their help," Briar explained urgently.

Suddenly, Rex aimed his wand directly at Briar, unleashing a powerful bolt of lightning. Briar attempted to evade the attack, but the bolt struck her arm with a searing intensity. Agonizing waves of pain surged through her body, leaving her breathless and weak. She collapsed to the ground.

"Briar!" Leon rushed to her side, pulling her upright and guiding her to safety behind a nearby cottage.

"Are you okay?" Leon asked, as he gently leaned Briar against the wall of the cottage.

"I feel so weak," Briar admitted, her voice barely a whisper.

"They are hiding behind the cottage!" someone shouted from the sky.

In an instant, fireballs rained down upon the cottage, setting it ablaze with terrifying speed. Briar and Leon had to run away as the flamed roof toppled to the ground.

Seeking refuge behind another cottage, Briar and Leon found themselves once again under attack as fireballs and arrows relentlessly pursued them.

"What should we do?" Leon shouted over the explosions. "Fight back!"

"No," Briar replied weakly, her voice barely audible over the chaos. "We can't fight them."

Amidst the chaos, Rex's voice pierced the uproar, rallying his troops with fervent determination. "Attack! I want the head of the enemy!" He released a powerful battle cry. Inspired by his words, the fairy army launched a more intense assault, sending more fireballs and arrows blindly.

Briar and Leon flattened themselves against the ground, narrowly dodging arrows and fireballs that whizzed dangerously close.

Briar and Leon flattened themselves on the ground as the arrows zoomed past their head. It was fortunate that the fairies weren't good at hitting the target, or else the princess and prince would have been dead a long time ago.

"Enough!" Leon declared as he rose to his feet, drawing his sword from its scabbard.

But Briar pulled him back down. "Don't be crazy," she said. "They will burn and stab you to death."

"We should fight back," Leon said, his eyes ablaze with fury. "A true hero never turns his back to a battle."

"Take a battle tip from me," Briar said. "They are large in numbers. They have fireballs, an unlimited number of arrows, and most importantly, they have magic. And the stupid fairy did something to me and I suddenly felt weak. Besides, if we fight back, it would look like we wanted to attack their land."

"Then what?" Leon asked.

"Wait till they get tired," Briar suggested. "Or set their village on fire."

As the fairy army continued their assault, unleashing another wave of fireballs, the once-peaceful village descended into chaos and destruction. Cottages, trees, and the very ground itself were consumed by flames.

In a panic, the fairies fled their burning homes. When they finally understood what was happening, they shouted at Rex to stop his army.

"You are burning us!" screamed a fairy, her once beautiful gown now engulfed in flames. Frantically, two other fairies rushed to her aid, desperately trying to extinguish the fire by dousing it with water.

"You will burn down the village!" shouted a lanky old fairy with transparent wings. "Stop the fight!"

"I'm in charge!" Rex screamed back, his voice echoing with authority. "It is my job to protect you."

"You have lost your mind!" the old fairy retorted.

Rex's gaze narrowed. "Stop interfering with my work or else," he threatened. With a flick of his wrist, he aimed a fireball at the protesting fairies, forcing them to retreat in fear.

As the chaos unfolded, Rex launched into an even more intense assault, his screams filling the air as he unleashed a barrage of fireballs upon the village. It seemed like if he could not hit Briar and Leon, he would hit his people.

From above, a voice exclaimed, "Look, they're here!" Briar and Leon glanced upwards to see a fairy soldier floating near the cottage where they had taken cover. With his spear aimed downward, the fairy soldier declared, "I have found the spies."

Before Briar and Leon could react, four fairies descended upon them, their wings beating frantically as they restrained the prince and princess. Leon struggled against his captors, but Briar lacked the strength to resist.

With a mischievous grin, Rex landed before them, his eyes gleaming with malicious intent. "How about we play a little game of 'off with your head'?" he taunted, holding a blazing fireball in his hand. "I've quite enjoyed playing hide and seek with you humans, but it seems the game is over now." He aimed the fireball directly at Briar and Leon.

CHAPTER 10

"Rex," said a sharp voice.

The young fairy stopped mid-attack, spun around, and let out a frustrated curse. "Why can't they just leave me alone?"

Two fairies were rushing toward them. The first, a tall fairy, wore a gown made entirely of vibrant yellow flowers, each petal shifting and rustling as if touched by a gentle breeze. Her blonde hair was elegantly styled in an elaborate bun, adorned with delicate, fluttering butterflies that seemed to dance in the air around her. The second fairy was draped in a gown that sparkled like a cascade of sewn blue and white crystals, glistening in the sunlight with an ethereal glow. Her long, wavy blue hair tumbled down her back like a waterfall, and in her hand, she held a wand topped with a large, gleaming blue crystal. Both fairies had piercing amber eyes, the same striking hue as Rex's.

Trailing behind the two fairies was the lanky old fairy that Rex had threatened earlier.

As they approached, the elderly fairy gestured towards Briar and Leon. "That's the human he captured and caused all the chaos," he said.

The two fairies gasped, their eyes widening in shock as they took in the sight of Briar and Leon.

"What are you doing with them?" thundered the yellow fairy, her voice ringing with authority and fury.

Rex straightened up, puffing out his chest as the fireball in his hand grew larger. "I caught the spies," he declared with a triumphant sneer. "They're here to assassinate our mother. If you hadn't interrupted, I would have killed them."

The blue fairy's eyes widened in horror. "Kill them?" she echoed, her voice trembling with disbelief. "They're just children!"

"And that makes them the perfect weapon, doesn't it?" Rex snapped, casting a venomous glance at Briar and Leon. "Who would suspect children? The fairy queen is clever and devious."

"Shut up, Rex!" snapped the blue fairy, her voice cracking like a whip. "Stop being obsessed with the fairy queen. She doesn't want our land."

"And you!" the yellow fairy turned her fierce gaze on the soldiers. "Release the children this instant."

The soldiers, their faces masked with uncertainty, looked from Rex to the two fairies, clearly torn between conflicting orders.

"I said leave the humans and go make yourselves useful by helping the villagers with the disaster my foolish brother has caused!" the yellow fairy shouted.

At once, the soldiers loosened their grip on Briar and Leon, the magical strands dissolving into thin air. Then, without another glance at Rex, the fairy soldiers turned and hurried off.

"Why did you dismiss my army?" Rex thundered, his chest heaving with barely contained rage. "I have the authority. I need their help with the spies!"

"We are not spying!" Briar interjected quickly, her voice trembling yet firm. The two fairies seemed like they wouldn't try to blast them with fireballs and listen to their side of the story.

"Silence!" Rex barked, turning on Briar with a fierce glare. He then faced the yellow fairy again. "I caught them, and I'll decide what to do with them."

"Never," the blue fairy retorted. "It is mother who will decide their fate. Now, stop creating more trouble for yourself and go use your army for something productive."

"And wait for mother to return and punish you," the yellow fairy added with a stern look.

Rex's face contorted with disbelief. "And what about the spies?" he asked incredulously. "You think I'll just leave them with you? Am I stupid? You two are so careless."

"Listen, Rex," the yellow fairy said. "We are older than you and have higher ranks. So, little brother, you must follow our orders. When mother returns, she will decide what to do with the humans. Now go."

Rex's eyes flared with frustration. He yanked off his helmet and hurled it to the ground with a loud clang. "I know you're taking advantage of your position!" he shouted, his voice cracking with bitterness. "You're jealous because I'm mother's favorite.

You want to steal the credit for capturing the spies, but I'll never let that happen. The entire village knows I caught them."

"The whole village also knows you set it on fire and nearly killed two humans who haven't been proven guilty," the blue fairy said pointedly.

Rex's face darkened with fury. He glared at his sisters, his jaw clenched tightly, then turned and stormed off, his wings flaring angrily.

The blue fairy turned her attention to the old fairy, who had been watching the argument from a distance. "Thanks for informing us," she said.

"Can't let him burn down our only home," the elderly fairy replied gruffly, shaking his head before turning to leave.

With the old fairy gone, the two sisters shifted their focus to Briar and Leon. "Who are you?" asked the blue fairy.

"I'm Briar Rose," Briar said.

"And I'm Prince Leon," Leon added, bowing slightly. "Also known as Prince Charming."

The fairies gasped, their eyes widening in amazement. "Sleeping Beauty and Prince Charming."

"If Rex had known that, he might have tried to kill you sooner," the blue fairy said.

Suddenly, Briar's vision blurred, and a wave of dizziness swept over her. She staggered, reaching out for support, and clutched Leon's arm as her legs threatened to give way.

"Are you all right, princess?" the yellow fairy asked urgently, rushing to Briar's side.

"Are you injured?" the blue fairy inquired, stepping closer, her eyes scanning Briar for any signs of harm.

"That stupid fairy hit her with a spell, and now she's weakened," Leon said angrily.

The yellow fairy's face contorted with rage. "A life-draining spell," she spat, shaking with fury. "Rex cast a life-draining spell on a human. What if she had died? Our reputation is already terrible enough as it is."

"What is a life-draining spell?" Briar asked, her voice trembling.

"The spell slowly drains the life energy from a person," she explained, pausing for a moment. "Until the person is dead."

"But you have nothing to worry about," the blue fairy interrupted quickly, moving closer to Briar. "Let me see." She pointed her wand at Briar's chest. Chanting softly, she released a warm, golden glow from the wand that enveloped Briar.

Briar felt the warmth spread through her body, a soothing sensation that seemed to chase away the cold tendrils of weakness. She tried to stand without any support, but her knees buckled. Before she could collapse, the yellow fairy and Leon caught her.

"It didn't work on her, sister," said the yellow fairy, her eyes clouded with concern.

"You mean you can't heal her?" Leon demanded, his voice rising in anger.

"Our sister Viviana is the best healing fairy," said the yellow fairy. "She will heal the princess."

"Let's go to her place," suggested the blue fairy.

"Wait," Leon said, his tone skeptical. "Why should we trust you? Who are you?"

"I'm Evalina," said the blue fairy.

"And I'm Lilliana," added the yellow fairy. "We are daughters of Viatrix. Unfortunately, Rex is our brother."

"Viatrix," Briar gasped, her breath catching as she tried to push away the unexpected wave of drowsiness that swept over her. "I need to see her."

"Sure, we will take you to mother," Evalina promised. "But first, let's treat you."

"Sure, we will take you to Mother, but first let's treat you," said Evalina.

Briar nodded, too weak to argue. She leaned on Leon as they followed the sisters through the village. The village was bigger than Briar had assumed. Thankfully, most of the village hadn't caught fire. As they walked by, the fairies stared at Briar and Leon in astonishment but remained silent since Evalina and Lillian were accompanying them.

"We're almost there," Lilliana said. As they approached, Briar saw a small castle nestled on the outskirts of the village. The castle's towers soared into the sky, each one topped with a vibrant red flag adorned with golden fairy wings. A massive stone wall encircled the castle, and fairy guards, armed with spears, patrolled carefully.

The guards at the gate gawked at Briar and Leon, their expressions a mix of curiosity and wariness. However, they said nothing and allowed them entry as Evalina commanded. The fairies led them through the gate and into a large, lush garden behind the castle. A clear pond shimmered in the center, reflecting the deep blue sky above.

As they stepped into the garden, Briar was overwhelmed by the fragrance of a myriad of herbs and flowers. The scents of lavender, basil, rosemary, sage, ginger, and thyme mingled in the air, creating a soothing, aromatic atmosphere. Briar noticed several herbs she couldn't identify, their colors and shapes as vivid and enchanting as the flowers of the enchanted garden. However, they seemed like they wouldn't attack Briar. But she couldn't be sure, so she kept her distance from the plants.

"Look, that's Viviana, our little sister," Lilliana said, pointing towards a fairy seated on the ground with her back turned. Viviana hummed softly to herself as she carefully dug a tiny hole in the soil and planted a seed.

Evalina approached her with a smile. "Hey, Viviana."

Viviana continued to hum, lost in her own world, her head bobbing up and down with the rhythm of her song.

"Viviana!" Lilliana called louder.

Startled, Viviana stopped humming and turned to look at her sisters. "Oh, Evalina, Lilliana!" she exclaimed, standing up and wiping her dirty hands on her gown. She shared the same delicate facial features and amber eyes as her sisters, but her short, dark hair set her apart. She appeared younger, with a sense of innocence and curiosity that seemed to radiate from her.

Her eyes widened as she noticed Briar and Leon. "Where did you find the humans? Who are they?"

"That's Sleeping Beauty and Prince Charming," Lilliana said.

Viviana let out a small yelp. "What?"

Evalina quickly recounted the events that had transpired, describing how Rex had cast a life-draining spell on Briar. "I tried to heal her, but the spell seemed too powerful," Evalina explained.

Viviana's expression softened as she turned to Briar, offering a reassuring smile. "Don't worry, princess. I'll fix it soon. Come with me."

Viviana guided them to a dome-shaped glass house at the end of the garden, nearly enveloped in thick ivy. The house was dotted with several windows and a circular door. The ivy clung to the structure like a protective embrace, and tiny flowers peeked through the greenery, adding splashes of color to the glass walls.

"This way," Viviana said softly as she produced a small, ornate key from her pocket. She slid it into the lock and twisted it with a satisfying click. The door creaked open, revealing the interior.

Inside, the room was spacious, adorned with plants that seemed to breathe life into the very air. Vines climbed up the walls, twisting and turning like serpentine guardians, while unusual flowers bloomed from every surface, their petals glowing faintly with an ethereal light. The air was thick with the heady scent of blooming flora and the subtle undertone of damp earth.

Viviana led Briar to a wooden bench near a large, round window that offered a charming view of the garden outside. "Please, have a seat," she said.

Briar hesitated for a moment, her gaze sweeping over the plants that surrounded her. She couldn't shake the memory of the flowers in the enchanted garden. But there was a calmness in Viviana's demeanor that made her want to trust the fairy. Taking a deep breath, she sat down.

"Let me see," Viviana said, taking Briar's hand. Her fingers were cool and soothing. She examined Briar's hand for a moment, her brow furrowing slightly before she gently released it.

"How bad is it?" Lilliana asked anxiously. She kept casting worried glances at her sister and Briar.

Viviana sighed. "It's bad," she admitted, reaching into her pocket and pulling out a slender wand. "But don't worry, it's nothing my plants can't heal."

Briar's heart pounded in her chest as Viviana placed the wand on her head. A faint warmth spread from the point of contact, radiating down her spine. "Stay still," Viviana said softly.

The fairy then lifted the wand and aimed it at the ceiling. Long, green ivies began to unravel and slither downwards like living tendrils. When the ivies touched her skin, Briar screamed and sprang from her seat, knocking over a few flower pots in her haste. Soil and shards of pottery scattered across the floor, and the room was filled with the earthy scent of uprooted plants.

"What happened?" Viviana asked, rushing to Briar's side.

Briar took a deep, shuddering breath, her cheeks flushing with embarrassment. The fear she felt in the enchanted garden had surged back to the surface. "I'm sorry," she said, her voice trembling. "It's just that I don't like magical plants. They... they remind me of those awful plants in the enchanted garden."

Viviana's expression softened. "Don't worry," she said, placing a comforting hand on Briar's shoulder. "These plants are here to help, not harm. I promise they won't hurt you."

Briar returned to the bench and allowed the ivies to coil gently around her hands.

Next, Viviana dropped few roots in a glass of water and handed it to Briar. "Drink this," the fairy said.

Briar hesitated, staring at the glass. The scent alone was enough to make her stomach churn, but she knew she had no choice. She pinched her nose and gulped down the liquid, grimacing as the bitterness hit her tongue.

"Good," Viviana said. "It will help to cleanse the toxins from your body. Just give it some time, and you'll start to feel better."

Briar nodded, her eyes watering from the bitterness of the drink. Despite the taste, she could feel a warmth spreading through her, a sign that the potion was beginning to work.

Viviana turned her attention to Leon. "Are you hurt?" she asked.

Leon shook his head, though he looked wary. "No, I'm fine," he said. "But... does your plant also eat humans?"

Viviana's eyes widened in surprise. "No," she said quickly. "These plants are meant to heal, not harm."

"The enchanted garden tried to eat us," he said.

Viviana gasped, her hand flying to her mouth. "You were attacked by the garden?" she asked.

"Yes," Briar confirmed, her voice shaky. The memories of the garden's thorny tendrils and carnivorous plants still haunted her.

"I'm surprised you are alive," Evalina said. "Those plants have been known to consume even fairies."

Leon nodded grimly. "The river tried to drown Briar as well."

"What?" Lilliana exclaimed, putting a hand on her forehead. "Princess, you are incredibly lucky to have survived."

Briar shuddered at the recollection and then remembered something unsettling. "I saw my reflections in the river," she said, her voice low. "Can they predict the future?"

"Rubbish," Viviana said, shaking her head. "The reflections you saw were the water hunters, nasty creatures. They can't predict the future, but they can mimic your form. They read your thoughts and use them against you, luring you into the water to steal your soul. Never get close to them again."

"Did they predict something for you?" Evalina asked, her eyes narrowing with suspicion.

"No," Briar lied, her voice firm despite the fear gnawing at her insides.

"Anyone want fresh pineapple juice?" Viviana asked, attempting to lighten the mood.

"Yes, please," Leon said eagerly, rubbing his throat. "Running from your bloodthirsty brother and his army has worn me out."

Viviana chuckled and disappeared for a moment, returning with five glasses of golden pineapple juice.

"Here you go," Viviana said, handing out the glasses. Briar took hers gratefully, savoring the sweet, refreshing taste that washed away the remnants of the bitter potion.

"This place is not safe for humans, especially ones as young as you two," Evalina said. "Why did you come here?"

"We need Viatrix's help," Briar said between sips. The sweetness of the juice was like a blessing, lifting her spirits.

"Mother's help?" Evalina echoed, her eyes narrowing in confusion. "Why?"

"To break the Curse of Thorns," Briar said. "We need the Book of Curses from your library."

"Curse?" Evalina's face darkened, and her sisters exchanged worried glances. The atmosphere in the room grew tense, the earlier warmth replaced by an icy chill.

Briar and Leon took turns explaining everything about the Wicked Fairy and the Curse of Thorns. They spoke of the suffering in Briar's kingdom, the fear that gripped the people, and the urgency to find a solution before it was too late.

The fairies were too stunned to speak, their faces a mixture of shock and anger. Finally, Lilliana broke the silence, her voice trembling with rage. "She cursed you again? Wasn't the sleeping curse enough? Hasn't she already caused enough havoc? Wasn't she satisfied with banishing us from our home?" Lilliana's eyes blazed with fury, and she looked like she could curse someone on the spot.

"It seems like she's vowed to bring mother shame forever," Evalina said coldly. Her eyes were hard, and she clenched her fists. "It revolts me to say she is our sister."

Briar's eyes widened in shock. "Sister?" she asked. "The Wicked Fairy is your sister?" The revelation was almost too much to grasp. She couldn't believe that the Wicked Fairy, the source of so much evil, was related to Evalina, Lilliana, and Viviana—the kindest fairies she had ever encountered.

Viviana's eyes filled with tears, which rolled down her smooth cheeks like tiny, glistening pearls. "She's our oldest sister," she said slowly. "The pride of our mother."

"She was," Evalina added grimly, her tone laced with bitterness. "Before she delved into dark magic, cursed an innocent baby girl, and sparked a war with the fairies."

"Because of her, we had to leave our home," Lilliana yelled. "Our Fairyland, our home."

Briar shook her head, still puzzled. "I don't get it," she said.

"Mowena—the Wicked Fairy you know—wasn't always like this," said Evalina, her eyes clouding with painful memories. "She was incredibly intelligent and ambitious. She aspired to become the next fairy queen. In Fairyland, when a queen retires, she and the elder fairies choose the next fairy queen. A deserving, capable fairy who possesses all the qualities of a ruler and passes all the trials."

"And Mowena was one of the contenders," Lilliana added. "She made it to the final round but failed the last test. Tara completed the final ritual and became the fairy queen."

"Because Tara deserved it," Viviana said. "She was more talented than Mowena and had all the qualities of a true queen."

Evalina shook her head, a sad smile playing on her lips. "Mowena couldn't accept it. She was furious. She believed she had been deceived and couldn't come to terms with the fact that she wasn't worthy of being queen. She thought if she read all the books and gained more knowledge, she could change the minds of the elder fairies. Mother, unable to bear her suffering, gave her full access to the magic library."

"A grave mistake," Lilliana said. She looked as though she wished she could turn back time and change everything.

"What we didn't know was that she wasn't just gaining knowledge," Viviana said, her voice trembling. "She was learning dark magic—the forbidden kind." She shuddered as if the very mention of it chilled her to the bone.

"After mastering dark magic, Mowena went to the fairy queen and challenged her to a duel," Evalina continued. "And of course, the fairy queen won. Mowena fled, only to show up at your christening and curse you. She did it just to prove her power, to show the world she was not to be trifled with."

"And then she launched an attack on Fairyland," Evalina said. "She took the lives of countless fairies."

Lilliana's eyes filled with tears of rage and sorrow. "The war between the fairy queen and Mowena went on for months. Many lives were lost. Eventually, the fairy queen managed to capture Mowena, but she escaped."

"The fairies blamed our mother for opening the library to Mowena," Evalina said. "They believed we were aiding her. In their anger and fear, they banished us from Fairyland. Mother accepted their decision, and our family and supporters followed us into exile. Because of Mowena, the whole world views us with suspicion and hate."

Viviana sobbed, burying her face in her sister's shoulder. "Those were dark times," she said through her tears. "The hate, the accusations—it was unbearable."

Briar felt a deep pang of empathy for the fairies. She knew all too well the pain of being hated for something beyond her control.

"We finally found refuge in the Midnight Forest," Lilliana said, her voice cracking with bitterness. "Living like monsters, hiding from the world."

"Mother was deeply wounded by it all," Evalina added, her eyes reflecting the same deep sorrow. "She couldn't bear the shame that Mowena, once her pride and joy, had brought upon us. She closed the library and vowed never to open it again."

Briar's heart sank. "Closed the library?" she asked, feeling the glimmer of hope slipping away.

Evalina nodded sadly. "Yes, Princess," she said. "She will never open it again."

CHAPTER 11

B riar's voice cracked as she tried to form the words, "She won't help me?"

"She will," Lilliana said with a reassuring firmness. "She will, princess. She absolutely will. We stand by your side." The fairy glanced at her sisters, who nodded in agreement.

Viviana moved to the window, her eyes searching the horizon. "Mother must have come back," she said.

"Let's go," Lilliana said, turning purposefully towards the door. "It's time to fix everything."

"Wait," Viviana said. "Let me help the princess first."

Viviana approached Briar, who was still entangled by the plants. The plants clung to her like stubborn serpents, their tendrils refusing to release their grip. With a wave of her wand, Viviana murmured a few words under her breath. The ivies loosened their hold, slithering back up to the ceiling.

"Do you feel better now?" Viviana asked.

"Yes," Briar replied. "Thank you." She stood without assistance, feeling a surge of strength flow back into her limbs.

Suddenly, the door burst open, and Rex stormed into the room.

"Mother, the spies!" he bellowed, his eyes narrowing as he pointed accusingly at Briar and Leon. "They attacked our land!"

A wise-looking fairy followed him into the room. She wore a dark green gown that seemed to shimmer with the essence of the forest. In her hand, she held a long wand encrusted with dazzling crystals that caught the light and reflected it in a kaleidoscope of colors. Her sharp, regal features mirrored Lilliana's, while her long blue hair, elegantly braided, resembled Evalina's. Her amber eyes, identical to her children's, sparkled with an ancient, formidable power.

Rex and his mother were accompanied by four fairy guards, each armed with spears.

"No, they didn't attack," Lilliana said defensively. "He attacked them. He hit a human with a life-draining spell."

"They are not some spy," Evalina added. "She is Sleeping Beauty, and the boy is Prince Charming."

Rex's mouth fell open in shock, his expression twisting into one of intense loathing. "That explains everything. They've come for revenge!" he shouted. "We should kill them now!"

"You can't lay a finger on them," Lilliana shot back, stepping protectively in front of Briar and raising her wand threateningly toward her brother.

"Enough," Viatrix's voice cut through the tension. Her children immediately quieted under her stern gaze. "I'll find out why they're here on my own." She walked closer to Briar. "Sleeping Beauty," Viatrix spoke softly. "Who sent you here?"

Caught off guard by the commanding aura emanating from Viatrix, Briar found herself momentarily speechless. Summoning her courage, Briar turned her gaze back to Viatrix. "No one. I came here because I want to meet you."

"Why?" the fairy asked.

"I... I want your help," Briar stammered, her voice trembling slightly under the weight of Viatrix's piercing gaze.

"Isn't the fairy queen aiding you?" Viatrix's tone was as cold as a winter breeze.

"The fairy queen cannot help us," Briar explained, her voice gaining strength as she spoke. She glanced at Lilliana and Evalina, who nodded encouragingly. "My kingdom is suffering from the Curse of Thorns, and only you possess the power to help me break it."

"Cursed!" Viatrix's eyes widened, and a flicker of something akin to fear flashed across her face. "Who cast this curse upon your kingdom?"

Briar didn't know how to answer the question without hurting the fairy's feelings.

"Who did this?" Viatrix's voice grew sharper.

"The Wicked Fairy," Briar blurted out.

The color drained from Viatrix's face, leaving her ashen. The room fell into a heavy silence, the tension thick enough to cut with a knife.

"Mother," Evalina stepped forward cautiously. "Are you okay?"

Viatrix blinked, as if awakening from a nightmare. She straightened herself, her expression hardening into an unreadable mask. "Yes," she replied curtly.

"Well," Lilliana said. "The princess needs our help to clear the mess, Mowena —" She stopped abruptly as Evalina and Viviana shot her warning glares. "I mean, we have to help her."

Rex, who had been simmering with barely restrained rage, finally exploded. "Are you serious?" he snapped. "You're asking our mother to help the enemy?"

The three sisters ignored Rex's outburst and closed around their mother.

"And mother, isn't it amazing?" Viviana said sweetly. "The ritual to break the curse is in your library."

Viatrix stood silent, her gaze distant as she stared through the circular window. For a moment, it seemed as though she was lost in contemplation, perhaps counting the leaves of a tree swaying in the breeze. After a prolonged silence, she turned her attention back to her daughters, her expression resolute. "No," she declared firmly. "I can't give you the ritual. I have closed off the library permanently and vowed never to enter it again."

Viatrix's words struck Briar like a blow. The princess's eyes widened in disbelief. "What?"

"You can't say no!" Leon said.

Ignoring the pleas, Viatrix turned to the guards. "Escort the children safely out of our village."

The guards seized Briar by the arms. As they began to drag her towards the door, the reality of the situation crashed down on Briar like a wave. Viatrix was not just denying her request. She was banishing her from the village, tearing her away from her last hope of saving her kingdom and her father.

"Please!" Briar cried out, struggling against the guards' hold. "You can't do this! My people need me!"

Briar wrestled free from the guards' grip, her heart pounding wildly as she bolted towards Viatrix. "You have to help us," she pleaded, her voice cracking with anguish. "You are our only hope. Please, please!"

Lilliana stepped closer to Briar. "What's wrong with you mother? How hard is it for you to give them the ritual?"

Viatrix's eyes flashed with anger, and she clenched her jaw tightly. "What part of 'I've closed the library' do you not understand?"

"But you can open it," Lilliana said, her voice rising in pitch. "The world will not end if you do."

Viatrix's expression hardened. "I don't want to be involved with humans," she declared. "It never ends well."

"Mother, we are already involved. We caused the problem." Evalina said.

Rex crossed his arms defiantly. "Mother, we don't need to help the humans," he said. "We didn't tell Mowena to go and curse them."

"You shut up," Lilliana snapped, her eyes blazing with fury. Her patience had clearly worn thin, and her usually gentle demeanor was replaced with a fiery determination.

Viatrix held up a hand. "No more arguments," she said sternly. "Guards, take the humans away."

"I will not let that happen." Lilliana stepped in front of the guards, her eyes challenging them to come closer.

Viatrix raised her wand. "Lilliana, move aside or I will command the guards to take you as well."

"I don't care if you throw me away," Lilliana yelled. Tears streamed down her cheeks. "This place is not home, and we get kicked out of our home because of you." Her words hung in the air, heavy with years of pent-up resentment.

Viatrix's face paled as if she had been struck. Her eyes widened a look of shock and hurt crossing her features. "Are you blaming me?"

"Yes!" Lilliana's voice rang out, echoing through the room like a thunderclap. "You've always been on Mowena's side. You even defended her dark magic. And now, see what she's done." Her voice grew louder, filled with a mixture of pain and anger. "We have no place to call home and no one respects us. Everyone despises us because of you and your wicked daughter." Lilliana's chest heaved with a heavy breath. The weight of her words finally released.

"Lilliana is right," Viviana said. She turned away as Viatrix tried to meet her eyes.

"I had no idea you felt that way about me," she whispered, her eyes shimmering with unshed tears.

"Mother," Evalina said calmly. "All we are saying is that it is also our responsibility to help the princess. We have a chance to make everything right. You can't turn your back on this responsibility."

"I'm not turning my back on anything," Viatrix said.

"Yes, you are," Evalina said. "The world will laugh at us if we refuse to help the princess. They already think we are with Mowena. If you don't give Briar the book, you'll prove them right. You'll show them that we are truly evil."

Viatrix's eyes darkened, her expression turning colder as she turned to leave. "I am not concerned with the world's opinion," she said.

"But we do!" Lilliana cried, rushing to block her mother's path. "We can't tolerate being treated like monsters simply because of your wicked daughter. And just because you taught her dark magic."

Perhaps Lilliana had said too much. Everyone in the room gasped, including the guards.

"I DIDN'T TEACH HER DARK MAGIC!" Viatrix roared, her voice shaking with fury. The walls seemed to reverberate with her words, and the temperature in the room felt like it had dropped several degrees.

"Okay, I'm sorry," said Lilliana, lowering her gaze. "But please, I beg of you, help the princess and her kingdom."

"Stop manipulating mother," Rex said as he walked over to Viatrix and took her hand. "Don't listen to them. I stand by your side. I know we should never help humans. They are with the fairy queen."

"Mother, this forest is not our home," Evalina said, her voice softer but filled with a deep longing. "We don't belong among these creatures. Our very existence is meaningless without Fairyland."

Viviana, her eyes brimming with tears, stepped forward. "We long for our home, mother," she sobbed. "Everyone feels the same way. We've been pretending not to care for a long time, but we can't anymore. We stayed silent because we love and respect you. But a fairy is nothing without Fairyland."

"Our safety is gone in this forest," Evalina continued. "Each day brings a fresh attack, each day we risk being kidnapped for our power. We want the safety of our home, the safety of Fairyland."

"Are we going to pass this cursed life onto our future generations?" Lilliana asked.

Viatrix stood like a statue, her face unreadable.

"We are tired of being seen as monsters," Lilliana continued. "It's not fair. Why are we being blamed? Why should the princess and her kingdom suffer because of us?"

"Mother," Evalina said, stepping closer to Viatrix, her eyes pleading. "The fairies blamed us for something we never did, and now we are blaming humans for something they never did. Humans are the victims here. Think of the innocent children mother. You love children."

Viatrix's face softened at the mention of children, a flicker of pain passing through her eyes.

"Mother, we can show the world that we care for humans," Viviana said. "We have kindness and goodwill in our hearts. The fairy queen must see that we deserve our place back in Fairyland, where we belong."

"Mother, please," the three sisters pleaded in unison. "Please, we beg you. Open the library. Give us the book."

Viatrix glanced around, unsure of what to do.

"Let's decide by voting," Lilliana suggested suddenly.

"What?" Rex spat, his face contorted with rage. "That's stupid! Mother, don't listen to them. They're manipulating you."

Viatrix looked conflicted, her brow furrowing as she considered her children's words. Her eyes darted between Lilliana's determined face and Rex's angry one.

"I am in favor of helping the princess," Lilliana said firmly, locking eyes with Briar. She stood tall and raised her hand high.

"Me too," Evalina chimed in. She glanced at Briar with a gentle smile before raising her hand.

"I want to help her," Viviana added softly, her hand rising to join her sisters'.

"No!" Rex bellowed, throwing both hands up in the air in exasperation. "I'm in favor of killing them."

Lilliana turned to the guards, her eyes pleading. "Your opinion counts as well. You are more than welcome to vote."

The guards shifted uncomfortably, glancing at each other in uncertainty. One guard, a tall fairy with a stern face, seemed to be thinking hard. He finally stepped forward and raised his hand. "Help the princess and her kingdom. We love helping," he said.

Encouraged by the first guard's bravery, the other guards followed suit. One by one, they raised their hands, their voices a chorus of support. "Help the humans," they said.

Briar's heart raced with hope. She knew the final decision rested with Viatrix. The room fell silent once more, all eyes turning towards the fairy. Briar's breath hitched in her throat, her fate hanging on the edge of Viatrix's decision.

Viatrix's gaze lingered on her daughters, their hands still raised in a silent plea. She looked around the room, taking in the hopeful expressions of her children and the guards. Her eyes met Briar's, and for a moment, the room seemed to hold its breath.

With a slow, deliberate motion, Viatrix raised her palm. The gesture seemed to hold the weight of the world. She took a deep breath, her voice trembling slightly as she spoke. "Fine," she said. "I'll give them the book."

A cheer erupted from Lilliana. "Yes!" she exclaimed, her face lighting up with a triumphant smile.

Briar's eyes filled with tears of gratitude. She stepped forward, her voice trembling with emotion. "Thank you," she cried. "Thank you so much. You've saved my kingdom, and I am forever in your debt.

CHAPTER 12

Suddenly, a golden key materialized in Viatrix's hand. The key seemed to radiate a soft, golden glow, casting a warm shimmer across the room. The fairy queen stared at the key.

"Mother," Evalina said softly, stepping forward. She extended her hand toward the key.

Viatrix's face was unfathomable as she placed the key in Evalina's hand without uttering a single word.

Evalina's face broke into a wide grin. "Thank you, mother," she said. Her fingers closed around the key, holding it as if it were a precious gem. Viviana smiled too, her cheeks wet with the remnants of tears, wiping them away with the back of her hand.

The room erupted into cheers and applause. All except for Rex, who stood apart, his arms crossed and his face set in a scowl.

"I'll be right back," Evalina said, nodding at Briar with a broad smile. She turned and quickly exited the room.

Leon turned to Briar with a wide grin. "Finally!" he exclaimed. "For a minute there, I thought we were doomed."

"Me too," Briar admitted. She felt an overwhelming sense of happiness welling up inside her. It was as if she had walked to the very edge of despair and then been pulled back into the light.

After what seemed like an eternity, Evalina returned, carrying an enormous book with a dark velvet cover. The book was ancient, its surface adorned with mysterious symbols and inscriptions in a language Briar didn't recognize. The dark velvet seemed to absorb the light, giving the book an aura of gravity.

Evalina approached Viatrix and handed the book over to her. Viatrix took it with a trembling hand, her eyes reflecting a flurry of emotions. Her fingers traced the contours of the symbols.

Briar's heart pounded in her chest. She prayed silently, her fingers digging into her palms. Please, don't change your mind. The fate of my kingdom rests in your hands.

Finally, Viatrix tore her gaze away from the book. Her eyes met Briar's, and for a moment, they seemed to soften. She took a step forward and handed the book to Briar.

"I hope you remember this help," Viatrix said, her voice firm.

Briar clutched the book to her chest. "I will. I promise," she said.

With a nod, Viatrix turned and left the room, her footsteps echoing softly. Rex shot them a final sneer, his face twisted in disdain before he followed his mother.

Lilliana and Viviana hugged each other tightly, their faces lighting up with happiness.

"At last, mother has made the correct choice," Lilliana said. She looked as though a heavy burden had been lifted from her shoulders.

"Mother is not heartless," Evalina said. "She may have turned cold, but she is not evil."

Briar turned to the three sisters, her eyes filled with tears of gratitude. "Thank you," she said. "If it were not for all of you, I wouldn't have gotten the book."

Lilliana smiled warmly at Briar. "You deserve it," she said.

Viviana clapped her hands together. "Well, are you going to look at the ritual or just stare at the book?" she asked playfully.

Briar felt a rush of excitement as she looked down at the ancient book in her hands. Taking a deep breath, she opened the book. She gasped. The silver pages of the book were empty. "There is nothing written here."

The fairies exchanged knowing glances before bursting into laughter.

"The rituals are right here, but as a human, you cannot see them," Evalina explained.

She took the book from Briar and tapped it gently with her wand. Instantly, crimson letters began to materialize on the previously blank pages, swirling and twisting into intricate patterns and symbols. The room seemed to hum with a faint, mystical energy as the ancient magic awakened.

Evalina flipped through the pages, her fingers gliding over the delicate parchment until she found what she was looking for. "The ritual for breaking the Curse of Thorns," she announced.

Briar leaned in to get a closer look. The page was filled with strange markings and cryptic runes that looked more like art than any language she could comprehend. The symbols seemed to dance on the page, their meaning just out of reach.

Viviana nervously bit her lip as she peered at the book. Her eyes darted back and forth. "What is written in it?" she asked.

Evalina began to read aloud. "To break the Curse of Thorns, one must embark on a quest to gather four essential magical items. The first item is the Ancient Book of Spells, a tome written by the ancient fairies themselves. The second item required for the ritual is the precious gold of a dragon. The third item is the mermaid flower, a delicate blossom that can only be found in the depths of the ocean. And finally, the last and most crucial item is a vial filled with the blood of a fairy godmother." She paused, looking up at the group, her eyes grave. "Once you have gathered these magical items, bring them to the sacred fairy shrine. It is there, under the moon's gentle rays, that the sacred circle will be illuminated with a divine energy. Arrange the items in the center. Place your hand on top. From the depths of your heart, you must summon the magic. As you do so, a powerful surge of energy will emanate from the items, ultimately breaking the curse," Evalina finished, closing the book with a soft thud.

"I hate things that involve blood," Viviana muttered, wrinkling her nose in disgust.

"Especially a fairy's blood," added Lilliana, her face contorting with a look of distaste.

Evalina, however, remained unfazed. "Anyway, princess," she said, turning to Briar with a reassuring smile, "you just have to collect four magical objects. Nothing you can't handle."

Briar's face fell. "And I don't even know what most of these magical items are," she admitted. She had believed that obtaining the ritual would solve her problems, but it appeared that her journey had only just begun. Time was running out—she had only three days left before her birthday, the deadline for breaking the curse.

Briar turned to Leon, hoping to find a reassuring smile or a spark of confidence in his eyes. But she saw only uncertainty. The prince scratched his head. "I'm just as clueless as you are," Leon admitted. "But I can help with the dragon."

"Why do you think we're here?" Lilliana grinned, her wings fluttering gently behind her. She took the book from Evalina's hands and began to scan the pages, her eyes flashing over the intricate script. "So, the first thing you need is the Ancient Book of Spells, which can be found here. The second magical item is the dragon's gold. That might be a bit more challenging," she said, her tone becoming serious.

Viviana nodded in agreement, her eyes wide with concern. "Dragons are obsessed with gold and treasure," she explained. "They hoard it in their lairs, deep within the caves of mountains. They guard their treasures with immense power, and many brave warriors have lost their lives trying to retrieve even a single coin."

Briar's heart sank at Viviana's words. "So, can't we get the gold?" she asked. The last thing she needed was for one of the essential items to be impossible to obtain.

"You can," Lilliana said. "My sister is just making it sound more complicated than it is."

Leon's eyes lit up with excitement. "I love fighting dragons!" he exclaimed, his enthusiasm causing Briar to glance at him in alarm.

Evalina shook her head, her expression stern. "Don't make that mistake. No matter how powerful you think you are, avoid dueling with dragons," she warned. "Dragons are wise and mystical creatures. They possess ancient knowledge and immense strength. But if you approach them with respect and ask them nicely, they might just help you."

"Mark that, Leon," Briar said. She turned back to the fairies. "But where can we find a dragon and his gold?"

"A dragon lives at the peak of the highest mountain in the forest," Lilliana said, pointing towards the east.

"Which mountain?" Leon asked. "This forest is full of mountains."

"I could point it out if only I had a map," Lilliana replied, looking over at Viviana.

"I have one," Leon said, pulling the rolled-up parchment from his pocket and handing it to Lilliana.

"That's perfect," Lilliana said, studying the map. Her finger traced a path through the forest until it stopped at the largest mountain on the eastern side. "There. This is the dragon's mountain," she said, tapping the peak.

Leon sighed. "And we have one problem," he said. "It's going to take us days to climb that mountain on foot. Even if I had my horse, it would take more than four days to reach the peak."

Evalina nodded in agreement. "Even with a horse, the journey would be long and arduous. The terrain is treacherous, and the higher you go, the colder it gets."

Briar's face fell. "What are we going to do?"

"Don't worry," Lilliana said with a mischievous grin. She waved her wand, and a red carpet with golden tassels materialized in the air, hovering just above the ground. The carpet shuddered as if waking from a deep slumber, then suddenly sprang to life, zooming around the room with a burst of energy. It knocked over a vase of flowers and sent a stack of books tumbling to the floor, causing everyone to duck in surprise.

Lilliana's hand shot up, and she grabbed the carpet. "This is my magic carpet. It can take you anywhere you want to go," she said, stepping onto the carpet with a flourish. "Fly," she commanded.

Instantly, the carpet rose into the air, gliding around the room with a smooth, almost playful grace. It circled the chandelier and swooped low over the table, sending papers fluttering in its wake. "Land," Lilliana said, and the carpet obediently descended to the ground, coming to rest gently at her feet. "This is how you use it."

Leon clapped his hands in delight. "Incredible! This is even better than a horse," he said.

Lilliana carefully folded the carpet and presented it to Briar with a smile. "You can keep it until your quest is finished. It will get you to the mountaintop in no time."

"Thank you," Briar said. The prospect of facing the dragon seemed less daunting now that they had a means of reaching the mountain quickly.

"So, the next magical object is the mermaid flower," Evalina said. "A flower that grows deep in the ocean, in the gardens of the merfolk."

"Can the carpet also swim in the sea?" Leon asked, a note of excitement in his voice.

"You don't have to go under the sea," Evalina answered. "A mermaid brought the flower from the sea and planted it on an island in the Southern Sea."

Briar's gaze fixated on the map, where the Southern Sea sprawled across the southern region in a vast expanse of deep blue. Tiny brown dots peppered the map, representing countless islands scattered like freckles on the face of the sea. "There are so many islands," Briar said, feeling overwhelmed as she took in the multitude of landforms. "How will we ever find the right one?"

Evalina smiled, her eyes twinkling. "Just look for the islands covered with cherry blossoms," she said, her finger delicately tracing a path on the map. "You'll see them easily from the sky, a splash of pink in the endless green of the sea."

"How long will it take us to get there?" Briar asked, her heart pounding with anticipation.

Evalina glanced at the map again, her eyes darting from the dragon's mountain to the Southern Sea. She counted on her fingers, her lips moving silently as she made her calculations. "It should take you about four hours on the magic carpet to go from the mountain to the sea," she concluded.

Briar breathed a sigh of relief.

"What about the fairy godmother's blood?" Leon asked, his brow furrowing with concern. "Do you think she'll be willing to give it to us?"

Lilliana's face lit up with a knowing smile. "Yes, she's quite helpful, unlike my mother," she said.

Evalina shot her sister an angry look. "Lilliana, you know mother is not an awful fairy."

"Yeah, yeah. She has a good heart," Lilliana replied, rolling her eyes. "But what does it matter if we can't see what's inside her?"

Evalina's expression hardened, her lips pressing into a thin line.

"You know I'm just joking," Lilliana said, a mischievous grin spreading across her face. "Mother has been sulky ever since Mowena's betrayal. She has all of us, even that fool Rex, but she behaves like she's childless. I don't understand why all her favorite children turn out evil. Look at Rex!"

"And the fairy shrine," Briar asked, pulling the fairy's attention back to the ritual.

"The fairy shrine is in Fairyland. It's a sacred place for fairies and is well known. You won't have any trouble finding it." Lilliana closed the book with a decisive snap. "So, there you have it, princess. Your problem is solved."

Briar nodded, repeating the names of the magical items under her breath until they were etched into her memory. She needed the Ancient Book of Spells, dragon's gold, the mermaid flower, and the fairy godmother's blood. She glanced at Leon, who gave her an encouraging nod.

"And the Ancient Book of Spells," Briar said. "Will your mother give us the book?"

"I'll talk to her," Lilliana said, her voice brimming with confidence. "If she's opened the library, why not help you properly? She has a reputation to clear."

Evalina's expression turned somber. "Mother can't give you the book," she said.

"Why not?" Lilliana asked.

Evalina looked at her sister, a hint of sadness in her eyes. "Did you forget mother traded the book with the witch for a place in the forest?"

Lilliana's eyes widened in shock. "She traded the Ancient Book of Spells? I thought she traded some dark magic book!"

"Mother didn't give the witch a dark magic book," Lilliana said. "Imagine the chaos that could have caused. The witch wanted the Ancient Book of Spells instead."

Lilliana's face twisted in anger. "How could mother trade such a powerful book with a witch?" she demanded, her voice rising.

Evalina tried to reason with her sister. "We needed a place to live," she explained.

"She could have given the witch something else," Lilliana argued, her voice trembling with frustration.

"The witch only wanted the book," Evalina replied.

"Still, mother shouldn't have done it," Lilliana said.

Viviana stepped between her sisters, her hands raised in a gesture of peace. "That's not our biggest concern right now," she said. "How are we going to get the book from the witch?"

"Simple," Lilliana said, her eyes gleaming with mischief. "You have to steal it."

CHAPTER 13

"Are you crazy?" Briar's voice echoed through the room. "I'm not going to steal a magic book from a witch. Stealing from a witch is like signing your death contract."

Lilliana sighed deeply as she crossed her arms over her chest. "Then forget about breaking the curse."

"There has to be another way," Briar insisted. She glanced around the room, hoping for support.

"Like what?" Lilliana placed a hand on her hip, raising an eyebrow skeptically.

"We can ask the witch to give us the book," Briar suggested.

Leon chuckled. "You must have misheard. It's a witch, Briar, not a kind old lady who bakes cookies. Not all witches are as nice as your friend Lavonna."

"That's exactly what I'm saying," Briar said. "Lavonna would probably forgive someone who stole something from her, but maybe this witch is dangerous. We need to handle this carefully."

"Well," Evalina began hesitantly, her wings fluttering slightly. "I don't think there's anything inherently wrong with stealing in this context."

"What?" Briar's jaw dropped in disbelief. She had always seen Evalina as the most level-headed and sensible of the fairies. "I can't believe I'm hearing this from you."

"I mean," Evalina continued, a touch of pink coloring her cheeks. "Stealing is bad, of course. But in this case, you're stealing for a noble cause. The book doesn't even belong to the witch. She has no rightful claim to it."

Briar shook her head, her curls bouncing with the motion. "Listen, the best way—or should I say the safest way, the way that won't get us all killed—is to go to the witch and talk to her."

"Talk to her about what?" Lilliana's eyes narrowed.

"Maybe we can negotiate a deal," Briar suggested. "Witches love trading. Maybe we can trade something with her for the book."

"Trading with a witch? Are you serious?" Evalina's voice was laced with astonishment.

"Why not?" Lilliana's voice dripped with sarcasm as she shot Briar a knowing look. "If you're willing to trade a part of your body, half your age, or maybe even your whole life. Or worse things you can't even imagine. I've got plenty of horror stories about trading with witches."

"Include ours," Viviana added, her voice somber. "Mother had to give the witch the Ancient Book of Spells. You can't win against a witch."

Briar bit her lip, the fairies' words weighing heavily on her. Deep down, she knew they were right. The tales of witches and their dark bargains were enough to make anyone think twice.

"Look, stealing is not that difficult," Leon said, his eyes gleaming with a mischievous light. "We'll break into her house, get the book, and leave. No problem. No trading our lives or anything." It was clear that he was with the fairies on this one. Leon always chose the side where there was trouble.

"Princess, do you want to save your kingdom or not?" Lilliana asked.

"Of course, I do," Briar replied. "I'm willing to do whatever it takes to protect my kingdom."

"Except get a book from a witch," Leon taunted.

Briar felt a surge of anger, Leon's words hitting her like a punch to the gut. "I'm not scared," she shot back.

"Yeah, we can see that," Leon said, a smirk playing on his lips. "I don't know about you, but I will get that book."

"You know what? Let's vote," Lilliana suggested, raising her hand high. "I'm in favor of breaking into the witch's house and taking what belongs to us."

Leon eagerly raised his hand, not missing a beat. "I agree."

Lilliana turned to Evalina. "What about you?"

Evalina hesitated, glancing between her sisters and Briar. "Well," she said slowly, raising her hand. "It's the right thing to do. Steal the book."

Briar felt a pang of disappointment at Evalina's response. She had hoped for support, but Evalina's vote made it clear where she stood. Briar turned to Viviana.

Viviana bit her lip, her eyes darting nervously around the room. After a moment of hesitation, she raised her hand. "Steal the book," she whispered.

Leon's face lit up with excitement. "You lost," he said triumphantly, looking at Briar. "You have to do it."

Briar shook her head, her mind racing. "I don't know if we should..."

Leon's face darkened, and he turned to the fairies. "Take me to the witch's house. I'll steal the book."

Briar's heart pounded in her chest. She knew Leon was a magnet for trouble. The thought of him inside a witch's house, meddling with magic and danger, made her shudder.

"Alright," she said, letting out a deep sigh of resignation. "No need to be so dramatic. We'll steal the book."

Lilliana flashed a confident grin at Briar. "I know you're brave."

"Hold on," Briar interjected, a wave of dread washing over her. "What if the witch catches us stealing?"

Lilliana's grin widened, a mischievous glint in her eyes. "She won't. Luckily for us, the witch is currently absent from her home."

Briar's eyebrows shot up in surprise. "How can you be so sure?"

"She happens to be our neighbor," Lilliana explained, leaning in as if to share a juicy secret. "And I enjoy keeping a watchful eye on her. During this season, she goes far away to gather potion ingredients. This is when she's weakest and most vulnerable."

Evalina and Viviana stared at their sister in astonishment.

"Lilliana?" Viviana's voice was laced with accusation. "Have you forgotten what mother warned us about? No snooping around the witch."

Lilliana shrugged nonchalantly, brushing off Viviana's concern. "Relax, Vivi," she said. "Rules are meant to be broken, right?"

"You can't just break the rules," Evalina said.

"You're overreacting, sis," Lilliana replied with a dismissive wave. "I just keep an eye on things from afar, that's all." She turned back to Briar and Leon, her expression brightening. "It's the perfect opportunity for you two, isn't it? It's like fate wants you to have the book."

Briar had a feeling the fairies were pleased with the idea of stealing the book. Yes, the sisters wanted to help Briar, but getting the book from the witch would give them some other kind of satisfaction.

"You can trust me and my research," Lilliana assured, placing a hand on Briar's shoulder.

Briar looked into Lilliana's eyes. "I trust you," she said. The fairies had risked everything, even banishment from their home, just to help her.

"So, our path is clear," Leon said.

"Actually, not so clear," Evalina interrupted, holding up a small, worn leather sack that seemed to appear out of nowhere. She extended it towards Leon, her eyes serious. "Offer this at the witch's door, and it will open for you."

Leon took the sack, his brow furrowing. "What's inside? It's heavy."

"Remember, only open it when you reach the door," Evalina said.

Leon nodded. "Alright."

"There's one more thing," Evalina added, her voice lowering to a conspiratorial whisper. "You might encounter frightening sights near the witch's hut. Don't let them scare you. It's just the witch's illusions meant to ward off unwanted visitors."

"Sounds like the witch does not like company," Briar said.

Lilliana smirked, a playful glint in her eyes. "You have nothing to worry about. The witch is away, and she's not going to return anytime soon. Just be careful of her guardian."

"Guardian?" Briar's eyes widened in surprise. "Great, just what we need! As if a witch wasn't dangerous enough on her own, now we have to deal with a guardian too."

"Relax," Lilliana said, waving off Briar's concern. "Evalina has a solution for that as well."

Evalina extended her hand, and with a gentle flick of her wrist, a small pouch appeared, shimmering faintly. "If the guardian shows up, use this." She handed the pouch to Briar. "You'll be fine."

Briar took the pouch, feeling its soft, mysterious weight in her hand. She tucked it into her satchel, her mind racing with a thousand thoughts. Something about this plan gnawed at her, a persistent doubt that she couldn't shake. But if this was the only way to save her kingdom, she had to see it through.

"The book you're looking for has a red cover adorned with silver moons and stars," Viviana added. "I thought you should know the details to recognize it."

"Thank you, Viviana," Lilliana said. "Those details will help you find the book. Another way to identify it is that when you hold it, you'll feel a surge of magic."

Briar nodded, taking a mental note of every word. "And where exactly does this witch live?" she asked, trying to mask the nervousness in her voice.

"She lives here, in the Midnight Forest," Lilliana replied, pointing to a dark, dense area on the map. "We can show you the path. Go whenever you're ready."

Leon gave a determined nod. "We're ready," he said, turning to Briar for confirmation.

"Yes, we're ready," Briar said. She didn't want to waste any more time overthinking this plan, despite the anxiety gnawing at her insides.

Lilliana clapped her hands together, a spark of excitement in her eyes. "Then let's get going."

They said goodbye to Viviana, who decided to stay in her garden and left the fairy village with Evalina and Lilliana. The forest felt less intimidating with the fairies by their side.

The fairies led Briar and Leon through a maze of trees and underbrush. The forest became denser and more shadowy with each step. The air was thick with the scent of pine and damp earth. The only sounds were the rustling of leaves and the distant hoot of an owl.

After what felt like an eternity of winding paths and looming shadows, Lilliana came to a sudden halt. "This is as far as we can go," she said. "Beyond this point lies the witch's territory. We can't go any further without breaching our border pact."

Briar glanced around, noticing the subtle shift in the atmosphere. The air felt heavier, charged with an unseen energy that sent a shiver down her spine. "This is the border?" she asked, her voice barely a whisper.

Evalina nodded, pointing to a line of ancient gnarled trees that marked the boundary. "Yes, here our territory ends. We have an agreement to respect each other's borders."

Leon's eyes narrowed as he peered into the darkness beyond the border. "We can take it from here," he said.

Evalina gestured towards a narrow, barely visible trail that snaked through the dense underbrush. "Follow this path," she said. "It will lead you to her hut."

"Can't we just fly?" Leon asked. He seemed tempted to unfurl the carpet and take to the skies.

"No!" the fairies cried in unison.

"The magic carpet is our magic," Lilliana said. "If you fly, she will sense it. The witch is attuned to magic in her territory. You can use the carpet once you're clear of her land, but until then, you must remain on foot."

Leon sighed. "Fine, we'll walk."

"Thank you for all your help," Briar said, her voice filled with genuine gratitude. "You've disobeyed your mother to aid me, and I cannot express how much that means."

Lilliana gave a dismissive wave, though her eyes softened. "We're doing what is right," she said.

"Good luck, Princess," Evalina added, her voice warm. Then, with a flutter of wings, the fairies ascended gracefully into the air, their forms disappearing among the trees and leaving a faint trail of sparkling light in their wake.

As they departed, Briar and Leon turned towards the shadowy path ahead. "I can't wait to break into the witch's house," Leon said. Briar rolled her eyes at him. Sometimes the prince was unbelievable. Their life was in danger, and it was only an adventure for him.

They set off, following the direction Evalina had indicated. The trail was narrow and winding, hidden beneath a thick blanket of grass and fallen leaves. Before long, a thick mist began to swirl around them, its ghostly tendrils creeping through the trees and wrapping around their legs. It grew denser with every step, transforming the forest into a shadowy, ethereal maze. Visibility dropped to almost nothing, and they were forced to move slowly, feeling their way forward with outstretched hands.

"This mist is unnatural," Briar said, her voice muffled by the heavy fog. "It's as if the forest itself is trying to deter us."

"Don't worry," Leon said confidently. "We'll find the way."

After what felt like an eternity of wandering through the mist, it began to thin, revealing faint shapes and shadows in the distance. Gradually, the fog lifted, revealing a clearing bathed in an eerie, muted light. At the center of the clearing stood a hut.

"I think that's the witch's hut," Leon said. He pointed to the dark shape looming ahead, its outline gradually coming into focus as the last of the mist dissipated.

As the fog cleared completely, Briar's heart skipped a beat and a cold dread settled over her. The hut was unlike anything she had ever seen. It stood on top of two enormous chicken legs, which twitched and shifted as if the hut were alive. The structure itself was a twisted, ramshackle thing, with crooked walls and a sagging roof, its windows glowing with an unsettling, flickering light. Surrounding the hut was a fence, not of wood or stone, but of human bones and skulls, their empty eyes staring out at the forest with a macabre, eternal gaze.

"Oh no," Briar gasped. "The witch is Baba Yaga."

CHAPTER 14

Briar's mouth went dry. Of all the witch's huts they could have gone to, it had to be the most dangerous one.

Briar remembered the tale of the man who walked into the hut without the witch's consent. Baba Yaga had severed his head and displayed it on her hut wall. People said the head was still there, adorned on the wall.

Briar felt a shiver run down her spine as she imagined her head covered in blood, hanging on Baba Yaga's wall.

She glanced at Leon and was happy to notice his shocked expression. It seemed like he never expected the witch to be Baba Yaga.

"The fairies forgot to tell us that the witch is Baba Yaga," Leon said in disbelief. He momentarily lost his composure as a hero. "What a surprise."

"I don't like this kind of surprise," Briar said. "Are you scared? After all, you are the one who was so eager to steal the book."

"Of course, I'm not scared," he snapped, but the tremor in his voice betrayed his bravado. Briar narrowed her eyes at him and he dropped his hero attitude. "Okay, maybe a little. But what choice do we have? We have to go to the witch's hut, no matter who she is." He cast a worried glance at the hut. "But you don't have to come inside if you're scared. I'll go and get the book."

"How many times do I have to tell you I'm coming?" Briar snapped. "Don't forget, it's my quest, not yours."

She marched toward the hut angrily and did her best not to look at the special fence around it. Who made a fence out of skeletons, anyway? The witch was dangerously creative. Her home decoration would give any guest a heart attack. Perhaps she didn't want any guests at all.

As Briar drew nearer to the hut, she noticed something unsettling. The skulls comprising the bone fence seemed to come to life, one by one, each turning its empty gaze toward her. To her horror, their eye sockets emitted an eerie red glow.

Briar halted in her tracks, her heart racing with fear. "Are those eyes really glowing and the skulls moving, or am I losing my mind?"

"It's true," said the prince. "But Evalina said it's just an illusion."

Ignoring the skull, they moved forward. But before they could advance farther, the ground beneath them began to tremble violently. It felt as though the earth itself was roiling with unseen turmoil. Then, with a spine-chilling screech, a horde of insects, scorpions, and snakes erupted from the soil. Within seconds, the ground was blanketed in a writhing mass of dark creatures, their skittering and slithering filling the air with dread.

With a shriek, Briar bolted back to the spot where they had stood moments ago, her heart pounding like a drum in her chest. She frantically brushed at her legs, even though nothing had touched her body. The insects made her feel like they were crawling under her skin.

Leon joined her, his expression mirrored Briar's shock and repulsion. Even the bravest of heroes was afraid of creepy crawlies.

"What in the world is this?" Briar said.

"An illusion," Leon replied, his gaze fixed on the writhing mass of insects that seemed to multiply by the second.

"Illusion or not, they're revolting," Briar wrinkled her nose in disgust as the insects continued screeching. "And they're everywhere. How are we supposed to reach the hut?"

Leon's eyes lit up with an idea. "The flying carpet," he suggested eagerly. "Let's fly."

Briar grabbed her satchel. "And alert the witch we are here."

Leon's enthusiasm faltered. "Ah, yes," he said. Well... now we have only one way to reach the hut."

"What?"

"Walk above the insects."

"Are you serious?" Briar's eyebrows shot up in disbelief.

Leon nodded. "I know it sounds crazy, but it's our best chance. I'm certain it's just an illusion. If we don't at least try, we'll be stuck here forever. And with each passing moment, those creepy crawlies are multiplying."

"I can't do it," Briar protested, her skin crawling at the mere thought of stepping into the writhing mass below.

"You have to believe me," Leon urged. "Or trust in what the fairies told us. It's just an illusion."

Briar shook her head, torn between fear and determination. "I... I don't know if I can."

"Come on," Leon insisted, already striding towards the insect-covered ground.

Briar followed him, wishing to be anywhere but here.

Leon grabbed her hand. "It will be okay."

Briar only nodded. At this time, she couldn't be positive. She kept her eyes ahead and didn't dare to look down.

As her feet touched the ground, Briar's worst nightmares came to life. The sensation of insects crawling over her skin sent shivers down her spine, and the unexpected touch of a slithering snake only intensified her terror. It was a sensation beyond words, an indescribable horror that gripped her very being.

"Run," Leon yelled.

Briar closed her eyes and ran. She had never run so fast in her life.

As soon as they reached the bone fence, the insects disappeared. Briar looked down at her legs. The snake and all the insects that were clinging to her body and gown vanished with a poof of dark smoke along with a horrible tingling feeling.

"See? I told you it was all an illusion. Just a clever trick by the witch." Leon chuckled. "If it wasn't an illusion, we would have died the second we placed our feet there. The scorpion and snake were poisonous. Few even bit me."

"You were right," Briar nodded, feeling a rush of relief flood through her.

"Let's go. The hut is waiting for us," he said, facing the hut. "What do you think, you chicken legged hut? You are smarter than us."

"I am," a ghostly voice responded from within the depths of the hut.

Briar's grip on Leon tightened. "Did... did the hut just speak?"

Leon's expression mirrored Briar's disbelief. "I must admit, I wasn't expecting that. But if the rumors are true and this hut can walk, then I suppose it can speak as well."

"Children, do not dare to come close," the hut's bark echoed through the air

"It's probably just another trick of the witch. Don't let it distract you." Leon said, calm and collected, "Ignore it."

"How can I ignore it?" she exclaimed. "A talking hut!"

"Concentrate on our mission," Leon urged, leading the way as they crossed the threshold of the bone gate and entered the front yard. "It's just a voice. It can't harm us."

"Will you listen to my warning and retreat peacefully, or shall I remove you forcefully from my territory?" the hut warned.

The princess and prince ignored it and continued walking.

"You brainless children," the hut bellowed. "Prepare to face the consequences of your recklessness!"

Suddenly, a horde of figures materialized before them, obstructing Briar and Leon's paths. Their hair hung in tangled masses over their ashen faces, their nails gleaming like daggers in the light. Eerie yellow eyes pierced through the darkness, casting an unsettling glow. Clad in moss-covered attire, they exuded an odor of decay reminiscent of rotting flesh. These were the undead, a creature that hunted the graveyard, loyal servants of Baba Yaga.

Briar swallowed hard. Leon gripped her hand firmly, as he positioned himself at the forefront.

"I wish some stories just remained stories," Briar whispered, as she watched the walking corpses, their skeletal hands reaching out and their eyes empty of life. The tales said Baba Yaga raised the dead to guard her hut, but Briar had never imagined it would be like this.

The dead moved with a horrifying synchronization. Their teeth were bared like a pack of ravenous wolves ready to pounce. Their skin hung loosely over their bones, and their eyes seemed to fixate on Briar and Leon with an insatiable hunger.

"Children, return or the dead will tear your flesh from your bones," boomed the hut.

Briar and Leon stood their ground, undeterred by the chilling threat.

"Throw them out of our territory!" the hut bellowed.

"Briar, the pouch!" Leon shouted.

With her heart pounding in her chest, Briar fumbled to pull out the pouch that the fairies had given them. Her fingers trembled as she untied the delicate strings. When she peered inside, her heart sank.

"Powder!" she exclaimed in utter disbelief. "It's just powder!"

"It must be something magical," Leon said, but he didn't sound that confident.

Before she could say anything, a cadaverous man lunged at her, his hands like iron clamps around her throat. He dragged her away from the hut, his grip tightening with every step.

"Get off me!" Briar choked out. She struggled to breathe, her vision narrowing as the world blurred around her. She reached into the pouch and grabbed a fistful of the mysterious powder.

With a silent prayer for it to work, she flung the powder into the man's face.

For a heart-stopping moment, nothing happened. The man continued to drag her. But then his grip loosened. A guttural scream of agony tore from his throat as dark smoke began to rise from his body. His flesh seemed to melt away, consumed by fire, until he was nothing more than a pile of ash on the ground.

Briar staggered back, stunned by what she had witnessed. The pouch of powder, now clutched tightly in her hand, was her lifeline.

"Briar! Help me!" Leon's voice broke through her daze.

She turned to see the prince pinned to the ground by a swarm of the dead, their jaws snapping at his flesh, their eyes glowing with hunger. Leon struggled beneath them.

Without a second thought, Briar ran to him. She scattered the powder over the creatures, and they recoiled in agony, their bodies convulsing as they were consumed by the same dark fire. The smell of burning flesh filled the air as they disintegrated into ash.

Leon scrambled to his feet, brushing the blackened remains from his clothes. "Thanks, Briar," he said.

Briar nodded, her eyes locking onto the hut where a new line of the dead had assembled, their eyes glowing with a malevolent light. She stepped forward, her heart pounding in her chest, and drew another handful of the magical powder.

She raised her arm and faced the grotesque assembly. "Didn't you see what happened to your friends?" she shouted. "They were turned to ash. If you don't leave, that will be your fate as well."

The dead hesitated, exchanging uncertain glances with each other.

"I'll count to three," Briar warned.

"ONE."

"TWO."

"THREE!"

All the dead vanished. Briar couldn't help but smile triumphantly as she watched the undead retreat into the shadows.

"Hey, cowards!" the hut bellowed, its voice echoing through the forest and reverberating like a thunderclap. "Come back! Stop them! Baba Yaga will punish you!"

Briar carefully placed the powder back into the pouch. Beside her, Leon adjusted his grip on the sack that the fairies had given them. Then they walked closer to the hut.

The hut towering twenty feet above them like a giant monster. Up close, it was even more unsettling,

"Go back, children," the hut warned. "This is your last warning."

"Stop it," Briar said, rolling her eyes. She turned to Leon. "Leon, give it the thing and shut it up already."

Leon reached inside the sack, pulling out an object that dripped with a dark, viscous fluid. Briar's eyes widened in horror as she realized what it was.

A hear! A freshly removed, still-beating heart.

Briar let out a scream, her hands flying to her mouth. Leon's grip faltered, and he nearly dropped the grotesque offering.

"Hut, we offer you this," Leon said quickly, his voice strained as he tried to hide his revulsion. "Open for us."

The hut fell silent, and then its windows seemed to squint in delight. "Oh! A heart! I love hearts!" it said dreamily, its voice now tinged with a sinister glee.

"Just. Take. It," Leon said, holding the heart out at arm's length, his face pale and eyes wide with disgust. It was clear he was struggling to keep from vomiting.

The heart vanished from his hand as if snatched by an invisible force. The hut gave a shudder of satisfaction and began to lower itself, the creaking of its woods growing louder. The ground seemed to tremble as the hut settled onto the earth, and the door swung open with a creak that sounded like a monstrous yawn.

Briar and Leon exchanged a tense nod. The air around them felt heavy with anxiety, but there was no turning back now. Together, they stepped into the yawning maw of Baba Yaga's hut.

CHAPTER 15

The moment they stepped inside, Briar felt a shiver run down her spine. The interior of the hut was like something out of a nightmare. Bones and skeletons littered the floor, casting eerie shadows in the dim light. Alongside the bones were rows of cabinets filled with potions, some of them broken and in disarray. Crystal balls glimmered ominously from one cabinet, while another overflowed with mystical amulets.

Brooms lay forgotten in a corner, covered in dust. It was clear that the witch didn't bother with mundane tasks like cleaning. Cobwebs draped everything in sight, giving the room a sinister atmosphere.

In the center of the room, towering over the flickering flames of the fireplace, stood a chair crafted from weathered wood. It was an odd sight among the horrid surroundings. Leaning on the wall beside the fireplace were three skeletons with rotten flesh still attached to them.

"It is disgusting." Briar controlled herself from puking.

"My nanny used to tell us that Baba Yaga's hut is enchanted," Leon said. "It's only ugly on the outside and once you enter, it is a whole different world. Treasure chests full of gold and diamonds and rubies. And that's why people are dying to come here."

"Well, it's ugly on the outside and as well as the inside," Briar said.

"Only the good rumors about Baba Yaga are false," he looked at the room with disappointment. "I was expecting to see her lavish lifestyle."

"Let's forget about it and look for the book," Briar said taking a deep breath to steel herself for the task ahead. She glanced around the cluttered room, feeling a bit overwhelmed by the chaos before her. "Where do we even begin?"

She looked up at the ceiling and screamed. Suspended from the ceiling were heads, their hair tied with ropes to form a grotesque chandelier of sorts. Each head bore a wrinkled face, their eyes shut tight, and their lips twisted into unsettling grins.

She pointed a trembling finger upward. "What are those?"

Leon's face went white. "Deadheads," he muttered, his voice tinged with unease

Briar squinted at the wrinkled faces dangling above. "Are they... alive?" she asked.

"Relax," Leon reassured her. "There's nothing to fear. The heads are dead."

Briar's gaze darted around the room, but everywhere she looked, she was met with disturbing sights. The anxiety coursing through her veins refused to decrease, her heart racing and her hands trembling uncontrollably. "We need to find the book. I can't stand being in this place any longer."

"I'll search over here," Leon offered, indicating the right side of the room. "You check the other side."

Briar nodded and headed toward a small bookshelf tucked away in the corner. She carefully examined each book, flipping through their pages one by one. None of them seemed to match the description of the Ancient Book of Spells that the forest fairies had described.

After replacing the books on the shelf, she turned to Leon. "Did you have any luck?" she asked, hoping that he had found something useful.

"Look at this." Leon held up a small wooden wand with intricate carvings. He twirled it around, playing with it.

"Leon," Briar marched to him angrily and snatched the wand from him. "We are here for the book."

"Briar," he said, reaching for the wand again. "I stumbled upon this while searching. It might come in handy. Let me keep it."

"No," Briar replied firmly. "We're here for the book, not to play with random objects. Haven't you learned your lesson in the garden?"

"Oh, come on," Leon said with a laugh. "It's just a harmless wand. it's not going to eat us."

"You can't be sure," Briar insisted, handing the wand back to Leon and urging him to return it to its place. She resumed her search for the book, feeling the room grow darker as the sun began to set. Briar was determined not to spend the night in the witch's hut.

As Briar carefully maneuvered around the large glass jars containing the preserved body parts, one jar slipped from her grasp and crashed to the floor. Yellowish liquid splattered everywhere, filling the air with a pungent, acidic smell. To her horror, the teeth preserved inside the jar began to scurry away.

"Warning!" the hut bellowed. "You can't destroy the property."

"It's not my fault," Briar protested. "The jar was slippery."

"You're inside?" the hut questioned, sounding surprised. "Who let you in?"

"You did," Leon replied. "When we gave you a heart."

The hut gasped as if it had just realized its mistake. "Yes, heart. I love heart. But I should not have let you in. If my mistress found out, she would be furious. Get out, children."

"We are not going anywhere," Leon said stubbornly.

Suddenly, Briar had an idea. "Leon," she said, delighted. "I know how to find the book."

"How?" the prince asked.

"I'll tell you," she said and pulled the prince to a corner, away from the hut. Then she realized it was useless as they were inside the hut. It would hear them anyway. The walls literally had ears.

She cupped her hand around his ears and whispered, "The hut will give us the book."

"But why?" The prince whispered back.

She cupped her hands around his ears again. "The hut let us in, but it shouldn't have. Now watch what I'm doing."

The prince nodded as Briar walked back to the jars of preserved animals. "Hut, where is the Ancient Book of Spells?"

"You dare to enter Baba Yaga's hut and ask for her most beloved book," the hut said. "I'll never help you, intruders."

Briar smiled. "Are you sure?" She picked a jar that contained two brains joined by a greenish nerve and smashed it on the floor.

"Hey!" the hut yelled. "What are you doing?"

"Are you going to tell us, or should I break more?" she threatened, picking another jar.

"I can't betray Baba Yaga," the hut cried out.

"You already did," Briar said, her tone confident. "You let us in. Baba Yaga will not be pleased. And if we break all the things, she would be more furious. We just want to read the book. For a project. You know, for our school. That's all. Then we will leave."

She glanced at Leon, who wore a mischievous grin. "Yeah, just a little homework."

"I'll never help you," the hut protested weakly, its resolve faltering.

"Fine," Briar said, determination flashing in her eyes. "Let's get in more trouble."

She swiftly returned the jar to its place and dashed towards the nearest potion cabinet. With a firm grip, she yanked the glass door open and beckoned to Leon. "Leon," she called out. "Give me a hand with this. Let's make some noise."

The prince gladly joined her, grasping the other side of the cabinet.

They both feigned exertion as they pushed against the cabinet, deliberately letting a few potion bottles slip to the floor.

"One, two..." Briar counted, as they leaned the cabinet further and further.

"STOP!" the hut yelled. "YOU WIN!"

They carefully placed the cabinet back in its original position. Briar crossed her arms across her chest. "Where is the book?"

"Behind the skeletons," the hut said. "Inside the secret wardrobe."

Briar and Leon pushed aside the skeletons with decaying flesh, clearing the way to a hidden wardrobe. Briar yanked the door open. But instead of revealing the book, the door broke loose from its hinges and crashed down on top of her. Briar, unable to keep her balance, tumbled to the ground, pinned beneath the weight of the heavy wooden door.

"Leon!" the princess yelped.

Leon quickly rushed to Briar's side and helped her free herself from under the door.

"You broke the wardrobe!" the hut yelled.

"It was already broken," Briar replied, brushing dust off her gown.

She approached the wardrobe, hoping to find the Ancient Book of Spells. However, all she found inside were a few robes, peculiar black and yellow stones, and a sturdy iron chest.

Briar and Leon gripped the iron chest from either side and carefully maneuvered it to the center of the room.

With darkness enveloping the room, Briar called out to the hut. "Can we get some light in here?"

Reluctantly, the hut grumbled its agreement, and suddenly, candles scattered throughout the room burst into flame, casting a warm glow across the space.

Leon and Briar sat before the chest. It was miraculously cleaned and gleaming in the soft candlelight. It was secured by a large iron padlock.

"Can you break the lock?" Briar asked, twisting the padlock.

"No need for that," Leon replied calmly, retrieving a key ring from his pocket. It was a sight to behold, adorned with keys crafted from gold, silver, iron, and even bones.

Briar gaped at the prince. "Where did you get it?"

"Found it with the wand and decided to keep it. Don't get mad," Leon confessed with a grin.

"You know what? You have the potential to make a great thief," Briar chuckled. "But I'll not be mad if one of the keys unlocks the chest."

As luck would have it, the iron key slid smoothly into the padlock and turned with a satisfying click. Briar smiled triumphantly and lifted the lid of the chest.

Suddenly, a cobra raised its head, hissing menacingly at her.

The princess screamed, leaping away from the chest in terror.

The snake lazily slithered out of the chest and fixed its gaze on them.

"Go away!" Briar yelled, her voice trembling with fear. Leon swiftly slipped his sword beneath the snake, lifted it, and hurled it out of the window.

"I've had my fill of insects and snakes for one day," Briar declared, her nerves still on edge.

The chest was filled with numerous red velvet pouches. Despite Briar's warning, Leon opened one, only to find nails and hair inside. "I thought there would be diamonds," he muttered, disappointed, as he let the pouches fall to the side.

At the bottom of the chest lay a red book with silver moons and stars on the cover.

"Yes," Briar said, smiling. "The Ancient Book of Spells." As she reached out to pick up the book, a sharp pain shot through her hand as if a scorpion had bitten her. With a yelp, she dropped the book.

And to Briar and Leon's amazement, the book scurried away from them.

CHAPTER 16

"Did the book just run away?" Leon asked, gaping after it.

"It bit me!" Briar exclaimed, her hand swollen and red, pulsing with pain.

Leon's eyes widened as he inspected her hand. "That looks bad."

"It's fine," Briar said, shaking away the pain. "Where is the book?" She looked around for the book and found it wedged under a potion cabinet, trying to hide.

"Hey there," Briar cooed, crouching down to its level. "We're not going to hurt you. We just need to borrow you for a little while." She spoke softly, hoping to calm the book's nerves. Although she wasn't sure if the book understood her or not, she did her best to make the book feel safe. At least she was less scary than Baba Yaga.

"What is the book doing?" Leon asked.

"Hiding," Briar replied, her gaze fixed on the book. "Maybe it is scared."

"This place keeps getting creepier," Leon murmured.

"I promise we will not hurt you," Briar said gently, extending her hand towards the book.

The book hesitated, fluttering its pages nervously. Then, slowly, it inched closer to her.

"Yes," Briar clapped, encouraging the book. "Come here."

The book crept closer, its pages rustling slightly as it moved.

"Good book," Briar said as the book emerged fully from under the cabinet. "That's a good—"

Suddenly, the book jumped, smacking Briar squarely in the face.

"Ow!" she yelped, clutching her face in surprise. As she stumbled back, the book flipped open and sprinted away again, its pages fluttering wildly as if laughing at her. Briar stood there, momentarily stunned, before shaking her head and darting after it once more.

"Hey, stop!" Leon shouted, sprinting after the book as it darted into a potion cabinet. The prince lunged, throwing himself on top of the mischievous book.

However, the book slipped out from under him with a swift, serpentine motion, and Leon crashed into the cabinet. Shelves rattled, and potion bottles tumbled down, shattering around him in a cascade of glass and colorful liquids.

"Aww!" Leon yelled, groaning in pain and frustration as he lay amidst the broken glass and spilled potions, his clothes soaked and stained with various concoctions. The book, now perched on a nearby shelf, seemed to mock him with its flapping pages. Then the book jumped on the shrunken head chandelier.

"Why is the book running from us?" Leon shouted.

"Baba Yaga must have enchanted it to run away from anyone who tries to take it," Briar replied, pulling a wooden chair beneath the chandelier, her eyes following the book.

"I can't believe how much the witch loves that book," the prince said, shaking his head in disbelief as he picked himself up from the floor, brushing off potion residue.

"You will too, once you understand its value," Briar said, climbing onto the chair. "It's written by ancient fairies. It holds powers you can't even begin to imagine."

Briar climbed onto the chair and slashed at the rope holding one of the shrunken heads where the book had been resting. The rope snapped, and the head fell, but the book quickly leaped to another head.

Slash! Slash! Slash!

Briar cut blindly, sending shrunken heads tumbling to the floor, their creepy smiles seeming to grow wider as they rolled around.

Only one head remained, and the book perched atop it like a frightened cat.

"Give up now!" Briar yelled, slashing the final rope. The shrunken head fell, taking the book with it. Briar leaned to the side, reaching out to catch the book. For a fleeting moment, she had it in her grasp, but then the book bit her hand. She lost her balance and tumbled onto the pile of deadheads, the book slipping from her grip once again.

Briar cried out in frustration as the book escaped.

"Briar!" Leon yelled.

"After the book!" Briar yelled as she scrambled to her feet.

The book scurried up a cabinet containing large jars filled with preserved dead animals, knocking them to the floor in its nervousness.

"What did I say about damaging the property?" the hut roared, its voice echoing through the room as the jars shattered on the floor.

"Then tell the book to stop!" Briar shouted back at the hut.

"The book doesn't follow my orders!" the hut retorted.

The book, in a state of panic, was jumping from one potion cabinet to another, knocking over potions and causing a cacophony of crashes and splashes as the prince and princess chased it around the room.

"Stop that book!" Leon yelled, dodging a flying jar.

"I'm trying!" Briar responded, narrowly avoiding a potion bottle that fell from a top shelf.

The hut continued to scream in the background. "You're ruining everything!"

"If you can't help, just stay out of it!" Leon shouted at the hut as he lunged for the book, only to miss and knock over a stack of old spell books.

Briar dodged a falling jar and lunged at the book, managing to grab it for a brief second before it wriggled free, sending a cascade of potions raining down around her. "This is impossible!" she cried out in exasperation.

After numerous failed attempts to catch the book, Briar stopped. She knew it was pointless to keep chasing the book without a plan. They were wasting time. She scanned the room and spotted what she needed. A length of rope. Walking over to one of the shrunken heads, she carefully untied the rope binding its hair, doing her best to avoid touching the head itself.

"Leon, come here," she whispered, pulling him to the side as the book made another leap, this time into the wall.

"I've got a plan," Briar said, showing him the rope and quickly explaining her idea.

"You hide behind that cabinet," she instructed, pointing to a large, sturdy cabinet near the wall. "I'll chase the book toward you, and when I say 'jump,' you trap the book, and I'll tie it."

"Good idea," Leon agreed. He moved to the cabinet and crouched behind it, making sure he was out of sight.

Briar turned to face the book. It was clinging to the wall.

"Hey, book," Briar yelled, jabbing it lightly with her sword.

The pages fluttered nervously, and the book leaped to the floor. Briar poked it again, successfully turning it toward Leon's hiding spot.

"Yes!" Briar yelled, a grin spreading across her face. "Run!"

She sprinted after the book, which was now just a few feet away from Leon.

Three!

Two!

One!

"NOW!" Briar shouted.

Leon pounced on top of the book, pressing it to the ground with all his strength.

Briar dove in, quickly working on the rope, making knot after knot. Then she stood up with a smirk, dusting off her palms. "Got it!"

"Briar," Leon said from the floor.

"What?" she asked, her confidence waning at the tone of his voice.

"Untie me," he said.

Briar glanced down, horrified to see she had tied Leon's hands together, and the book had slipped away once again.

Briar let out a frustrated scream. "Enough!"

Leon struggled against the ropes, managing to free one hand. "Briar, the book is escaping!" he shouted.

"Stop!" Briar bellowed, sprinting with almost inhuman speed. With a swift kick, she sent the book flying, forgetting her promise not to harm it.

The magic book soared through the air before crashing into the wall with a resounding thud, sliding down to the floor.

For a moment, it lay there motionless.

Briar resisted the temptation to slam the book onto the floor again.

Leon, having freed himself, approached Briar with the rope in hand. Together, they bound the book tightly before Briar stowed it away in her satchel.

"Now, I just want to get out of this horrible house as soon as possible," Briar declared.

As they approached the door, it slammed shut in their faces with a resounding thud. Simultaneously, the windows all around the room slammed shut as well, the sound echoing in the confined space. Leon instinctively reached for the door handle and yanked it, but it refused to budge as if held fast by some unseen force. He tried again, putting all his strength into it, but the door remained stubbornly locked.

"What is happening?" Briar asked, her voice tinged with growing concern as she watched Leon's futile attempts to open the door.

Leon turned to her with a worried expression. "The door's locked," he said grimly, his voice echoing off the walls of the now eerily silent room. "We are trapped."

Chapter 17

"We can't be trapped," Briar yelled, panicking.

"It feels like we are," Leon grunted, straining to pull the door. But it remained stubbornly immovable as if it had fused with the wall. "The door won't budge."

"Hut," Briar yelled, her voice echoing through the empty halls. "Open the door!"

"No," the hut bellowed back, the walls trembling with its anger. "You lied to me. You are here to seal the book."

"Open the door!" Briar shouted again, her desperation growing. "Or else."

"You can't do anything," the hut taunted, its tone dripping with malice. "Break whatever you want. You can't scare me anymore. You can never escape. You are trapped inside me. Wait for Baba Yaga."

Briar's mind raced, her eyes darting around the room. Suddenly, she remembered the strange set of keys Leon had found earlier. "The keys!" she shouted, her voice filled with newfound hope. "Maybe they will open the door."

Leon's face lit up like a moon in the night sky. "Oh, yes!" He pulled the keys from his pocket, his hands trembling with excitement. "Luckily, I didn't throw them away." He raised the keys towards the door but then stopped, hesitation clouding his face.

"What are you waiting for?" Briar urged him. "Open the door!"

Leon gave her a troubled look, his brow furrowed. "The door has no keyhole."

"What?" Briar rushed to the door, her fingers tracing the smooth wood. The prince was right. There was no keyhole. "Maybe it's hidden. Let me try." She snatched the keys from Leon and began pressing them against the door, feeling for any hint of magic. She touched every inch of the door, from top to bottom, leaving no spot untried. Her movements grew frantic as nothing happened. "Come on," she muttered, pressing harder. "There has to be a way."

Furiously, Briar hurled the keys across the room, watching them clatter against the wall and fall to the floor. Her breaths came in short, furious bursts, her face flushed with anger and desperation. "This is hopeless!"

"Maybe the door needs some sort of offering to open," he suggested, scanning their surroundings for any clues.

"Where are we supposed to find a heart?" Briar's eyes welled up with tears. "Evalina didn't say we might get trapped inside. This wasn't part of the plan!"

"Maybe she didn't know," Leon said, trying to keep calm.

"I just want to leave this hut!" Briar sobbed, her frustration boiling over. She kicked the door with all her strength, her fists pounding against the wood. "OPEN!" she screamed, her voice echoing through the room. "OPEN!"

"Leave the book," The hut's voice reverberated through the space, cold and mocking. "And maybe you can go. I'll not tell Baba Yaga."

"Never!" Briar spat, her eyes blazing with defiance. "You have to open. I'll make you." She kicked the door again, her foot aching from the impact.

"Briar," Leon called softly, placing a gentle hand on her shoulder. "You're only hurting yourself. The door won't open if we take the book."

"And you know we can't leave the book." Briar threw one last futile kick at the door before Leon pulled her away.

"Relax," Leon said, guiding her to sit on the floor. He crouched beside her. "We'll think calmly. There must be a way out."

"The only way out is the door," Briar said. "And we have to break it."

"You can't break a magical door by hand," Leon replied, shaking his head. "And I don't think our swords will make any difference."

"This door will open," Briar said, a sudden spark of an idea lighting up her eyes. "I'll burn it." She paused, the thought solidifying in her mind. "We have to burn the door."

Leon looked at her, a mix of curiosity and skepticism on his face. "Well then, we'll need to build a powerful fire," he said, standing up and walking over to the fireplace. He gathered a few logs, glancing back at Briar. "But how do we make it strong enough?"

"This is a witch's house, Leon," Briar said, jumping to her feet with renewed energy. She dashed to the potion cabinets, her eyes scanning the shelves. "We don't need logs to build a fire."

"What do you mean?" asked the prince, following her.

"Wait and see," Briar said. Most of the potions had been destroyed, and she desperately hoped what she was looking for was still available.

As Briar searched through the remains of the cabinet, Leon peered over her shoulder. "What are you searching for?" he asked, his eyes scanning the mess.

"You will see," she answered, her hands moving bottles and jars aside with increasing speed. "It should be here."

"Tell me what you're looking for so I can help," he offered.

"Where is it..." she muttered, her eyes darting from one spot to another. Suddenly, she spotted a glass bottle of transparent liquid rolling on the floor. With a triumphant gasp, she picked it up and excitedly showed it to Leon. "This is our way out."

Leon didn't share her excitement. He looked at the bottle doubtfully. "A bottle will take us out?"

"This is not just any bottle," Briar said, waving the bottle in front of his face, the glass catching the dim light. "It's a potion. Look." She shook the bottle. The liquid inside swirled and gradually changed color. Briar gave it another vigorous shake, and the liquid turned a fiery red, bubbling like molten lava. It grew so hot that Briar had to wrap her cloak around it to hold it.

Leon's eyes widened in awe. "What is this?" he asked.

"It's an extremely powerful potion used to melt gold, silver, diamond, stone, and even bones," Briar explained.

"You mean like acid?" Leon asked.

"A thousand times more powerful than acid," she said. "The glass they used to store it is enchanted, or it would have melted as well."

"Why would anyone want to melt bone?" he asked, his face contorting with disgust.

"Am I a witch?" Briar snapped. "How should I know? It's witch business."

"How did you know all this?" he asked suspiciously

"Prince Leon, if you are trying to imply that I'm learning witchcraft," Briar said, her voice dropping to a dangerous whisper, "I will not hesitate to melt your bones."

Leon's eyes widened as if he seriously considered the possibility. "I was just curious," he said quickly.

"Well," Briar said, "I once saw Lavonna melting some crystals with it. It was fascinating, so I asked her about it. She explained that this potion is used for melting hard objects and how it works."

Leon looked at the potion, still skeptical. "Will it work on the door?" he asked. "The door seems magical."

"Of course," Briar said with a determined glint in her eyes. "The potion is magical, but this isn't enough. We need more."

They scoured the room, overturning broken shelves and sifting through the debris. Amidst the chaos, they discovered six more bottles of the melting potion. Baba Yaga had a substantial supply of this powerful liquid.

The hut fell eerily silent as if it were anxiously waiting for their next move.

"Let me throw it," Leon suggested as they approached the door, holding the bottles of the melting potion. "It might be dangerous."

Briar rolled her eyes. "I'm not that fragile princess anymore. Not that I ever was." She handed three bottles to Leon and kept three for herself. "Shake it until it turns red and hot."

They both shook their bottles vigorously. The liquid inside began to boil, transforming into a fiery red and radiating intense heat. Carefully, they removed the tight wooden corks. Hot vapor hissed out of the bottles, hitting their faces and bringing tears to their eyes.

"Ready," Briar said, holding her bottles at arm's length as they stood facing the door.

Leon nodded. And then they threw the liquid lava on the door.

As the potion splashed on the door, the hut erupted into howls and quakes. Briar staggered, the ground trembling beneath her feet. The very foundations of the hut seemed to convulse with agony, causing the remaining potions to crash to the floor from their cabinets.

Then they saw what was happening. The once-solid wood of the door sizzled and bubbled, a large, jagged hole forming in its center. The door melted away slowly, the hut's pained wails echoing through the room.

"Briar!" Leon's voice cut through the tumult, pulling her back to her senses. He reached out and helped her to her feet. "It worked."

The door had melted enough for them to jump through it. They sprinted to the door. Instantly, the chilly wind hit their face. It was dark outside, and they were several feet above the ground.

"We have to jump!" Leon yelled over the roar of the hut.

Briar nodded, her heart pounding in her chest. Anything to get away from the hut. She was ready to jump into the darkness of the forest. She checked to ensure the book was safely tucked away in her satchel, then turned to face the dark expanse of the forest beyond.

"NOW!" Leon's voice sliced through the air. Gripping each other's hands tightly, they launched themselves into the unknown abyss. They crashed to the ground with a bone-jarring impact, the force knocking the wind out of them. But miraculously, they didn't injure themselves.

With a grunt, Leon rose to his feet, his hand reaching out to help Briar up. Then they bolted away from the hut. The hut's agonized wails echoed behind them, fading into the distance as they sprinted away from its grasp.

Under the eerie glow of the moonlight, the forest took on a ghostly allure. Shadows danced and twisted among the trees, casting sinister shapes on the forest floor. Every rustle of leaves seemed to carry a whispered threat, and the night itself felt alive with unseen dangers.

Ignoring everything, they ran, leaping over boulders, ducking under thorny bushes, and dodging tree roots that seemed to reach out and trip them intentionally. Briar's breath came in quick gasps, her heart pounding in her ears as she clutched the strap of her satchel tightly. Inside the satchel, the book writhed, seeming to sense that they were running away from Baba Yaga's hut.

"The book is going wild in your bag!" Leon said, his voice strained as he stumbled over a root, barely regaining his balance.

"I know," she panted. "Just keep running!"

They tore through the forest, branches slashing at their faces and snagging their clothes. The mist began to thin, giving way to a familiar clearing bathed in soft moonlight. They finally stopped, doubling over to catch their breath, their chests heaving with exertion.

Briar glanced back, half expecting the hut to burst through the trees in pursuit. But the woods were still. She dropped to her knees, her legs trembling from the exertion and adrenaline. "I think... we're safe," she gasped, wiping sweat from her forehead.

Leon plopped down beside her, his face flushed and glistening with sweat. "It's the last time I'm ever visiting a witch's hut," he said.

"Oh, I thought it was an adventure for you," Briar wheezed, a small, wry smile tugging at her lips. "Stealing the book is so easy, isn't it?"

"Well," he replied, a mischievous grin spreading across his face despite his exhaustion. "On the bright side, we have the book. Mission accomplished."

Briar couldn't help but smile back. She gently patted the satchel, feeling the now-still book within. "We did it. We did it," she murmured, a sense of triumph flooding through her. For the first time since she had begun her journey, she felt a genuine surge of hope. She had the first object needed for the ritual. The curse seemed less daunting, almost within reach of being broken.

They sat in the clearing for a few minutes, savoring their hard-earned victory and sharing a canteen of water. The moon's calming rays pierced through the treetops.

"What's next?" Leon asked, taking a long swig from the canteen and passing it to Briar.

"The dragon's gold," she replied. After successfully retrieving the book and escaping Baba Yaga's dreaded hut, the prospect of facing a dragon seemed less terrifying.

Leon's eyes lit up with excitement. "A dragon! Now this is what I call a quest. What's a quest without a dragon, after all?"

"I'd rather not see the dragon if we can avoid it," Briar said.

Leon glanced around the clearing, considering their options. "Should we make camp here or move on? We need to rest."

Briar surveyed the area, the sense of peace here calming her frazzled nerves. "I don't think Baba Yaga's hut can find us here. We should be safe enough for the night. Let's stay."

Suddenly, the ground beneath them began to tremble, a rhythmic thudding reverberating through the earth. The noise grew louder, each thud sending a shiver up Briar's spine. She looked at Leon, her face pale with dread. "What is that?" she whispered.

Leon's eyes widened as the thudding grew nearer, the sound like giant footsteps pounding the forest floor. "I don't know, but it doesn't sound good."

Then, through the trees, they saw it—a monstrous silhouette hobbling towards them, its spindly legs jerking and twitching with each step. Briar's blood ran cold as she recognized the grotesque figure.

"Oh no," she breathed.

Leon and Briar screamed in unison as Baba Yaga's hut, perched atop its grotesque chicken legs, emerged into the clearing.

CHAPTER 18

"Look! The hut!" Leon yelled.

"It's coming!" Briar yelled back, fear tightening her voice.

"Right at us!" Leon pointed out.

"To kill us!" Briar couldn't tear her gaze away from the lumbering hut.

Between the trees and over the rocks, the hut bounded toward them. Surprisingly fast for a hut with chicken legs.

"Return the book immediately!" The hut boomed. Its door, half-melted, swung with the force of its voice.

The magic book whimpered inside Briar's satchel.

"The book belongs to Baba Yaga," the hut yelled.

"The book belongs to the forest fairies," Briar shot back. "Your witch had taken it."

"Thieves!" the hut accused, its anger echoing through the trees.

In an instant, the windows burst open, and knives flew out from the hut.

Briar and Leon screamed, diving for cover. The knives zipped through the air, stabbing into the trees. One blade grazed Briar, missing her arm by a hair's breadth.

After the knives, the hut began hurling logs their way. And when it ran out of logs, it started flinging whatever else it could find.

The hut hurled a wooden chair, and it smacked Leon on the back. The force of the blow knocked the prince to the ground, the breath rushing out of him in a pained gasp.

Before he could recover, the hut dashed toward him. One massive leg rose into the air, poised to strike.

"Leon, get up!" Briar screamed. She darted toward him. Just as the hut's leg began its descent, Briar grabbed Leon by the arm, yanking him up with all her strength.

"I didn't know the hut could run!" the prince yelled, his voice strained with exertion as they stumbled onto a rocky path.

"Leon, it has legs!" Briar said as she dared a glance behind them. The hut barreled after them, its chicken legs navigating the rocky terrain with unsettling quickness. Shards of broken glass flew from its windows, whizzing past them and clattering on the forest floor.

"Return the book," the hut kept chanting. Its voice echoed through the forest. "Return the book."

Briar and Leon ran blindly, their surroundings swallowed by darkness. The pale light of the moon was consumed by the thick canopy of trees, leaving them in near-complete darkness. Navigating the forest in daylight was challenging enough. Now, it felt like an impossible task.

Briar's breaths came in wheezing gasps, her legs burning with exhaustion. It felt like they had been running for hours. The hut showed no signs of slowing down. Why would it? It was magical. And the hut wouldn't give until it got the book. It ran after them, yelling and waking up the wild animals of the forest. Briar was scared it would wake up more trouble for them.

"We can't run from the hut forever," Briar yelled. "And it knows every inch of the forest by heart. We have to do something."

"I want to chop its legs off," Leon said furiously. "Yes, let's do that."

"I don't know if chopping the legs will hurt it," Briar replied. "It's magical."

"But it cried when we burned the door," the prince pointed out.

"Oh yes. I didn't think about that," Briar said, her mind racing. The hut was just a few feet away from them, its monstrous legs thudding heavily on the ground.

"If the hut doesn't have legs, it can't follow us," Leon said menacingly, his hands tightening around the hilt of his sword.

"I don't want to cut the entire leg," Briar said softly. Despite the danger, she felt a pang of pity for the hut. It was only doing its job, following orders from Baba Yaga.

They stopped running and turned to face the hut, their hearts pounding. The hut reached them, its windows gleaming with a malicious light. It seemed pleased that they had stopped running.

"So, ready to give up?" the hut said smugly, its voice echoing with a sinister glee.

"Yes," Briar said, gripping the handle of her sword tightly.

"We are tired of running," Leon said, pretending to be sad.

"We want to give up," Briar added as they walked toward the hut.

The hut laughed, a chilling sound that sent shivers down their spines. "You foolish humans. You thought you could steal from Baba Yaga."

"Yes, we are fools," Briar nodded. They were standing just next to the chicken legs now, their swords at the ready.

"Very well," said the hut. "Now return the book. Maybe we can think of a less painful punishment for you."

"Certainly," Briar replied, her voice steady despite the pounding of her heart. She looked at Leon and nodded.

Quickly, they drew their swords and lunged at the chicken legs. The blades struck with a sickening thud, sinking into the tough, leathery flesh. Black blood gushed out, coating the ground in an inky pool. The hut howled in agony, its cry reverberating through the forest and shaking the trees.

Birds burst from the branches, their frantic chirping filling the night air as they fled the commotion. Briar yanked her sword free. The hut's wails continued to pierce the silence.

"Hurry!" Briar shouted, glancing at Leon who stood transfixed, watching the hut writhe in pain.

"But the legs aren't broken," Leon protested, pulling his sword free with a grunt.

"It's injured. It can't follow us anymore," Briar insisted, already sprinting away from the hut.

"Baba Yaga!" the hut cried out in a desperate, haunting wail. "Baba Yaga! Baba Yaga!"

"Yeah, keep yelling. The witch will never help you," Leon taunted, catching up to Briar.

Suddenly, a dark shadow swept over them, blotting out the pale light of the moon. Briar looked up, her breath catching in her throat. The sky was clear and star-studded but against the backdrop of twinkling stars, a sinister figure shot toward them with alarming speed.

Briar gasped, her eyes widening as she took in the sight before her. A woman was riding a mortar and pestle, a broom trailing behind her, sweeping the air automatically. Hanging from the side of the mortar was a large fishnet, and within it, the forms of what seemed like a human and a horse struggled in vain.

The woman descended, her mortar and pestle coming to rest on the ground with a dull thud. She fixed Briar and Leon with a glare that could freeze blood. She was a gaunt, wrinkled old woman with a large hooked nose and bloodshot red eyes. Her green robe flowed around her like a shroud, adding to her menacing presence. She was more gruesome than all the stories described her.

Unmistakably, they were facing the infamous, child-eating, heartless, most evil witch of all time. They were facing Baba Yaga.

Briar and Leon stood rooted to the spot, their breath caught in their throats as the witch sneered at them, her eyes gleaming with malice.

"Baba Yaga," a voice whimpered from behind them. "Save me."

All of them turned to see the hut, its chicken legs buckling, attempting to drag itself towards the witch. With a final groan, it collapsed to the ground. Life seemed to drain from its structure.

Briar closed her eyes.

As if it wasn't enough, the Ancient Book of Spells suddenly sprang from Briar's satchel. The book flipped through the air and landed at Baba Yaga's feet.

Baba Yaga let out an angry scream that reverberated through the entire forest, causing the trees to shiver and the ground to tremble beneath their feet. Her eyes blazed with fury, and her hooked nose flared with each enraged breath.

The witch raised her fist, and the blue stone on her ring began to glow, crackling with electric energy that danced around her gnarled fingers like restless serpents. She shouted an incantation in a guttural, ancient language and pointed the ring directly at Leon and Briar.

Before Briar could react, a bolt of blue lightning shot from the ring, striking her with such force that it felt like being hit by a speeding carriage. The impact was so powerful it knocked the air out of her lungs, and she was sent flying backward.

Everything around Briar blurred into the darkness. The last thing she saw was the witch's horrible face. The world faded into a void, the sounds of the forest and the witch's laughter growing distant and faint.

CHAPTER 19

Briar slowly opened her eyes, the world around her a blur of pain and confusion. Every inch of her body ached as if she had been crushed beneath a mountain, each movement sending a fresh wave of agony through her. She tried to sit up but found her wrists and ankles bound tightly with coarse rope. The fibers dug into her skin, leaving angry red marks.

She struggled for a few seconds and then pushed herself into a sitting position. Her muscles protested, and her head throbbed with a dull ache, but she forced herself to survey her surroundings. Briar winced at the sight of the room, remembering the chaos they had caused during their desperate struggle to escape. Broken jars and scattered herbs lay in disarray, their pungent smells mingling to create a nauseating scent that hung heavily in the air. The dim light from a flickering candle cast eerie shadows that danced around the room, making it difficult to distinguish between objects and their ghostly silhouettes.

The events of the night hit Briar like a lightning bolt. Baba Yaga had captured them, and they were now inside the hut. Panic surged through her veins as she remembered the monstrous sight of the hut lumbering through the forest, chasing them down. They had been so close to escaping, but now they were at the mercy of the witch.

Briar glanced around desperately, searching for Leon. Her heart sank when she saw him slumped against a wall near a pile of skulls, his face pale and eyes closed. He looked lifeless, and for a terrifying moment, Briar feared the worst. But then she noticed the faint rise and fall of his chest, a small but significant sign that he was still breathing.

Next to him lay another figure—a boy with bronze-colored skin and striking silver hair. He was also bound with thick ropes, his arms and legs tied in an awkward position. Beside the boy was a magnificent white horse, tangled in the net. The horse's coat shone with an ethereal light.

Briar's heart raced as she took in the scene. The boy and the horse seemed just as trapped as she and Leon were. Who were they, and what had brought them into this dreadful mess? Her thoughts were interrupted by the distant sound of a voice—a harsh, guttural murmur that sent a shiver down her spine. It was the witch, speaking in an arcane language that Briar couldn't understand.

The candle flickered, and shadows danced around the walls. Now they would face the consequences she had feared. The witch's angry face loomed in front of her. The anticipation of what the witch would do to her and Leon was killing her slowly. It was more painful than the actual death.

She turned her attention back to Leon. "Leon," she whispered urgently. "Leon, wake up."

When the prince didn't answer, she crawled towards him, her movements hindered by the ropes biting into her wrists and ankles. The room around them seemed to close in, the shadows cast by the flickering candle growing longer and more ominous.

As Briar reached the prince, she nudged him gently with her knee, her eyes searching his face for any sign of life. He remained still, his face pale and expressionless. A knot of worry tightened in her chest. She poked him again, more insistently this time. When he still didn't respond, she kicked him hard on the bottom.

Leon's eyes flew open, and he sat up with a start, his mouth gaping as if ready to scream. His eyes darted around wildly, taking in the dim, cluttered room.

"Don't shout," Briar hissed. The last thing they needed was to alert the witch.

Leon turned to her. "Briar," he stammered, his voice hoarse. "The witch..."

"Got us," Briar finished.

Leon's shoulders slumped, and he leaned back against the wall, closing his eyes in defeat. "I'm sorry," he said softly. "I know this is all my fault."

Briar raised an eyebrow. "Why?"

"I... I should have listened to you when you said it was a bad idea," Leon said, his voice cracking with regret. "We're in this mess because of me."

For a moment, Briar was at a loss for words. Part of her wanted to lash out, to tell him that yes, it was his fault and that they wouldn't be in this dire situation if he had listened to her. But she couldn't bring herself to kick him while he was already down.

"Stop saying sorry whenever something goes wrong," she said. "It's not always your fault."

Leon didn't meet her eyes, his gaze fixed on a spot on the floor. "You can blame me," he muttered. "We're going to die because of me."

Briar felt a spark of anger flare up inside her. "Excuse me," she snapped, her eyes flashing. "Who is dying?"

"Us," Leon said, his voice filled with a resigned despair. "Do you think the witch will let us go after what we did?"

"I'm not going to die," Briar said firmly. "At least not until I break the curse. Death has to wait."

"That's motivating," Leon said, a bitter smile tugging at the corners of his mouth. "But not true."

Briar's mind flashed back to the foreboding words of the reflections in the river. They had hinted at her death. Was she destined to die here, in Baba Yaga's clutches? The thought sent a chill down her spine, but she quickly pushed it aside.

"No!" she told herself fiercely. The forest fairies had assured her that the reflections' words were nothing but tricks, meant to lure her into despair. She wouldn't let herself be swayed by their dark prophecies. She would escape, she would find the magic book, and she would break the curse. She had to believe that.

"That sounds very brave," Leon said. "But the witch is Baba Yaga. Even the fairies are scared of her. And we're just two humans."

Briar studied Leon's face, noting the lines of worry etched into his features. His usual bravado was gone, replaced by a look of hopelessness that was painful to see. "What happened to you?" she asked. "Why are you talking like a failure?"

Leon lowered his eyes, unable to meet her gaze. "Because I am," he whispered, his voice filled with a sorrow that made Briar's heartache. "I failed you, Briar. I failed everyone. I thought I could handle this, that I could be the hero. But now look at us. We're prisoners, and it's my fault."

Briar stared at the prince, her heart sinking at the sight of his dejection. Where was the confident, reckless hero she had depended on? The one who had navigated the treacherous forest, faced countless dangers, and kept her spirits high with his daring optimism? Seeing Leon so defeated felt like a crushing blow to her resolve. She needed his strength now more than ever, and his despair was infectious, dragging her down into a pit of hopelessness.

"Leon," she said softly. "You're not a failure. We both made mistakes, and we both ended up here. But blaming yourself won't help us get out. I hate seeing you like this. You are brave. That's what makes you special. Don't let that go. The witch wants you to be weak, to give up."

Leon's eyes flickered with a glimmer of hope. "You think I'm brave?"

"Of course," she said, her voice firm. "Everyone knows you're brave. Our entire kingdom loves you. Remember, you are their hero. They look up to you."

"But I got us into this mess," he said, his voice breaking with regret.

Briar shook her head vigorously. "Forget that. That was the past. What matters is now. Let's not give up. We can still find a way out of this."

A faint smile touched Leon's lips, and he nodded. "Okay," he said, his voice stronger now. "What's the plan?"

"Listen, I'll untie you, and you untie me, and we'll figure out what to do next," Briar said.

Before Leon could respond, the door burst open with a deafening crash, and Baba Yaga stormed in. Her eyes were burning with fury, and a dark aura seemed to fill the room. Briar noticed that the melted door had been replaced with a new one.

The witch's eyes locked onto Briar, and she felt a chill run down her spine. Baba Yaga moved slowly, deliberately, with the Ancient Book of Spells floating ominously behind her, its pages rustling.

"So, the thieves are awake," Baba Yaga said, her voice dangerously calm. The wooden chair beside her slid across the floor with an eerie creak and stopped next to Briar and Leon. The witch sat down, her bony fingers drumming on the armrests, and the Ancient Book of Spells jumped into her lap, purring like a cat as she stroked its cover.

"Destroyed," Baba Yaga said. "Years of hard work ruined." Her eyes swept around the room, taking in the chaos and destruction. Her gaze settled back on Briar.

"Do you know what it took to mend my hut?" Baba Yaga continued, her voice rising slightly. The intensity of her stare made Briar feel like she was being physically crushed.

"I could have killed you right then and there," the witch said, her voice dropping to a whisper that sent shivers down Briar's spine. "Do you know why your bones haven't joined my fence yet?"

Briar couldn't bring herself to look the witch in the eye. The weight of Baba Yaga's gaze was unbearable, and the words seemed to twist around her heart, squeezing it tight.

"You arouse my curiosity," the witch continued. "I want to know why and how you dared to enter my hut. Many brave warriors would think hundreds of times before setting foot in here. You two are either incredibly brave or have a death wish."

The witch leaned in closer, her hooked nose nearly touching Briar's face. The stench of decay and rot emanated from her, making Briar's stomach churn. Baba Yaga's eyes were dark pools of malice.

"If I had killed you in my anger, it would have been quick," Baba Yaga said. "But now, I'll take my time. I'll kill you. Very, very painfully."

It felt as though someone had poured a bone-melting potion into Briar, her insides turning to jelly with each word Baba Yaga spoke.

"Don't you agree, my dear hut?" Baba Yaga called out.

The hut groaned in response. "Give them hell," it replied.

"Hut, you'll be able to walk again," Baba Yaga cooed, her tone unsettlingly tender. "Heal, my lovely, heal."

The witch leaned back in her chair. Her wrinkled hand rose in a gesture of command. Her eyes, cold and merciless, locked onto Briar and Leon. "Now, do you have a death wish? Tell me."

Briar and Leon exchanged a terrified glance. The air seemed to grow colder, the shadows in the room lengthening and closing in around them.

"Speak!" Baba Yaga bellowed, her voice a thunderous roar that sent a spray of spittle flying from her lips. "Why did you break into my hut?"

Briar's throat felt like it was full of sand, each attempt to speak coming up dry and rasping. She opened her mouth, but no sound emerged. Her voice caught in a stranglehold of fear.

"To steal your book," Leon blurted out.

Briar's heart sank. He wanted to die, she thought.

"Let me handle this," she said, shooting him a warning glance.

Turning to face the witch, Briar cleared her throat, willing herself to be brave. "I... I need the book," she said. "You were, well, away, so we decided to borrow it." She shivered under the witch's unblinking stare. "We didn't mean to steal it."

Baba Yaga rocked in her chair, her eyes narrowing to slits as she scrutinized Briar. "And what will you do with my book?"

Briar took a deep breath, summoning all her courage. "Break a curse and save my kingdom," she said.

Baba Yaga's eyes narrowed further, a flicker of dark amusement crossing her face. "I do not care what happens to you or your kingdom," she said, clutching the book to her chest as if it were a beloved pet. "My book. My dear book. They are trying to take you away from me. Should I let you decide what punishment you want to give them?"

The book flipped its pages eagerly, the rustling sound like the whispering of spirits eager for blood.

"Hut, suggest some punishment?" Baba Yaga called out, her tone almost playful.

"Feed them to the bear," the hut responded. "I want to see the bear tearing them apart."

Baba Yaga's lips curled into a smirk. "Oh, the bear," she mused. "The hut is suggesting I feed you to the bear, as I did to that unfortunate man who dared to enter my home." Her eyes gleamed with sadistic pleasure as she pointed to a grisly head mounted on the wall, the hollow eyes staring lifelessly into the room.

Briar recoiled, her stomach churning at the sight. So, all the rumors about Baba Yaga were true.

"But feeding you to the bear would not be nearly painful enough," Baba Yaga said, stroking her chin thoughtfully. "I want to inflict a pain a thousand times worse than the pain you caused my hut. The right punishment for stealing my book."

Briar's mind raced, desperately trying to imagine a fate more horrific than being torn apart by a bear.

"It's not your book!" Leon shouted suddenly. "You are the thief! You took it from the forest fairies!"

Baba Yaga was in front of Leon in an instant, her movements a blur of speed and fury. Her hand shot out, seizing Leon by the throat, her nails digging into his flesh and drawing blood. "So, the forest fairies sent children to retrieve the book," she hissed. "The book is mine, boy. Mine!"

"Leave him!" Briar cried as she watched Leon's face turn an alarming shade of red, his eyes bulging as he struggled for breath.

The witch released Leon, who collapsed to the floor, gasping and coughing. Baba Yaga wheeled around, her eyes blazing with fury as she grabbed a fistful of Briar's hair, yanking her head back. "You will get your punishment," she snarled, her face inches from Briar's. "I'll do what witches are famous for. I'll cook you. You will go to my stomach, and your bones will join my yard."

Baba Yaga strode over to Briar's satchel, her eyes gleaming with malevolent delight as she rummaged through it. She pulled out the flying carpet. Her smirk widened into a grin of pure malice. She tossed the satchel aside, and it landed near the silver-haired boy.

"The flying carpet," the witch said, her gaze locking onto the enchanted fabric with a look of predatory glee.

"Give it back!" Briar yelled. "That's not yours!"

Baba Yaga pointed a gnarled finger, adorned with the blue ring, at the carpet. Flames erupted from the ring, licking hungrily at the fabric. Within moments, the flying carpet was reduced to a pile of smoldering ashes.

Lilliana's magic carpet was gone. Briar's hope of completing her quest crumbled to dust, her heart sinking into a pit of despair.

Baba Yaga turned toward the fireplace, a triumphant gleam in her eye. "Start the fire," she commanded, her voice echoing through the hut. "I am finally going to cook after a long time."

Chapter 20

Princess Briar Rose had often pondered the various ways she might meet her end. Cursed as a child, she imagined herself lying in bed, drifting off into a peaceful, eternal sleep. Sometimes she envisioned herself falling from the castle wall or being bitten by a snake in the forest. On better days, she hoped for a natural death in her old age, surrounded by loving grandchildren and great-grandchildren. But never, in her wildest imaginings, did she think she'd be cooked and devoured by a witch.

No, she couldn't accept such a fate. Giving up without a fight was for cowards, and Briar was determined to be the brave princess she had always aspired to be. Perhaps, she thought, there was still a chance to reason with the witch. Talking might have been a better strategy than storming into Baba Yaga's hut uninvited.

"Baba Yaga," Briar called out, her voice steady despite the fear gnawing at her insides. "Can we talk this through? Settle the matter peacefully?"

The witch turned to look at Briar with cold, calculating eyes. "Everything is settled," she replied. "I'm cooking you."

"I have a mission," Briar insisted. "I can't die now. I'll repay you for any damage we've caused."

Baba Yaga's expression remained unchanged, her eyes narrowing slightly as she regarded Briar.

"You can't kill us," Briar shouted. "It's unfair!"

The witch ignored her, her attention shifting to an enormous cauldron, its blackened sides already beginning to warm over a crackling fire. The cauldron was big enough to fit two people, and Baba Yaga cackled gleefully as she began chopping vegetables with swift, precise movements. "Ah!" she exclaimed, addressing the hut. "We're having a feast today! Isn't it wonderful?"

Briar's stomach churned at the sight of the witch. "Do you hear me? You can't eat us! I'm a princess, and my father will throw you in the dungeon!" Briar's voice wavered, and she knew her threat sounded weak, even to her ears.

The witch cackled again, louder this time, a sound that reverberated off the walls and seemed to fill the entire hut with malevolent glee. "Your father will never know what happened to you," she sneered.

"You can't do this!" Briar yelled, struggling against the ropes.

"It's okay, Briar," Leon said gently, his voice calm.

Briar shot him a sharp look, her eyes blazing with frustration. "She's going to cook us, Leon! How can you say it's okay?"

"We'll figure something out," Leon replied, though his voice trembled with uncertainty.

"When? After she digests us?" Briar retorted.

Leon had no response.

Briar leaned back against the wall, her body shaking. "Why do we always end up in a mess?" she muttered.

Leon looked at her with sympathy. "You can't always make things right," he said softly. "It's okay to mess up sometimes."

"Thanks," Briar replied, a bitter laugh escaping her lips. "That's very motivational."

At that moment, the silver-haired boy began to stir. He sat up slowly, his eyes wide and green, filled with a dazed confusion. His features were strikingly handsome, even in the dim light.

"Hello," he croaked, his voice hoarse. "I seem to be bound. Would you kindly untie me?"

Leon raised his bound hands, showing the ropes that held him captive. "We'd love to help, but we're tied up as well."

The boy's gaze swept around the room, taking in the surroundings. "Where are we?" he asked.

"We're about to be eaten by a witch," Briar replied.

"I'm sorry," the boy said, confused.

"There," Briar nodded towards the witch, who was merrily chopping vegetables and tossing them into the cauldron.

The boy's face went as white as his hair. "Oh, no! Baba Yaga! She tricked me"

"Tricked you?" Leon asked, raising an eyebrow. "I thought we were the only fools here."

The boy looked around frantically, his eyes landing on the horse, still ensnared in a net and lying unconscious on the ground. "Knight!" he exclaimed, panic rising in his voice. "If anything happens to him, I will never forgive myself."

"Why is everyone so depressed?" Briar muttered.

"That's what happens when you're about to die a painful death," Leon said dryly.

"Who are you?" Briar asked the boy.

"I'm Theodore," he replied, his voice steadier now. "I'm the youngest healer in the world, blessed by the fairy queen to serve humankind." He managed a small, strained smile.

"Nice to meet you," Briar said. "Why does the witch want you?"

"She wants to eat my horse," Theodore replied.

"I thought she wanted to eat you," Leon said.

"The witch is growing weak," Theodore explained. "She needs to gather as much magic as she can. My horse, Knight, is magical. She would never have caught me if she hadn't disguised herself as a dying old woman. People like Baba Yaga make it hard to believe in humanity."

"She's not human at all," Leon pointed out.

"I would have forgiven her if she wanted to eat me," Theodore said, his eyes glistening with unshed tears as he gazed at his horse. "But why innocent Knight? The poor horse."

"You said your horse is magical," Briar said, her curiosity aroused despite the grim circumstances.

"Yes, he is a magical horse from Fairyland," Theodore answered. "Knight can fly."

Briar's eyes widened with wonder. "Your horse can fly?" she repeated. "I thought they were only in tales."

Theodore smiled gently, the corners of his mouth lifting with a touch of pride. "He is as real as you and me. The fairy wanted me to reach my patient as soon as possible, so they gifted me Knight. He is a miracle."

"We need a miracle now, or we will go straight into the witch's stomach," Leon said.

"No, we can't lose hope," Theodore said. "Faith is the most important thing. That's what I tell my patients. We must not lose hope."

"It's nice that you're optimistic," said Leon, his eyes flickering nervously toward Baba Yaga, who was muttering to herself as she stirred her bubbling cauldron. "But being optimistic isn't enough. How are we going to escape her?"

Theodore's gaze remained steady. "We'll fly away," he said simply. "With my horse."

Briar's face lit up, hope blooming anew in her heart. "Yes! That's an amazing plan."

"You're forgetting one crucial obstacle in this plan. The witch Baba Yaga." Leon said. "Even if his horse can fly, we can't just escape her magic."

The small balloon of happiness that had inflated in Briar's heart burst with Leon's words. He was right. The witch's magic was powerful, and they couldn't simply fly away from her.

"So what?" Theodore said. "Are we just going to get eaten?"

"I don't mean that we should give up," Leon said. "We need a strong plan. First, we need to understand how powerful our enemy is and what weapons she has."

"The spell book and the magic ring," Briar said, her eyes narrowing as she glanced at the witch.

"And the ring isn't hers," Theodore added. "She killed the original owner to get it."

"What about her weaknesses?" Leon asked.

"She's already weak," Theodore replied, his gaze fixed on the witch. "Her magic is failing her, which is why she wants to consume Knight."

"So, she's only powerful if she has the ring and the book," Briar said thoughtfully. "If we can separate her from the book and the ring..."

"Exactly," Theodore nodded.

They exchanged determined glances, a silent understanding passing between them.

"Look at the book. The witch had left it in the chair." Briar pointed, as the witch placed the book on the chair and went to add more logs to the fire. The book appeared to be sleeping.

"She still has the ring," Leon said.

"I'll get the ring," Briar said.

"What?" Leon asked, his eyes widening in disbelief. "How?"

"Don't worry," Briar replied.

"Briar, if you're planning something stupid that could end in death, drop the plan immediately," Leon said, his voice laced with concern.

"Leon, it's your method, not mine," Briar replied with a smirk, her eyes twinkling with mischief.

"But first," Theodore interjected, holding up his bound hands. "We are tied up."

"I think I can do something about that," Briar said. "Theodore, can you give me my satchel?"

Theodore nodded, shifting awkwardly to kick the satchel toward Briar. It made a loud scraping sound as it slid across the floor, causing Baba Yaga to glance suspiciously in their direction. Briar quickly moved in front of the satchel, raising her voice to divert the witch's attention.

"Let us go!" she shouted.

Baba Yaga threw back her head and laughed wickedly. "You're not going anywhere," she sneered, turning back to her cauldron.

Still facing the witch, Briar sat down with her back to the satchel. She managed to open it with her hands bound, groping inside until her fingers brushed against the cool hilt of the dagger. She held the blade with a firm grip, scooting behind Leon, and started to cut the ropes. It was a slow, painstaking process, every movement filled with the fear of accidentally cutting him. Finally, after what felt like an eternity, the rope snapped, and Leon's hands were free.

Leon quickly set to work, freeing Briar. Once Briar was free, they turned their attention to Theodore, working together to release him from his bonds.

"Leon," Briar whispered urgently, her eyes locking onto him. "You get the book." She turned to Theodore. "And you wake your horse." She handed him the dagger to cut the net and prayed it wasn't enchanted.

At that moment, Baba Yaga turned to face them, her eyes narrowing with suspicion. The room fell into an eerie silence, and all of them froze, doing their best to look hopeless and bound. Theodore quickly hid the dagger behind his back.

"Now, now," the witch said, a twisted smile spreading across her face. "You are ready to be cooked."

The witch hobbled toward them, her twisted cane tapping rhythmically on the stone floor. Briar's heart pounded in her chest. It was now or never. She had to act. She couldn't let them end up in the cauldron.

Without warning, Briar sprang to her feet. With a fierce, determined cry, she leaped at Baba Yaga.

CHAPTER 21

Briar and Baba Yaga crashed onto the floor, the impact reverberating through the room. Quickly, Briar scrambled on top of the witch, straddling her with her knees pressed firmly into the witch's sides. Baba Yaga's ancient eyes blazed with fury as she looked up at her.

"What are you doing girl?" Baba Yaga spat, her voice a harsh rasp.

"Trying to escape," Briar grunted, tugging at the ring on the witch's gnarled finger with all her might. The ring was embedded with a dark blue gem that seemed to pulse with a sinister energy.

The witch clenched her fist. "No one escapes Baba Yaga," she hissed. Her breath smelled of decay. From this close, Briar could see the cruelty etched into every line of her face, making the witch even more horrifying.

"Leon!" Briar shouted. "The book!"

In a blur, Leon dashed to the chair where the book lay. He grabbed it, hastily tied it with a piece of rope, and stuffed it into his satchel. "Got it!" he called back.

"LEAVE MY BOOK!" Baba Yaga screamed, her eyes wild with fury as she struggled beneath Briar. She tried to shove Briar off, her strength surprising for someone who looked so frail.

Briar seized the moment of distraction, wrenching the witch's hand towards her and prying at her fingers, desperate to free the ring. Baba Yaga's eyes locked onto Briar's, a fierce, burning gaze that seemed to pierce into her soul. "Don't make your death more painful, girl," the witch snarled. She twisted her wrist violently, trying to break Briar's grip.

"I don't want to die," Briar gritted out through clenched teeth, her face contorted with effort. She fought to maintain her hold, her fingers digging into the witch's leathery skin.

With a sudden, vicious move, Baba Yaga drove her knee into Briar's stomach, knocking the wind out of her. Briar gasped, pain exploding through her body as she was thrown off the witch and landed hard on the cold floor.

Baba Yaga scrambled to her feet. "Stupid girl," she spat, raising her hand and aiming the ring directly at Briar. "I will—"

Before she could finish, Briar was on her feet. Summoning every ounce of strength, she launched herself at Baba Yaga, driving her knee into the witch's chest. The force of the blow sent the witch stumbling backward. Without giving her a chance to recover, Briar swung her fist, connecting solidly with Baba Yaga's face. The witch's head snapped to the side, but she quickly recovered.

"You dare strike me?" Baba Yaga roared, grabbing Briar's hand with a grip like iron and twisting it sharply. Pain shot up Briar's arm, causing her to cry out. The witch's grip tightened, and with a vicious snarl, she hurled Briar across the room.

Briar slammed into the wall, her vision blurring with the impact. She collapsed to the ground, pain radiating through her body. Baba Yaga, trembling with fury, aimed the ring at her, dark magic crackling at its stone. "Prepare to die, foolish girl," she shouted.

As a bolt of lightning shot out from the ring, Briar instinctively rolled to the side. The lightning bolt struck the wall, blowing a jagged hole. The hut roared in agony, the walls shaking with the force of the blast.

Desperate, Briar's eyes darted around the room, landing on a skull lying amidst the clutter. She grabbed it and, with a surge of adrenaline, hurled it at Baba Yaga. The skull struck the witch square in the face, causing her to stagger backward with a howl of rage.

Seizing the opportunity, Briar dashed forward, grabbing Baba Yaga's hand. Ignoring the revulsion that churned in her stomach, she bit down on the witch's leathery palm. Baba Yaga shrieked in pain.

With a final, desperate yank, Briar pulled the ring free. She scrambled to her feet, clutching the ring, feeling a strange surge of power coursing through her veins.

"GIVE IT TO ME!" Baba Yaga demanded, her voice a thunderous roar of fury. She looked more dangerous than ever, her eyes glowing with an unearthly light.

"After we leave," Briar shot back. "Theodore, get the horse ready!"

Across the room, Theodore and Leon were frantically trying to free the horse from the net. Theodore wielded the dagger Briar had given him, hacking at the thick ropes with all his strength. Leon had managed to create a small hole in the net, but it wasn't yet large enough to pull the horse free.

"Hurry up!" Briar urged, her eyes darting between her friends and the enraged witch. Panic clawed at her insides. What if they couldn't free the horse in time? What if the horse didn't wake up? How would they escape?

"You are not going anywhere," Baba Yaga screeched, advancing towards Briar, her hand outstretched. "Give me my ring!"

"No!" Briar shouted back, clutching the ring even tighter. She felt a strange, exhilarating power thrumming through her, bolstering her courage. "You're not getting it back." She turned to the prince. "Leon, quick, we don't have much time!"

Leon was a blur of movement, his hands a flurry of activity as he worked to free the horse. Tossing his sword aside, he yanked the net from the horse's body and, with a grunt, hurled it into the roaring fire the witch had built in the corner of the room, its flames hungrily consuming the tangled mess.

"You can't escape," Baba Yaga repeated.

Briar took a step forward, her heart pounding. "That's exactly what we're going to do." She brandished the ring, aiming it directly at the witch. "Be a good girl and stay still, or I'll hurt you."

"The horse isn't waking up!" Leon's voice cracked as he knelt beside the still form of the horse, shaking its massive head and splashing water over its face in a desperate attempt to rouse it.

"Then what do we do?" Briar shouted back, panic rising in her throat. The room was filled with the acrid smell of the net burning, and the walls seemed to close in on them.

"We have to leave without the horse," Leon called.

"No!" Theodore cried out. "I can't leave my horse!"

"Give it to me, girl," Baba Yaga's voice sliced through the chaos. She turned to the skeletons lining the walls, her bony fingers pointing at them. "Get my ring, my dear children."

With a sickening creak, the skeletons sprang to life. Their hollow eyes glowed with a malevolent light as they turned their skulls to face Briar and began their slow, menacing advance.

Briar's heart pounded. She pointed the ring at the advancing skeletons, her hand trembling. "Attack!" she shouted, her voice echoing in the tense silence of the room.

For a heartbeat, nothing happened. The skeletons kept advancing, their bony hands reaching out, and panic tightened around Briar's chest like a vice.

Briar gripped the ring. "Burn them," she commanded, her voice a desperate plea.

But still, nothing happened.

Baba Yaga cackled, her laughter a grating, high-pitched sound that seemed to fill the room. She clapped her hands together, mocking and triumphant. "Magic doesn't come to everyone, girl. Now give it to me and get ready to be cooked."

Briar's blood boiled with frustration and fear. She clenched her fist around the ring, her knuckles turning white. This had to work. It was their only way out. Lavonna's words echoed in her mind. "Magic is inside us. We just channel it through objects." Briar closed her eyes, forcing herself to relax, to calm her mind. She focused inward, summoning the magic from the depths of her heart, visualizing it flowing through her veins and into the ring.

But nothing happened.

"Wear the ring," Theodore shouted.

Briar slipped the ring on her middle finger. She took a deep breath and pointed the ring at the skeleton. "Burn them."

Suddenly, a warm, tingling sensation filled her body. Her eyes snapped open, and a jet of blue light burst from the ring, striking the skeletons. They exploded into pieces, their bones scattered across the room in a cloud of dust and ash.

Briar stood, wide-eyed and breathless, as the remnants of the skeletons clattered to the ground. A sense of triumph surged through her, mingling with the adrenaline that still pumped through her veins.

"NO!" Baba Yaga shrieked. Her eyes widened with a mix of astonishment and rage. "You can't use my ring!"

"It's not your ring," Briar retorted, her newfound confidence steadying her voice. "Like everything else, you stole it."

As she pointed the ring at the witch, her gaze flicked to Theodore. He was beside the horse, desperately trying to wake it by placing something—a vial of liquid, perhaps—into its mouth. Leon splashed water over the horse's face.

Briar turned her focus back to Baba Yaga just in time to see the witch flick her hand, a bolt of lightning crackling at her fingertips. "Die, you little pest!" Baba Yaga spat as she hurled the lightning towards Briar.

Briar ducked. The bolt sizzled past her and slammed into the wall, leaving a smoking, charred hole. The hut roared in pain, the walls shuddering with the impact. Briar's heart raced. She had underestimated Baba Yaga, assuming the witch had no magic of her own—a mistake that could easily cost her life.

With a snarl, Baba Yaga sent another bolt of lightning hurtling toward Briar. "You think you can defy me? I'll tear you apart!"

Briar's eyes widened in terror, but she forced herself to focus. She felt the power of the ring thrumming through her. She raised her hand, the ring glowing with an intense blue light.

"Stop!" she shouted, her voice echoing with a newfound authority.

The ring flared, and a brilliant beam of light shot out, intercepting the witch's lightning bolt in mid-air. The two forces collided with a deafening explosion, filling the room with blinding light and a wave of scorching heat.

Baba Yaga staggered back, her eyes wide with shock and rage. The witch started to mutter a spell.

Briar focused intently on the ring. She visualized immense lightning bolts erupting from it, each one larger and more powerful than anything the witch could conjure. "Attack! Attack! Attack!" she shouted.

The ring shuddered, vibrating with a force that seemed to resonate through her entire body. Suddenly, lightning bolts began to erupt from the ring in rapid succession, each bolt crackling through the air with deafening intensity.

The bolts hit all around the room, scorching the walls and setting the potion shelves ablaze. The air filled with the acrid stench of burning wood and potions. Baba Yaga let out an ear-splitting scream.

"Watch out!" Leon yelled, ducking as a bolt of lightning zoomed past them, narrowly missing his head.

One of the lightning bolts struck the horse. With a sudden, violent jolt, the horse leaped to its feet, electricity crackling around its body. Its eyes, now wide open, glowed with a strange, otherworldly light.

"Knight!" Theodore cried, engulfing the horse in a tight embrace. "Oh, thank God you're okay!" He buried his face in the horse's mane.

The horse shook itself vigorously, sending Theodore stumbling backward. Its body seemed to pulse with energy.

Briar, meanwhile, was struggling to control the ring. It had become an uncontrollable force, firing lightning bolts in all directions. The weight of the ring and the power surging through it made her sway from side to side, her arms trembling with the effort of holding it steady.

"Stop! Please, stop!" Briar cried. She closed her eyes and concentrated as hard as she could, willing the ring to cease its relentless assault. Gradually, the ring's vibration slowed, and finally, it stopped firing.

When Briar opened her eyes, she was met with the sight of thick smoke filling the room. She glanced down at her hair and saw that it was singed, smoke rising from the ends.

Across the room, Baba Yaga looked like a giant, grotesque fireball. Her hair was ablaze, and her eyes burned with a fiery rage. The witch's bony hand was clenched into a fist, and she began muttering a spell under her breath, her voice a low, malevolent hiss.

But Briar didn't give the witch the chance to finish. Now that she had the hang of the ring, she commanded it with confidence. She aimed it at Baba Yaga and, with a flick of her wrist, ropes of energy shot out, wrapping around the witch from head to toe. The ropes tightened, turning Baba Yaga into a mummified figure, her eyes the only part of her left uncovered.

"No! Release me!" Baba Yaga screamed, her voice muffled by the ropes. She thrashed against her bonds, but they held firm.

"Briar, quick!" Leon shouted.

Theodore had already mounted the horse, which was pawing at the ground, eager to be off. Briar ran to them, her heart pounding. Leon reached down, grabbed her hand, and helped her scramble onto the horse's back. Then he swung up behind her, holding on tight.

"Don't let them go, my dear!" Baba Yaga roared from the floor.

The doors and windows slammed shut with a deafening bang, trapping them inside.

"Now what?" Theodore shouted, his voice filled with panic.

Briar pointed the ring at the roof. With a surge of magic, she blasted a hole through the ceiling. The hut shuddered and roared in protest, and the witch's screams grew louder.

The horse unfolded giant white feathered wings from its sides, a sight that would have been majestic under different circumstances. With a powerful beat of its wings, it lifted off the ground, rising towards the open sky above.

As they soared upward, Briar glanced back at the witch, who was still writhing on the ground, her face contorted with rage. The princess pulled out the ring from her finger. "Witch, take your ring back! I don't want to steal it." She tossed the ring down towards Baba Yaga.

The ring fell into the boiling cauldron below, and in the next instant, it exploded with a thunderous boom, sending a shower of sparks and debris through the air.

"What? No! That's not what I meant..." Briar gasped, her eyes widening in horror.

"Next time I see you," Baba Yaga's thunderous voice bellowed from the wreckage, "I will eat you without bothering to cook!"

Briar shivered at the witch's words, an icy dread settling in her stomach. But they didn't linger to hear more. The horse's powerful wings carried them higher and higher, away from Baba Yaga's hut and the threat of being cooked alive.

CHAPTER 22

Briar clung tightly to Knight's silky mane as they soared higher and higher into the starry night sky. The cool wind whipped her hair around her face, but she welcomed the sensation. It was a reminder that they were alive and far from the clutches of Baba Yaga. The sense of relief was overwhelming. The towering trees of the dark forest below shrank away, and Briar felt the weight lifting from her heart.

The sky was a deep, velvety blue, with millions of twinkling stars that seemed almost within reach. The moon, bright and serene, cast a silvery light. Hundreds of feet above the ground, Briar felt a peculiar connection to the heavens, as though the stars were close enough to touch.

It was the first time she had ever enjoyed the night in the forest. Below them, the forest sprawled in all directions like a thick, dark blanket. The tall mountains in the distance rose majestically, their peaks brushing against the sky. As she gazed down, her heart lurched at the sight of the vast wilderness. The forest was more formidable than she had realized, a perfect haven for hiding dangerous creatures.

Knight's wings beat rhythmically, creating a gentle, almost musical sound that soothed Briar's nerves. She leaned back against Leon, her eyelids growing heavy with exhaustion. The steady motion of the horse's wings and the peaceful night began to lull her into a light sleep.

Suddenly, an unfamiliar voice broke through the serene moment, startling Briar awake. "So, are you guys going to thank me or not?"

Briar sat up, eyes wide with astonishment. The voice hadn't come from Leon or Theodore. It had come from the horse.

"I saved your lives, you know," the voice continued.

Briar blinked in disbelief as Knight turned his head back, squinting at them with a knowing expression. "Y-you can talk?" she stammered, barely able to believe her ears.

Knight let out a snort, his eyes rolling slightly. "Do you expect me to neigh like some common horse?" he asked.

"I've never met a talking horse before," Briar said.

"Well, now you have," Knight said, turning his head back to focus on flying. "I was born in Fairyland, raised by fairies, and then dragged away to live with this guy." He jerked his head slightly toward Theodore.

Theodore chuckled, patting Knight's neck affectionately. "Knight is a special horse, and the fastest in the world."

Knight huffed. "I'm more than just a fast horse. I have feelings, too, you know. And I miss Fairyland."

Briar giggled, her astonishment giving way to delight. "Wow, Knight! You're fantastic."

"Not that fantastic," Leon said, who had been silently listening to the horse the whole time. "My horse back home can run faster than you can fly."

Knight let out an angry grunt and, without warning, increased his speed dramatically. They shot forward like an arrow, and Briar, Leon, and Theodore were flung against each other, clutching desperately to avoid being thrown off.

"Theodore, slow him down!" Briar yelled over the roaring wind.

"Knight, slow down!" Theodore shouted, trying to regain control.

Ignoring his master completely, Knight surged ahead, the stars above blurring into streaks of light as they hurtled through the sky.

"Please, Knight!" Briar cried out, her grip tightening around Knight's mane. "Please slow down!"

Gradually, Knight slowed his pace, returning to a more manageable speed. "Does your horse run faster than this?" he asked Leon, his voice dripping with smugness. "Or do you want me to show you my maximum speed?"

"My horse—ouch." Leon started to respond, but Briar elbowed him sharply in the ribs, shooting him a warning look.

"Do you want to go back to Baba Yaga?" she hissed. "Don't insult the horse unless you want to fall and break every bone in your body."

Theodore clapped his hands, laughing. "That was terrific, Knight! You should save that speed for emergencies."

"At that speed, you'll have an emergency," Knight retorted. "Anyway, I'm the fastest horse in the world, magical and non-magical, included."

Briar couldn't help but smile. Knight was indeed a unique horse—one who could fly, talk, and had an attitude to match. His name suited him perfectly.

"I hope your speed is faster than Baba Yaga," Leon said, a hint of unease in his voice. "She's powerful. Do you think Knight can outrun her mortar and pestle?"

Knight grunted, clearly unimpressed. "I can outrun anything," he muttered, though his confidence seemed a bit forced.

Briar's mind drifted back to the witch. "Do you think Baba Yaga will follow us?" she asked. She had bound the witch, but the rope might not hold her for long.

She glanced down nervously, half-expecting to see the chicken-legged hut emerging from the sea of trees, with Baba Yaga flying after them in her magical mortar and pestle.

"Not now," Theodore replied. "Her hut is damaged. She's bound, and you've destroyed her ring. Plus, we have her spell book. By the time she starts looking for us, we'll be far away."

"The witch must be brewing up some recipe that includes us," Leon added, his tone dark. "She was furious."

"So," Briar said thoughtfully. "Anyone would have been angry if their house was destroyed."

Leon's eyebrows shot up in surprise. "You feel bad for the witch?"

"Of course," Briar replied, turning to face him. "What we did was wrong. We barged into her home and destroyed it. It's natural for her to be angry. I'd feel the same if someone did that to me."

Theodore chuckled, giving her a wry smile. "So, you would have naturally tried to eat the intruders?"

Briar shot him a playful glare. "Well, maybe not eat them, but I'd be upset."

"The witch deserves what she got," Leon said firmly. "She's terrorized people for so long. Kidnapping children, eating the m... Now she will think before she tries to eat any human. Cause they bite back."

They all laughed, the tension from their escape finally easing. It felt good to laugh after everything they had been through.

Knight took them to a clearing near a small pond, and they all agreed to stay there for the night.

"Even a magical horse needs to freshen up," Knight said with a dignified snort. He galloped into the pond to clean himself.

Briar looked down at her dirty gown. It was smudged with dirt and remnants of their adventure, but she was too tired to care about getting cleaned up. She glanced over at Leon and Theodore, who were busy setting up camp.

"How do you carry so many things in your satchel?" Briar asked, marveling as Theodore pulled out a variety of items from his seemingly small bag.

Theodore smiled, his eyes twinkling in the moonlight. "The fairies gave me this satchel. It can store an entire house inside and remain light as a feather."

"The fairies seem to like you," Leon remarked. "A flying horse, a magical satchel... What's next?"

"There are a few perks to serving humanity," Theodore replied with a grin, continuing to unpack the satchel.

Leon eyed the satchel wistfully. "I wish I had a magical satchel. I could have packed more chocolate cakes."

"Well, I don't have cakes," Theodore said, pulling out cooking pots and pans, "but I can whip up a nice meal."

It turned out Theodore had an entire kitchen hidden away in his magical bag. He produced bread, butter, a jar of milk, and a variety of fresh vegetables. Briar helped him chop tomatoes, potatoes, and green peas for a hearty vegetable soup, while Leon headed to the pond to catch fish.

The prince returned triumphantly, holding two large fish. "Can you do something with these?" he asked, offering the fish to Theodore.

"Certainly," Theodore replied, taking the fish and examining them. "These will make a fine addition to our meal."

Briar looked at the fish suspiciously. "What if they're magical?" she asked. The encounter with Baba Yaga had left her wary of eating anything that might be enchanted.

"Then we'll have a magical feast," Leon said with a mischievous grin. "Who knows, maybe we'll end up cooking a mermaid!"

Theodore laughed and expertly cleaned the fish, seasoning them with salt and spices. He wrapped the fish in large leaves and placed them under the hot coals to cook.

As the aroma of cooking fish and soup filled the air, Briar's stomach growled loudly. "It smells amazing," she said, her mouth-watering. "I don't care if it's magical or not. I'm starving."

Knight trotted over, his white coat gleaming in the moonlight, and eyed the food hungrily. "You're having a picnic, and you didn't think to invite me?"

"Here you go, Knight. Enjoy." Theodore handed the horse a sack of apples, which Knight devoured with gusto.

With the food ready, they gathered around the fire and dug in.

Briar took a bite, savoring the delicious, tender fish. "This is fantastic," she said.

As they ate, Theodore turned to Briar. "So, why did Baba Yaga capture you?"

Briar let out a dry chuckle. "She didn't capture us. We went to her hut to steal her spell book."

Theodore's eyes widened in shock. "What? Are you crazy? Didn't you know how dangerous she is?"

Leon, looking guilty, stopped eating and stared at the ground. "Blame me. It was my idea."

Briar shook her head, placing a reassuring hand on his arm. "I'm not blaming you, Leon. I needed the book." Briar turned to Theodore. "Have you ever heard about Sleeping Beauty?"

"Yes," Theodore said.

"Me too," Knight chimed in, his ears perking up.

Briar took a deep breath and said, "I'm Sleeping Beauty."

Theodore nearly choked on his soup. "You're what?" he sputtered.

Briar smiled and gave a small, regal bow. "I know, I'm famous."

"So, you're the princess who slept for a hundred years?" Theodore asked, his voice filled with awe.

Briar nodded. "Yes, that's me."

Theodore seemed almost giddy with excitement. "How did it feel? Sleeping for a hundred years must have had some effect on you!"

"Sleeping felt like sleeping," Briar replied, shrugging. "I don't remember much, and I felt fine when I woke up."

"Hey, don't forget, I'm part of the story, too. I'm the hero who broke the curse. I'm Briar's true love. I'm Prince Charming!" Leon said.

Knight, chewing on an apple, looked at Leon skeptically. "Prince Charming, huh? I was expecting someone taller, more handsome, and heroic. What a disappointment!"

Leon's face turned red. "Excuse me? I'm Prince Charming! The fairies didn't think I was a disappointment. I had the charm to break the curse, and I'm plenty tall!"

Knight snorted. "You only broke the curse because the fairies helped you."

"I found the castle myself!" he shouted, his voice echoing through the clearing. "I—"

"Leon, Knight!" Briar cut in sharply. "Let's not argue about the past."

Leon, seething with anger, dropped back onto the ground and resumed slurping his soup.

Theodore, trying to ease the tension, cleared his throat. "So, the curse was broken by—"

"I broke the curse!" Leon shouted again.

Briar held up her hands, signaling for calm. "The point is," she began, looking directly at Theodore, "the Wicked Fairy cursed my kingdom again. The Curse of Thorns is spreading, and we have until my birthday to break it." She then explained the dire situation they were in, and how they had only just begun their quest to gather the objects needed for the ritual to save her kingdom. "The Ancient Book of Spells was the first object, and we had no choice but to steal it from the witch."

Theodore listened intently, nodding as he processed the information. "I don't think you did anything wrong," he said finally. "You stole the book to save your kingdom and its people. I would have done the same if it meant helping someone."

"So, when are you going to break the curse? I love it when curses get broken," Knight asked.

"We've only just started," Briar said. "Right now, we have one object. The next thing we need is a dragon's gold."

Theodore's eyes widened with surprise. "Do you know any dragons?" he asked. "Dragons aren't exactly easy to find."

"There's a dragon that lives in this forest," Briar replied. "The fairies had given us a magic carpet to reach the mountain, but Baba Yaga burned it."

"And Briar didn't let me bring my horse, which is incredibly fast, by the way. So now we have to walk," Leon said.

Knight let out a hearty laugh. "Well, good luck climbing a mountain in less than a day on foot," he said with a smirk.

"It's impossible," Theodore said. "But don't worry Knight and I will take you."

Briar blinked in surprise. "What?"

"Why?" Knight asked.

Theodore turned to Briar. "Princess, you helped me escape the witch. I owe you a debt. The least I can do is help you."

Briar shook her head. "No, Theodore. I can't put your life in danger. You have responsibilities, patients who need you."

Theodore waved her concerns away. "Right now, I don't have any patients. And healing an entire kingdom is far more important."

"We don't need your help," Leon said.

"They don't need our help," Knight said.

"The fairy would want you to help them, Knight," Theodore said, turning to his horse.

Knight sighed and grumbled, "Fine."

Theodore's face lit up with a smile. "So, it's settled. We'll accompany you on this great task."

"You don't have to do this, Theodore," Briar said.

The healer shook his head firmly. "Even if you refuse, I'll follow you. So, you might as well accept our help."

Briar let out a frustrated growl. Why were boys so stubborn and childish?

"So, the dragon's mountain is next?" the healer asked, putting his bowl back and rubbing his hands.

"I haven't given you permission to come with us," Briar said.

"I don't need your permission for great work," Theodore said. "I'm here to serve humanity. Right Knight." He looked at Knight, but the horse looked away. "Knight can take us to the mountain in a few hours."

Briar thought about it for a minute. She didn't have an option now. Knight could help her. And she would try her best to keep them out of danger.

"Okay," she said. "You can come with us."

Leon pulled Briar aside. "We don't know them. We can't trust them."

Briar met his eyes. "They're willing to risk their lives for us, Leon. I trust them."

She turned back to Theodore. "If you're going to come with us, you need to make a promise."

Theodore looked intrigued. "What promise?"

"The same promise Leon made before we left our castle," Briar explained. "When I say back off, you guys have to listen to me and let me handle things."

Knight nodded. "I have no problem with that. Theodore, promise the princess."

Theodore placed a hand over his heart and nodded solemnly. "I promise."

Briar allowed herself a small smile. "Alright, let's break this curse."

Chapter 23

As the first light of dawn broke across the horizon, Briar and her friends mounted Knight and took to the skies. The morning air was crisp as they soared over the vast expanse of the forest. Briar was grateful for the swift flight, knowing it spared them the grueling trek through the dense woods and rugged terrain below.

In the light of the rising sun, the forest transformed into a breathtaking tapestry of greens and blues. Rivers wound like silver threads through the lush canopy, and ponds shimmered like jewels scattered across the landscape. Briar leaned over Knight's side, marveling at the beauty below. Her heart lifted at the sight of a herd of deer grazing peacefully on a sprawling meadow. However, as they flew closer, one deer looked up, and its eyes flashed red, sending a shiver down Briar's spine. She realized with a jolt that these were no ordinary deer. They were creatures of darkness, cloaked in a guise of innocence.

"Did you see that?" Briar said.

Leon nodded. "Nothing is as it seems here."

The journey continued, and soon they reached the towering dragon's mountain, the tallest among the surrounding peaks. Its jagged summit pierced through the thick, swirling clouds, reaching toward the sky like a spear. The mountain was cloaked in dense, ancient forests that stretched from the base to the top.

Knight circled once before descending toward the peak, where a massive cave mouth gaped like a dragon's maw. As they landed, the heat hit them like a physical blow. The air was thick and suffocating, making it hard to breathe. Briar wondered if it was the altitude or the dragon's fiery breath that made the air so unbearably hot.

"My job here is done," Knight announced as Briar and her friends dismounted. "This place gives me the creeps. Many heroes have met their end here, lured by the dragon's treasure."

"Thanks for the pep talk," Leon said dryly as he adjusted his sword.

Knight huffed. "Just thought you should know."

"I'm not scared," Briar declared, though her voice wavered ever so slightly.

"Well, I am," Knight retorted, shaking his mane. "I've seen dragons up close. They can burn you with a single breath. Turn you into a crispy snack before you even know what's happening. And I have no intention of meeting such a fiery end. I'm only two hundred and four years old. So young!" The horse turned a wary eye toward the cave entrance, a dark void that seemed to swallow the light. "I'll stay out here, where it's safe."

Theodore frowned at the horse. "Knight—"

"It's alright, Theodore," Briar interjected, placing a reassuring hand on Knight's flank. "Let him stay. We'll manage."

Knight let out a relieved snort. "Thank you, princess. You're the sensible one." He turned to Theodore, his eyes narrowing. "You should stay with me, healer. What will happen to your mother and your farm if you get yourself killed there?"

"I'm not a coward like you," Theodore shot back, his tone icy.

"Just not as wise," Knight said with a smug shake of his head. "Good luck in there. You'll need it."

"Hurry up," Leon called from the cave entrance.

Briar took a deep breath, pushing aside her fear. With a last glance at Knight, she followed Leon into the darkness of the cave, her heart pounding with a mix of dread and determination.

The tunnel narrowed as they delved deeper. The walls pressed in on them, making the air thick and stifling. The light from their torches flickered, casting eerie shadows that danced along the rocky passage. The deeper they went, the more oppressive the heat became, wrapping around them like a suffocating blanket.

As they descended, a faint red glow began to illuminate the tunnel, casting an otherworldly light on the rough stone walls. Briar's breath caught in her throat as they rounded a corner and saw the source of the glow. Liquid lava pulsed through the rock, snaking along the walls like fiery veins. The heat radiating from the molten rock was intense, making the air shimmer with waves of unbearable heat.

"Lava?" Briar asked as sweat trickled down her forehead.

"Dragons like to live close to lava," Leon replied, fanning himself with one hand. "They thrive in these hot temperatures."

The heat surged again, enveloping them in a stifling wave that made the very air seem heavy. Within moments, their clothes clung to their bodies, soaked with sweat, and Briar felt as though she were trapped inside a giant oven, each breath a struggle against the suffocating heat.

Theodore reached into his satchel. "I think I have something that might help us deal with this temperature," he said, pulling out a knobby root. He snapped it into three pieces and handed one to Briar and another to Leon.

"Chew on this. It's a cooling root. Very useful for traveling in the summer heat," he explained, popping a piece into his mouth.

Leon eyed the root with skepticism, turning it over in his fingers. "Are you sure this works?" he asked.

"Why don't you find out for yourself?" Theodore replied, already chewing.

Briar hesitated only for a moment before biting into the root. A surprising mix of flavors burst into her mouth—spicy ginger, sharp black pepper, refreshing mint, and an icy tingle that spread through her throat and chest. As the juice trickled down to her stomach, a blissful chill enveloped her, as if she had been plunged into a pool of cold water.

"Wow," Briar exclaimed, feeling the coolness spread through her limbs. "This is incredible, Theodore."

Leon finally took a cautious bite. "Not bad," he admitted.

The healer grinned. "Let's just hope it lasts."

They continued down the narrow, winding tunnel, careful not to touch the scorching walls. The lava oozing from the stone ceiling dripped like molten rain, sizzling as it hit the ground.

Finally, the tunnel ended abruptly in front of an iron door, its surface etched with ancient runes that seemed to pulse with a dim, malevolent light. Briar's heart pounded in her chest as she stared at the door, Knight's warnings echoing in her mind. The horse had been right—dragons were not to be underestimated. One wrong move, and they could all meet a fiery end.

"Wait," Briar said, as she placed a hand on Leon's arm. Leon and Theodore had already risked so much for her. She couldn't drag them further into danger. "Remember the promise you guys made to me?"

Leon, who had already drawn his sword, looked at her with confusion. "Yes, I promised to support you."

Theodore nodded in agreement. "We're in this together, Briar."

"I know," Briar said. "But you also promised that if I told you to back off, you would."

Leon's eyes narrowed as realization dawned. "What are you saying? No way. I can't let you do this alone. I'm coming with you."

"The prince is right," Theodore added. "We can't let you face the dragon by yourself."

"NO!" Briar shouted, her voice echoing through the cavern. "You two are going back to Knight and waiting for me. I'll find the dragon's treasure alone. I've already seen both of you nearly die because of me in Baba Yaga's hut. I can't risk losing you here."

"It's not your fault Baba Yaga captured me," Theodore pointed out.

"I'm a dragon expert, remember?" Leon insisted, his eyes flashing with determination. "You need my help."

Briar clenched her fists, her nails digging into her palms as she struggled to keep her composure. "Both of you, get out of the cave," she ordered. "That's final. If you don't, you can't come with me on my journey anymore."

Leon's face twisted with frustration. "But—"

"No buts," Briar interrupted, her eyes fierce. "Leon, you never listen to me. You always make reckless decisions." She hated to say it, knowing it would hurt him, but she had no other choice. "You're being foolish, and I can't risk you doing something stupid near the dragon and ruining everything."

Leon gave her a pained look. "I'm foolish."

"Yes," Briar lied. But she had to stop the prince.

Leon's expression darkened, and he looked away, staring at the ground. The silence stretched between them. Without warning, Leon turned and sprinted to the massive door, flinging it open and slipping through before Briar could react.

"Leon!" Briar cried, her heart lurching as she and Theodore rushed after him. "Why can't you ever listen to me?"

But Leon didn't look at her. He stood transfixed, his eyes wide with shock. Briar turned to see what had captured his attention and stifled a scream.

They stood on the edge of a narrow stone bridge that stretched across a vast chasm. On the other side, a pair of massive, ornate doors loomed, their surfaces intricately carved with dragon motifs.

A river of molten lava roiled beneath the bridge, its angry, glowing surface bubbling and hissing. The heat from the river was intense, radiating up in waves that distorted the air and made the very ground seem to tremble.

"Oh!" Briar whispered, clutching Leon's arm for support. "This is it. The dragon's lair." The other side of the bridge seemed a lifetime away, and the massive double doors loomed distant, taunting her with their inaccessibility. How were they ever going to reach them?

Briar made the mistake of looking down again. The sight of the churning, fiery lava far below sent a wave of dizziness through her, and her legs wobbled like jelly. She quickly squeezed her eyes shut, clutching her chest as her heart pounded wildly

"I wish we had Knight with us," Theodore muttered.

Leon peered over the edge, his face pale under the heat. "What if this is just an illusion?" he said.

"Real or illusion, we still have to cross it," Briar said firmly, trying to steel herself against the overwhelming fear. She took a deep breath, squared her shoulders, and took the first tentative step forward, her boots scraping against the hot, rough stone. Leon and Theodore followed closely behind.

As the three of them timidly made their way across the narrow bridge, a sudden gust of wind howled through the cavern, nearly knocking them off. Briar's arms flailed wildly as she struggled to maintain her balance. With nothing to hold on to, she dropped to her knees, balancing herself on all fours, the scorching stone searing her palms, causing blisters to form instantly.

After the wind subsided, Briar gingerly rose to her feet, her hands aching from the burns. She pulled out her sword, using it as a makeshift walking stick to steady herself as she continued toward the other side. Time seemed to stretch into an eternity, the unbearable heat pressing down on them despite the cooling root Theodore had given them.

"We're almost there," she muttered to herself, though she wasn't sure if she was trying to convince Leon and Theodore or herself. Her throat was dry, her lips cracked from the relentless heat.

Finally, after what felt like a lifetime of terror, they reached the end of the bridge. Briar let out a shaky breath of relief as they stepped onto the solid ground in front of the massive doors.

"Please, no more bridges," she whispered fervently, glancing up at the imposing doors that stood before them.

Leon pushed open the door with all his strength. It groaned loudly on its hinges, revealing a yawning, pitch-black tunnel beyond. The oppressive heat of the lava river was replaced by a cool, damp chill that seeped into their bones. Briar's sigh of relief was audible as she stepped inside.

"Well, a dark tunnel is better than another bridge over a river of lava," she said, trying to keep her voice light despite the lingering fear gnawing at her insides. The darkness enveloped them as they moved forward, swallowing the faint light from the lava behind them.

"Theodore, do you have anything we can use as a light?" Leon asked.

"Nothing," Theodore replied, shaking his head. "I left my torch outside. We didn't think we'd need it here."

Briar's skin prickled with unease. The darkness felt suffocating, almost alive, and she couldn't shake the feeling that they were being watched. The hairs on the back of her neck stood on end as she glanced nervously around, her eyes straining to pierce the blackness. "Did you see that?" she whispered urgently.

"What?" Leon asked.

"The eyes," Briar said, her voice a trembling whisper. "I swear I saw eyes on the walls, watching us."

An icy shiver ran down her spine as something whispered in her ear, the words unintelligible but filled with malice. She yelped as long, sharp nails scratched down her back, sending a bolt of fear through her. Her sword slipped from her grasp and clattered to the ground with a loud clang that echoed through the tunnel.

"What happened?" Leon asked.

"There's something in here with us," Briar said, her voice shaking as she retrieved her sword. "I can feel it."

"I can feel it too," Theodore said.

"Let's stick together," Leon suggested. He took Briar's hand in his and reached for Theodore's.

They moved forward, their hands gripping tightly as they navigated the twisting tunnel. The darkness pressed in on them from all sides, and the feeling of being watched grew stronger with every step. Briar's heart raced as shadows seemed to flicker and dance just beyond her vision, and the whispered voices grew louder.

After what felt like hours of stumbling through the dark, Briar spotted a faint glow ahead. It was a small, flickering light that beckoned them forward.

Ignoring the creeping fear that clawed at their minds, they broke into a run, the soft glow growing brighter with each step. The whispers and shadows seemed to recede as they approached the light, and finally, they reached another massive door. Briar's heart sank at the sight. How many more doors would they have to pass through?

"Please, let this be the last one," she murmured, pushing the door open with trembling hands.

As the door swung wide, they were blinded by a brilliant, golden light that filled the room beyond. Blinking against the sudden brightness, Briar gasped as her eyes adjusted to the dazzling scene before her. They stood at the entrance of a vast chamber, its walls lined with gleaming treasures that glittered in the golden light.

CHAPTER 24

The vast chamber stretched before them, a glittering expanse of wealth that seemed to defy imagination. Treasure chests overflowed with gleaming gold coins, jewels of every hue sparkled, and statues crafted from pure gold stood sentinel among the riches. Briar couldn't help but be awestruck by the wealth that surrounded them. It was a sight beyond anything she had ever seen, even in the grandest halls of her kingdom.

"This chamber has enough gold to make a few kingdoms rich," Theodore remarked, his eyes wide with wonder as he surveyed the room.

Briar nodded in agreement, her gaze lingering on the golden statues of kings and knights that lined the chamber walls. "It's... breathtaking," she whispered. She was a princess, but she had never seen so many treasures in her life before.

Leon looked around with a frown. "Where is the dragon?" he asked. "I thought he would be waiting for us, ready to attack."

"Maybe the dragon left the cave," Briar suggested hopefully, though her heart hammered in her chest at the thought of facing the fearsome creature.

"Is that a dragon?" Theodore asked, pointing to a small golden castle tucked away in a corner of the chamber. A miniature figure perched atop one of the castle towers.

Leon strode over to the castle and plucked the golden dragon from its perch. "A real one would have been much better," he remarked, turning the figurine over in his hand.

"Leon!" Briar exclaimed. "Your habit of picking up everything is going to get us into trouble someday."

The prince rolled his eyes. "And I hate your habit of snatching everything I find," he retorted.

"Stop finding problems," Briar said. "We need to stay focused."

Suddenly, the figurine shuddered in Briar's hand. With a loud clatter, she tossed it away, watching in horror as it began to shake and tremble on the floor. Then, to their astonishment, the dragon statue began to grow, its form shifting and expanding until it towered over them like a colossal titan.

"I'm free!" the dragon roared, its voice reverberating through the chamber like thunder. Flames danced in its eyes as it basked in its newfound freedom, and Briar's heart sank as she realized the danger they were in.

Leon drew his sword, his face set in determination. "I'll kill—"

But before he could finish his sentence, Theodore clamped a hand over his mouth. Briar and Theodore quickly pulled Leon behind the statues of the golden kings and knights, their hearts pounding in their chests as they crouched in the shadows.

The dragon was one of the most beautiful creatures Briar had ever seen. His golden body was covered in shiny scales that looked like emeralds and rubies, sparkling with green and red colors. Down the length of his graceful tail were sharp, polished spikes. From his broad shoulders grew huge, bat-like wings, their leathery surfaces reflecting the light like liquid gold. As he moved, his wings opened smoothly, casting shadows around the room.

"I'm free!" the dragon continued to roar, its voice echoing off the chamber walls. Flames licked at the air as the creature unleashed its fiery breath, the temperature in the chamber rising to unbearable levels. ·

"Let me go." Leon's voice came out muffled. The prince struggled to throw Briar and Theodore off of him.

"Don't get us killed," Briar hissed in Leon's ear and gripped him.

"Where are you humans?" the dragon said.

Briar exchanged a terrified glance with Theodore. Was the dragon searching for them? Would it hunt them down and destroy them?

Then, to their astonishment, the dragon's voice softened, filled with gratitude and wonder. "Where are you, my savior?" it called, its tone almost pleading. "Please come out and let me thank you."

"Savior," Briar mouthed the word, her heart pounding in her chest.

"The dragon wants to thank us," Theodore whispered.

"He wants to kill us," Leon hissed back, as he struggled to free himself from Theodore's grasp.

Briar peeked from behind the enormous statue of a king, her face half-hidden in the shadows. "Are you talking to us?" she called out.

The dragon's head snapped toward her with a sudden, piercing gaze. His eyes, the color of burning embers, squinted slightly. "Yes," he rumbled. "Are there any other humans here?"

Briar shook her head vigorously, her hair swaying in the faint, scorching breeze that flowed through the cavern. "Only us," she replied.

"Please, come out," the dragon requested.

Briar shook her head again, clutching her cloak tightly around her. "What if you burn us?" she asked.

The dragon laughed, a deep, resonant sound that bounced off the cavern walls, sending small rocks and dust raining down from the ceiling. "I'll never hurt you. I promise," he said, his laughter dying away into a series of gentle rumbles.

Briar knew that magical creatures took their promises very seriously. Besides, she needed his gold. She glanced at Theodore, who gave a small, encouraging nod. Reluctantly, they both turned to Leon, forcing him to lower his sword back into its sheath.

The three of them emerged from their hiding place. They stood a safe distance from the dragon, their hearts racing.

The dragon stared at them for a long, contemplative moment. "Welcome to the golden chamber of mighty dragon Donovan, young humans," he said. He stepped forward with surprising grace for his size and bowed his massive head low. "Thank you for freeing me."

Leon raised an eyebrow. "What are you talking about?"

"You saved me," the dragon answered.

"How?" Briar asked.

"By breaking the curse," the dragon explained, a hint of sadness creeping into his voice.

"Which curse?" Briar asked.

"A painful curse that had trapped me in this cave for years," said the dragon, his eyes darkening with the memory. "Many years ago, I was a greedy dragon. Full of hunger for treasure and gold. I didn't care about anything. You know, I was a bad boy. I was selfish. I was obsessed with gold. And in my greed, I made a great mistake. I killed two fairies because they refused to give me the golden castle they were guarding." He nodded sadly toward the gleaming castle at the back of the cavern. "I stole the castle and brought it to my cave. Later, an angry fairy, who was the mother of the two fairies I had killed, followed me into my cave and cursed me to turn into a golden statue forever." The dragon's breath came in heavy, sorrowful sighs, and sparks flew out of his nostrils with each exhale. "Then I realized what had happened. Yes, I love gold, but being trapped here for an eternity? That sounded bad. So, I begged the fairy for mercy. Thankfully, she was kind. She said the curse would only be broken when a human would come into my cave, not inspired by greed but with goodwill in their heart. And the human's touch would break my curse."

He looked up at the ceiling, his gaze distant and filled with sorrow. "A lot of humans came into my cave over the years, but they were all greedy. They would jump into the treasures the moment they entered the chamber. Some came in groups and they would fight among themselves, killing each other in their greed. I saw in them a reflection of my past and was disgusted with myself for ever being like that." The dragon sobbed, and huge, glistening droplets of tears rolled down his scaly cheeks, splashing onto the ground below. Briar stared in astonishment, more so because the dragon's tears were made of water, not fire as she had imagined. She never thought such a majestic creature could cry at all.

"I felt so lonely," the dragon sniffed. "Yes, there are the ghosts of the people who died in the cave, but they were too depressing to talk to."

"There are ghosts?" Theodore exclaimed, his face pale with fear.

"Yes, the tunnel is haunted by them," the dragon said. "They are nasty."

"I don't like ghosts," Theodore said, clutching his hands tightly together as if trying to ward off some invisible threat. "And I don't have any roots or magical herbs to chase them away."

"At last," the dragon said, a deep huff escaping his nostrils, sending a warm breeze across the room. "My wait is over. You three came into this cave with goodwill in your heart and broke my curse. Now I can finally escape this cave and leave behind the gold that once ensnared me."

The dragon's eyes softened as he gazed at them, the once imposing figure now seeming almost gentle.

"You should thank Leon," Briar said, pointing toward the prince. "Technically, he touched you first."

The dragon's massive head swung slowly toward Leon, and he lowered himself into a respectful bow. "Thank you, handsome boy, for breaking my curse," the dragon rumbled.

Leon's eyes twinkled with a mix of pride and amusement as he winked at the dragon. "I'm good at breaking curses," he said with a roguish grin. "I'm Prince Leon, at your service."

"I'm Princess Briar Rose," Briar added.

"And I'm Theodore the Healer," Theodore said, giving a polite smile.

"It's a blessing to meet you all," the dragon said. "But what brings you to my cave?"

"Well," Briar said. She was pleased that the dragon's curse was broken, but her curse still needed to be broken. "My kingdom is cursed and I'm on my way to break it, and that's why we are in your cave."

"A curse?" The dragon shuddered as if the mere mention of a curse brought back unpleasant memories.

"Yes," Briar continued. "The Wicked Fairy cursed my kingdom not because we did anything to her. She's evil. The people of my kingdom are turning into monsters."

"Sometimes, I wish I could snatch the fairies' wands and burn them to ashes," the dragon growled, a fierce burst of flame escaping his mouth. Briar ducked swiftly, feeling the searing warmth pass overhead.

"To break the curse, I need to complete a ritual," Briar said.

"Breaking a curse is so difficult. I can feel your pain," the dragon said sympathetically. "How can I help you?"

Briar blinked in surprise, hardly daring to believe her ears. The dragon was offering his help. "You want to help me?" she asked, her voice trembling slightly, as if afraid she was imagining the words.

"Yes," the dragon answered. "It will be a great start to my new life. Then I'll go in search of my ultimate peace."

"Can I take a small piece of your gold?" Briar asked hesitantly, as she glanced around the cavern, filled with piles of glittering treasure.

"Take as much gold as you want," the dragon said. "The whole chamber is yours."

"What?" Leon asked, his eyes widening in astonishment. "You want to give us the gold? Don't you want to duel or anything?"

The dragon exhaled deeply, a gust of hot air washing over them like a furnace. "I have no desire to fight, nor for gold or anything else," he said wistfully, his gaze distant, as if looking at some unseen horizon. "Now, all I seek is peace."

"Is he truly a dragon?" Leon whispered to Briar.

"Take the gold," the dragon urged. "We don't have much time."

Briar took a tentative step forward, her heart pounding as she approached a chest overflowing with glittering chunks of gold. Each piece gleamed with an almost magical light, casting flickering reflections on the cavern walls.

"Wait," Leon said sharply, yanking Briar back by the arm. "What if he's playing a game? He could pretend to be nice and then, when we least expect it, he'll attack us."

"I'm not planning anything," the dragon said. "I truly want to help you, young humans, as you helped me. I know it's hard to trust a creature like me, but please, believe me."

"If he attacks me," Briar said, turning to Leon with a determined look in her eyes, "you can kill him."

Briar took a deep breath and walked cautiously toward the chest. She picked up a small chunk of gold, feeling the warm metal against her skin. She clutched the gold tightly, a smile of victory spreading across her face as she turned to her friends.

Suddenly, the golden chamber began to rumble. The ground beneath their feet shook violently, sending ripples through the piles of treasure.

Chapter 25

"What is happening?" Briar shouted, her voice barely audible over the deafening roar of the cave collapsing around them. The golden walls of the chamber were cracking, and the ground buckled violently beneath their feet. Treasure chests toppled over, spilling their contents of gold, diamonds, and glittering gems, which scattered and rolled in a chaotic frenzy.

The ground heaved again, throwing Briar off balance. A massive chandelier, which had once bathed the room in a soft glow, now shattered from the ceiling and crashed to the floor just a few feet away from her, sending shards of crystal flying in all directions.

Amidst the chaos, the dragon surveyed the room with a casual, almost disinterested air. "Now that the curse is broken, the cave is closing," he said, his voice calm. "It will bury all the treasures and my suffering."

"And us!" Leon shouted as a portion of the ceiling smashed onto the floor, crushing several treasure chests beneath its weight.

"We are doomed!" Theodore cried, his face pale with fear as giant cracks spider-webbed across the floor. "We're going to be buried alive! We'll die and become ghosts!"

"No," the dragon replied. "You think I'd let that happen?" He lowered himself, offering his back. "Hop on. I'll give you a ride."

For a moment, Briar could only stare at the dragon in disbelief, but then the ground buckled again, and she sprang into action. She sprinted toward the dragon and leaped onto his back. "Come on, hurry!" she urged the boys.

Theodore followed quickly, scrambling up behind Briar. But Leon stood as if frozen, seemingly oblivious to the chaos around him.

"Leon, quick!" Briar yelled.

"What if he kidnaps us?" Leon called back.

"At least he'll take us out of here!" Theodore shouted, his eyes fixed on the ceiling, which threatened to collapse at any moment. "Prince Leon, if you don't hurry, we'll have to leave you behind!"

"Oh, you seem eager to leave me," Leon shouted, just as two golden statues toppled over, sending him sprawling to the ground. His crown slipped off his head, rolled across the floor, and disappeared amidst the scattered treasure.

Pushing the statues aside, Leon clambered to his feet, clutching his head. "My crown!" he shouted.

"Leon!" Briar shouted. "We have to go, now!"

"I can't leave my crown!" Leon protested, frantically searching through the debris. Rocks rained down from the ceiling, but he seemed oblivious, his focus solely on retrieving his lost crown.

Briar's heart ached for him. She understood the significance of the crown. But they had no time. "Leon, please! If we survive this, you can get another crown!"

Desperation etched on his face, Leon kicked aside golden goblets and jewels, his search growing increasingly frantic. It was clear he was losing hope.

Briar leaped down from the dragon and dashed over to him. Leon was struggling to push a heavy statue of a knight aside, trying to peer beneath it. Rocks tumbled down around them furiously. The ceiling was dangerously close to collapsing.

"Leon," Briar yelled, grabbing his arm and yanking him away from the statue. "Forget the crown. We need to go, now!"

He looked at her, his face flushed and eyes filled with tears. "But my crown..."

"The kingdom will give you another crown," Briar said firmly, not waiting for his response. She pulled him toward the dragon with all her strength.

"Quickly!" Theodore shouted, reaching down to pull both of them onto the dragon's back.

The dragon scanned the room one last time, a wistful expression on his massive face. "Farewell, my dear treasure. It was a pleasure collecting you." He turned his head to Briar, Leon, and Theodore. "Are you ready?"

"Yes!" Briar and Theodore shouted in unison. Leon grumbled under his breath but didn't argue further.

With a powerful thrust, the dragon shot out of the chamber just as the ceiling caved in, smashing to the floor with a thunderous crash. The narrow tunnel ahead was a labyrinth of rock and debris, making it difficult for the dragon to spread his wings fully. The confined space and falling rocks slowed his progress.

Briar, Leon, and Theodore flattened themselves against the dragon's back, ducking as the jagged ceiling scraped against their heads. The ground trembled violently beneath them, the deafening sound of rock grinding against rock filling the air. Lava explosions echoed through the tunnel.

The dragon grunted, pushing himself to fly faster through the collapsing tunnel. Rocks and debris rained down, and the dark shadows of the cave seemed to close in around them.

Dark shapes emerged from the walls, ceiling, and floor—shadowy fingers reaching out to grasp them. Chilling voices echoed through the tunnel, sending shivers down Briar's spine.

"Die! Die! Die!" the ghosts chanted, their voices a haunting chorus.

"You die again!" Briar shouted back.

"The ghosts are chasing us!" Theodore's voice quivered with fear.

"Fear not," the dragon said confidently. "The dead cannot harm you."

Dust and debris filled Briar's eyes, making it hard to see. It felt as though the tunnel was narrowing, trying to trap them inside. Suddenly, a massive boulder crashed down ahead of them, blocking their path. Briar's heart pounded in her chest, terror clawing at her insides.

"Oh, my god!" Theodore cried.

"Donovan, do something!" Briar yelled.

The dragon let out a low growl. "Hold on tight!" he bellowed.

With a surge of power, Donovan reared back and unleashed a torrent of fire. The flames engulfed the boulder, reducing it to molten rubble. The dragon pushed forward, barreling through the debris with a roar of determination.

The tunnel shook violently as the dragon surged through the collapsing cave, his powerful wings beating against the air. The heat from the lava and the pressure of the collapsing rocks made the journey feel like an eternity.

As they soared over the lava river, Briar kept her eyes tightly shut, feeling the intense heat radiating from below. She knew without Donovan's intervention, they would have perished in the fiery depths below or been buried alive by the collapsing cave.

When they finally left the treacherous river behind, the tunnel widened, allowing Donovan to fly more freely. The light spilling from the cave entrance ahead grew brighter, beckoning them toward safety. With powerful beats of his wings, Donovan accelerated, the wind rushing past them like a hurricane.

Just as they burst out of the cave into the open air, the entire structure collapsed behind them with a thunderous roar. Knight, who had been anxiously awaiting their return, neighed loudly and darted forward to meet them.

Donovan landed gracefully on the ground, his large wings folding neatly against his back. Briar, Leon, and Theodore dismounted shakily, their bodies covered in dust and bruises.

"Thank you, Donovan," Briar said, tears of relief welling in her eyes as she hugged the dragon's scaly neck. "You saved us. You're truly amazing."

Knight, who had been observing the scene with wide eyes, finally found his voice. "What... how..." He stammered, looking from Briar to the dragon in disbelief.

Theodore stepped forward, a proud smile on his face. "Knight, meet Donovan. He's the dragon who helped us escape the collapsing cave." He turned to the dragon. "And Donovan, he's Knight, my horse. He is helping me serve humanity."

"Hello, Knight," the dragon said sweetly.

"Hi," said Knight cautiously, maintaining a safe distance from the dragon "Oh, um, thank you for your help," Knight said tentatively.

"Please, it was my pleasure to assist," Donovan replied warmly, his voice echoing with sincerity. "Your dedication to serving humanity is admirable, Knight."

Knight straightened up, now more at ease. "Yes, it feels good to help others."

Donovan turned his gaze skyward, a nostalgic smile playing on his lips. "Ah, the open sky after so long. It truly is a treasure." He then focused on Briar. "I hope you break your curse soon. It was a great pleasure to meet you all, my friends. And once again, thank you from the bottom of my heart for breaking my curse. Now, I must seek my peace. Farewell."

With a powerful beat of his wings, Donovan soared into the sky, his form dwindling into the distance. Briar, Leon, and Theodore watched him go.

"He didn't seem so bad after all," Knight mused, breaking the silence that followed Donovan's departure.

"I almost wish he was," Leon muttered under his breath.

"He gave us gold," Briar said with a grin, reaching into her satchel and retrieving the small chunk of gleaming metal. "We now have two items for the ritual."

"What's next?" Knight asked.

"The mermaid flower," Briar replied. "Knight, please take us to the Southern Sea."

Knight nodded and flapped his powerful wings, lifting off into the sky. Briar unfurled the map, but Knight nudged it away with his nose.

"The map is for humans, not for me," Knight said proudly.

Theodore chuckled softly. "Knight has the map of the world imprinted in his mind."

"The Southern Sea?" Knight asked, glancing back at them. "But didn't you say you wanted to go to Fairyland?"

"Yes," Briar confirmed, "but first, we need to find the mermaid flower."

"Alright," Knight said, a touch of disappointment in his voice.

Briar, Leon, and Theodore settled onto Knight's back, feeling the wind rush past them as they soared through the open sky. Knight increased his speed.

"Once I'm done helping you," Knight said, his voice resolute, "I'll go in search of my peace."

CHAPTER 26

"I don't understand why dragons are always painted as evil creatures," Theodore said as they soared through the sky, the cool breeze a welcome relief from the blistering heat of the cave. "This one is quite the gentleman."

"Yes," Bria nodded in agreement.

"Well, we've got the gold," Leon said, a triumphant gleam in his eye. "That's two magical objects for the ritual down."

Briar patted her satchel with a smile. "Yes, we're halfway there." The princess was confident, but she knew better than to underestimate the challenges that lay ahead. Gathering the mermaid flower and the blood of the fairy godmother would be no easy task.

Hours passed as they flew, the harsh landscape of the Midnight Forest gradually giving way to lighter, more inviting surroundings. The mountain grew smaller and smaller in the distance until it was no more than a smudge on the horizon.

"Ladies and gentlemen, we have officially left the fearsome forest behind us!" Knight announced. "And I must say, I have no intention of ever flying over it again."

Their journey took them over the sea, a vast expanse of shimmering blue that seemed to stretch on forever. Briar gazed down in wonder, marveling at the waves crashing against the shore, the tiny seashells dotting the sandy beach, and the boats lined up along the coastline. In the distance, a village nestled close to the water's edge came into view.

"It's so beautiful," Briar whispered, inhaling the salty air deeply. "I've never seen a sea before."

"Really?" Theodore asked, turning to look at her.

Briar nodded. "There's no sea in my kingdom. Just rivers."

They flew over a series of islands, each one unique. The first was a barren outcrop, devoid of any vegetation. The second, smaller island was alive with the cacophony of seagulls squawking and diving for fish.

"Seals!" Briar shouted with glee as they glided over another island teeming with the large, lazy creatures, lounging and rolling around on the rocky shore. Briar's face lit up at the sight.

"How lucky they are," Knight mused. "All they do is sleep and eat."

"Most animals do just that," Leon said with a chuckle.

"Not me," Knight huffed. "Now, which island are we aiming for?" he asked, steering them closer to a large island covered in a dense forest of coconut trees. A broken ship lay abandoned on the shore, its tattered sails fluttering in the wind.

"We need to find the Mermaid Island," Briar explained. "The fairies told me there's a magical flower there that we need for the ritual. They mentioned the island is full of cherry blossoms." She squinted at the horizon, searching for any sign of the pink flowers.

"Oh, the True Love Island!" Knight exclaimed. "I love love."

"Is that what it's called?" Briar asked, puzzled. "The fairies called it Mermaid Island."

"Are mermaids dangerous?" Leon asked. "Most stories depict them as friendly, but there are also tales of them being deadly."

"It depends on their mood," Knight replied. "But mermaids don't live on Mermaid Island anymore. Long ago, two lovers named Eira and Elvis lived there, and that's why it's sometimes called True Love Island."

"Who are Eira and Elvis?" Briar asked.

"You don't know?" Knight seemed genuinely surprised. "Or their love story?"

Briar glanced at Leon for help, but the prince merely shrugged. "No," she admitted, feeling a little embarrassed by her ignorance.

Knight let out a dramatic sigh. "Of course, you don't. It's not as famous as a prince and princess love story."

"Yes, I remember the story," Theodore chimed in. "It's quite a sad one."

Briar's curiosity deepened. She wasn't typically interested in love stories, but if Knight was so enthusiastic, there had to be something special about it. "Knight, please tell us the story," she urged.

"I'm not a storyteller," Knight said, feigning reluctance.

"Oh, come on," Leon teased. "You're dying to tell the story. Quit the act and just go on."

Knight heaved a loud, exaggerated sigh. "Fine, since you're all so desperate to hear it. But you should pass it down to future generations. It's a tale worth remembering."

Just then, a massive splash echoed from the sea below. They all looked down to see something enormous swimming just beneath the surface, its body creating huge ripples. Without warning, a gigantic shark burst from the water, its mouth gaping wide open as it shot toward them like a giant arrow.

They all screamed in unison, panic rising as the shark's jaws seemed to close in on them. At the last moment, Knight soared higher, and the beast's teeth snapped shut on empty air before it plunged back into the depths.

"Oh, I forgot about those," Knight muttered.

"Forgot about the sharks?" Leon asked incredulously, clutching his chest. "How could you forget about something like that?"

Knight shrugged. "My mind was on more pleasant things, like Eira and Elvis."

Briar's heart pounded in her chest, the near miss of the shark leaving her breathless. The creature was enormous, its massive jaws capable of swallowing an entire ship. She could hardly believe they had escaped unscathed.

"Anyway," Knight said, steering clear of the water to avoid any other creatures of the sea that might be lurking below. "Once upon a time, hundreds of years ago, there was a girl named Eira. She lived in a village by the Sea. Eira was the most beautiful girl in the entire kingdom. Her eyes sparkled like the sea, and her hair flowed like the warm sands of the beach."

Knight continued. "Eira's beauty didn't go unnoticed, and it made her the target of jealousy, especially among her so-called friends. They pretended to care for her, but one day..." He gasped dramatically, causing Briar to lean forward in anticipation.

"What happened?" she asked, unable to hide her eagerness.

"They tied her hands to a large rock," Knight said, his voice grave. "They took her out to the sea in a boat and threw her overboard. She sank beneath the waves and drowned."

"She died?" Leon exclaimed. "Isn't there a happy ending to this story?"

"Patience," Knight scolded with a huff. "I'm not giving you any spoilers."

"Please, Knight, continue," Briar urged.

Knight resumed his tale, his tone now softer. "Eira's lifeless body drifted into the realm of the mermaids. A young mermaid named Elvis, who was on patrol, discovered her. His friend suggested handing her over to the mermaid king, but Elvis knew that meant certain death for Eira. Instead, he took her to his home. With the help of an old mermaid healer, they nursed her back to health. Elvis kissed Eira to grant her the ability to breathe underwater." Knight continued. "As time passed, they fell deeply in love. They lived happily together, but their joy was short-lived. The mermaid king eventually learned about Eira. Fearing she was a human spy, he had her arrested and thrown into prison. Elvis pleaded for her release, but the king refused and ordered her execution. But Elvis wasn't ready to give up on his true love. He broke her out of prison, and they fled."

"They escaped?" Briar asked.

"Yes, but not without consequences," Knight said. "The mermaid army pursued them relentlessly. During their escape, Elvis lost his sight in a fierce battle. Life became incredibly difficult for them after that. They had to keep running, and finding a safe place was nearly impossible, especially since Elvis needed to stay close to the water. The mermaid king, furious at their defiance, sent a sea serpent to kill them."

Briar gasped, clutching Knight tightly. "Did they survive?"

Knight nodded. "The serpent bit Elvis, and he was on the brink of death. Eira wept and kissed him one last time, and miraculously, the venom left his body. Their love was so powerful that it saved him. Touched by their love, the serpent decided to help them. It became their protector and found an island where they could live safely."

"What a story," Leon said, his voice barely a whisper. "But did they ever find peace?"

Knight continued. "Eira went on a quest to find a way to heal Elvis's blindness. She couldn't bear to see him suffer. The sea serpent took her back to the mermaid realm, and they stole a magical mermaid flower. The flower kept withering on land, but Eira refused to give up. She tended to it day and night until, finally, it bloomed. Its magic healed Elvis, restoring his sight. They built a home on the island and lived happily ever after."

Briar sighed, a wistful smile on her lips. "That's a beautiful story, Knight. Even better than a prince and princess's love story."

Knight's eyes filled with tears. "They lived happily until they died. Humans age faster than mermaids, so Elvis eventually gave up his mermaid magic. They died together peacefully."

As Knight finished the story, tears streamed down his face. Leon sniffled softly behind Briar, trying to hide his emotions. She turned to him.

"Are you crying?" she teased.

"No," Leon said quickly, wiping his tears on his sleeve. "Theodore is the one crying."

"Not me," Theodore protested, though his voice cracked with emotion.

Briar shook her head at them. She should have been crying too, but she felt strangely comforted by the story's ending.

"Don't be sad," she said. "They found their happy ending."

"But I can't help but think of all the years they spent in pain," Knight sobbed.

Briar smiled at him. "Don't you see? All the struggle was worth it. They were together, and that's all that mattered."

"Yes," Knight murmured.

Soon, an island appeared on the horizon. It rose majestically from the sea, resembling a giant pink flower floating on the water. As they descended, Knight landed gracefully outside a small house surrounded by a white picket fence.

"This is their house," he said.

Theodore patted Knight gently. "Let's go."

They climbed down, with Knight leading the way. He was an emotional guide, pointing out every detail that had once belonged to Eira and Elvis. The house was small but charming, its walls covered in climbing roses. The air was filled with the sweet scent of cherry blossoms, and the sound of waves crashing against the shore provided a soothing backdrop.

Inside, the house was filled with memories of the couple. There were seashells and trinkets collected from their adventures, and a well-worn book of fairy tales lay open on a table, its pages yellowed with age.

"These were Eira's favorite stories," Knight said, his voice trembling. "She loved happy endings."

Briar picked up the book, tracing her fingers over the delicate illustrations. "She must have been a wonderful person," she said softly.

"She was," Knight agreed, his eyes misty. "And so was Elvis. They were truly meant for each other."

Leon wandered around the room, his gaze lingering on a faded portrait of Eira and Elvis. "They look so happy," he said.

"They were," Knight said. "They found their paradise here, on this island."

Briar felt a warmth in her heart as she looked around the house.

Knight led them out of the house. "This is their grave," Knight said softly, his voice barely above a whisper. With delicate care, he plucked a few roses from a nearby bush with his mouth and placed them reverently on the tombstone. The stone was almost hidden beneath a blanket of cherry blossoms and leaves.

Briar, Leon, and Theodore followed suit, each laying a flower on the grave.

Knight struggled to hold back his tears. "I now understand why they say love is in the air," he said, his voice cracking with emotion. "This place is overflowing with love. Every flower, every tree, every blade of grass, and every pebble—it all whispers of love."

Briar nodded. "Where is the mermaid flower?" she asked.

"In the garden," Knight said. He led them down a winding path, the air growing cooler and more fragrant with each step. They soon arrived at a secluded garden, where a towering tree stood at the center, its branches heavy with the most extraordinary flowers Briar had ever seen. The petals seemed to be made of transparent blue crystal, catching the light in a way that made them shimmer like diamonds. At the center of each flower was a pearl-like bud.

"That is the flower you need," Knight said.

Briar walked slowly towards the tree, her eyes wide with wonder. Just as she reached out to touch one flower, something stirred in the shadows behind the tree.

From the darkness emerged an enormous snake, its scales glistening like polished onyx. The serpent slithered forward, uncoiling its massive body with a slow, deliberate grace. As it moved, the sound of its scales scraping against the ground sent a chill down Briar's spine. The snake's body seemed to go on forever, each coil revealing another until it finally came to a stop in front of her. Five heads, each with piercing green eyes, rose into the air, swaying menacingly.

Briar took an involuntary step back, her heart pounding in her chest. The middle head of the snake lowered towards her, its green eyes locking onto hers with a predatory intensity. She felt rooted to the spot, unable to move or even breathe. The snake's forked tongue flicked in and out.

"Oh, I forgot to tell you about Venom," said the horse casually. "He is the snake that helped Eira and Elvis. He's the guardian of the flower."

"Humans," the snake hissed, scrutinizing Briar with an intensity that made her skin prickle. "A girl and two boys," the serpent continued, its eyes flicking toward Leon and Theodore with a disdainful glare. "And... a horse? A horse from Fairyland. Why have you come here?"

"We need the flower," Briar said, her voice trembling but determined. She took a deep breath, willing herself to stay calm.

"The flower," the snake hissed. "You greedy humans."

"No, no, Mr. Venom. We don't want to misuse the flower." Briar said. "We need it to save a kingdom—to break a curse."

"Whatever your reasons, you cannot have the flower," the serpent said, its head moving in a slow, serpentine dance. "The tree only grants flowers for true lovers. Do you have your true love with you?"

Briar swallowed hard, then reached for Leon's hand, pulling him close. "Yes. My true love is with me. This is Prince Leon."

Leon smiled, squeezing her hand reassuringly. "Yes, we are true lovers."

The serpent's eyes narrowed, its middle head tilting to the side as if in deep thought. "How do I know that?"

"I broke her sleeping curse with a true lover's kiss," Leon said confidently. "Surely that proves our love is real."

"So, you claim," the serpent said, its heads bobbing skeptically. "But I require more proof."

"We are true lovers," Briar insisted, her voice firm. "Don't you know the story of Sleeping Beauty?"

"I am familiar with it," the snake replied, its eyes narrowing further. "But I cannot simply take your word for it. I need proof."

"What more proof do you need?" Leon asked. "Isn't breaking the curse enough?"

"More," the serpent hissed, its eyes glinting with a dangerous light. "I must be certain."

"What can we do to prove our love?" Briar asked.

The serpent seemed to consider this for a moment, its heads swaying in unison. "There is one way to find out," he said finally. "Are you willing to undergo a trial?"

"We are willing to do anything," Briar and Leon said in unison.

The serpent nodded slowly, its eyes gleaming with an unsettling light. Without warning, the serpent struck, its middle head moving with lightning speed. Briar barely had time to gasp before Leon cried out in pain, clutching his forehead. He staggered backward, then collapsed to the ground, unconscious.

CHAPTER 27

"Leon!" Briar cried, dropping to her knees beside the fallen prince. Leon lay motionless, his skin turning an eerie shade of blue, and his breathing was shallow and labored.

Theodore rushed to Leon's side, his bag clinking as he knelt and quickly checked the prince's pulse. His brow furrowed with concern. "He's alive, but the poison is spreading fast. It's incredibly strong," he said.

Briar turned her fiery gaze toward the serpent. "Why did you bite him?" she yelled, her voice trembling with a mix of anger and helplessness.

The snake lifted its five heads. "You said you wanted to prove he is your true love," he hissed. "You wanted the flower."

Briar's mind raced, but all she could think of was Leon and how to save him. "Just suck your poison out of him," she pleaded.

"I can't do anything," the snake replied, shaking all five heads simultaneously. "It's like an arrow. Once shot, it never returns. But you can help him."

"How?" Briar asked desperately, her eyes widening as she watched Leon's face, now a deepening shade of blue.

The middle head of the snake shot forward, its narrow eyes gleaming with malicious delight. "That's my favorite part," he said gleefully. His forked tongue flicked out. "The mermaid king once ordered me to bite Elvis. I did. But when Eira kissed him, he woke up, alive. If the boy is your true love, kiss him, and the poison will not harm him. Hence, it will be proven he is your true love, and you will get the flower."

Briar's eyes widened in disbelief. "He needs medicine! Like an anti-venom or something. Not a kiss."

"Only an act of true love can save him," the snake said smugly, his many eyes narrowing with twisted amusement. "Don't you know love is the best medicine?" The snake chuckled, a sound that sent shivers down Briar's spine. "And if you want the anti-venom," the snake continued, nodding toward the dark, churning sea in the distance, "it's inside the sea. Go get it. But I won't be to blame if he dies before you return."

"Kiss him, Princess," Knight urged.

"I don't think it will help him," Briar said doubtfully, her eyes filling with tears as she watched Leon's body convulse. She clutched his cold hands, her heart aching with fear.

"It's magic," Knight insisted. "Don't make it more complicated. Just kiss the prince."

Briar looked down at Leon, lying on the cold, hard ground, his body shaking with pain. What if it didn't work? What if she couldn't save him? What if he died?

"I don't like him that much, but didn't he once save you from the sleeping curse?" Knight reminded her.

"Yes, he did," Briar answered.

"He came with you to this dangerous forest to help you, despite the risks," Knight added. "To stand by your side."

Briar nodded, tears welling in her eyes. "Yes, he did."

"Just kiss him," Knight urged again.

"Sometimes, magic works better than medicine," Theodore said.

"Just kiss him," Knight repeated.

Briar felt frozen, her mind a whirlwind of fear and doubt. "What if he...?" she whispered, her voice trailing off as tears streamed down her cheeks.

Knight pushed her closer to Leon. "Trust in your love," he said softly. "Do it now."

Briar took a deep breath, her heart pounding in her chest. She loved Leon so much. She prayed silently for a miracle as she leaned down toward Leon, her lips trembling. She kissed him gently, her lips meeting his cold, soft ones. She held on for a few precious seconds, hoping, praying for the magic to work, and then leaned back, her heart racing with anticipation and fear.

They all waited, their breaths held in tense silence. The prince didn't move.

Seconds stretched into what felt like an eternity. Still, nothing happened.

Briar's heart tightened with despair. "Where's your magic?" she screamed at the snake, her voice filled with anguish.

"There," the snake said calmly, nodding toward Leon. "Your generation has no patience."

Briar turned her eyes back to Leon. Slowly, miraculously, the blue tinge of poison began to fade from his skin. The color returned to his cheeks, a healthy flush replacing the deathly pallor. The prince's eyes fluttered open, confusion filling his gaze.

"What happened?" Leon asked, struggling to sit up. He touched his forehead, wincing slightly. "Did the snake bite me?"

"It is proven," the snake declared with a sly smile. "You two are true loves. Your kiss has saved him."

"You kissed me?" Leon asked. He looked at Briar, his eyes wide. Briar's gaze darted away, avoiding his. "Really?"

"You didn't want me to?" Briar asked.

"Yes... No... I mean, yes. I want you to kiss me." Leon took a deep breath, the color returning to his cheeks. "Or maybe I would have died, I guess."

Briar shook her head, exasperated. Boys were so confused. She whirled to face the snake. "What if he didn't wake up? What if he had died?"

"Then you would have no flower," the snake responded simply, its many heads nodding in unison. "Now take it."

The giant snake slithered back, its scales rustling against the ground as it moved, making space for Briar to stand under the ancient, gnarled tree that held the precious flower. The princess raised her hands, and a single, delicate bloom drifted down, landing softly in her palm. It felt magical, a gentle warmth spreading from the flower to her hand. The petals were smooth and hard, like glass. She wouldn't have been surprised if the flower was made of pure crystal.

"Do something useful with it," the snake said, its voice fading as it slithered back into the shadows of the tree, the leaves rustling softly as it disappeared.

Briar stood there for a moment, cradling the flower in her hands, her heart filled with relief. She had the flower, and she had saved Leon.

"His venom seems exceptionally strong," Theodore observed. "I wish I could collect a sample of it to study its properties."

"Theodore, you have no true love to kiss you awake," Knight teased, flicking his tail and letting out a playful snort.

Theodore sighed wistfully, his eyes clouded with a hint of sadness. "No, I suppose I don't."

Knight seemed reluctant to leave the mystical island, and the horse had a greedy curiosity to explore every nook and cranny. His hooves danced eagerly on the rocky ground as he contemplated their next destination. But when he realized that Fairyland was their next stop, his eyes brightened with excitement, and he couldn't hide his anticipation.

"I haven't visited Fairyland in months!" Knight said, his voice brimming with joy. "I can't wait to see all my old friends, bathe in the crystal waterfalls and feast on the giant apples that grow there."

Briar shared his excitement, her heart pounding with anticipation. She only needed one more magical artifact to break the curse. She wished Knight could fly faster.

"Prince Leon," Theodore said. "How did you feel when the snake bit you? What kind of pain did you experience?"

Leon touched his forehead where the bite marks had almost disappeared. "I felt... nothing. No pain at all. It was as if I just... fell asleep suddenly. It was strange."

"Powerful magic," Theodore mused.

"Honestly, that stupid snake," Briar grumbled. "What if we weren't true loves?"

"You always seem to doubt that," Leon said, his voice softening with a hint of sadness. "Do you think the fairy who blessed us made a mistake?"

"I didn't mean it that way," Briar said quickly, her eyes earnest. "You know how these blessings and curses work—they always have loopholes. I just thought it was all connected to the sleeping curse. But anyway, I'm glad you're with me, and glad that you're my true love." She smiled warmly at him.

"You mean that?" Leon asked, his eyes widening in surprise.

"Yes," Briar laughed. "Or else I wouldn't have gotten the flower."

Leon's expression softened, and he let out a sigh of relief.

"But I'm serious," Briar continued, turning to face him fully. "Now that I've seen you nearly die, I need to tell you this. Because of you, I survived in the Midnight Forest. You've been a constant support. You're brave, loyal, generous, and you have a kind heart."

"You forgot to mention handsome," Leon said with a playful grin.

Briar rolled her eyes at him, though a small smile tugged at her lips. "Handsome or whatever."

Leon's grin faded, replaced by a thoughtful expression. "But you said I'm not smart and that I always get us into trouble."

"I said that so you wouldn't follow me to the dragon's cave," she explained. "But you did anyway."

"Oh," Leon said, looking a bit sheepish. "I thought you thought I was stupid."

"No, you're the best," she said sincerely, her eyes meeting his.

"Well, you're the best," Leon replied, his smile returning.

"See, the love magic of this island is already working on you two," Knight chuckled. "Look over there—a cloud shaped like a heart."

They all turned to look, but the clouds were not heart-shaped. The setting sun bathed them in shades of red, orange, and purple, casting a beautiful, otherworldly glow. Below them, they saw sprawling farmlands, vast fields of corn, and quaint little villages, their roofs shimmering in the fading light.

"We should reach Fairyland by midnight," Theodore said, his eyes scanning the horizon. "I've visited the fairy godmother there twice."

"You know, Theodore, sometimes I'm a bit jealous of you," Briar said. "You've traveled to so many amazing places."

Theodore laughed heartily, the sound echoing across the open sky. "It's one perk of being a healer."

"We're going to Fairyland! We're going to Fairyland!" Knight chanted.

As the sun dipped below the horizon, leaving a dim twilight in its wake, stars began to twinkle in the darkening sky. They flew over rugged terrain, the ground below them a patchwork of crags and deep crevices.

Suddenly, Knight shuddered, his wings beating erratically. The group clutched each other, trying to steady themselves as the horse vibrated uncontrollably.

"What's happening, Knight?" Theodore asked, his voice tinged with worry.

Knight flapped his wings harder, his body trembling as if struggling against an invisible force. "Something's pulling me down," he said, his voice panicked and strained.

Briar's eyes widened in fear. "Are you okay, Knight?"

"I don't know!" Knight cried, his wings beating frantically. "I can't control it!"

Before they could grasp what was happening, Knight's wings stopped mid-flap, and the horse went limp, his body losing all tension. With a sudden lurch, they were plummeting toward the rocky ground below, the wind howling in their ears as they fell at a terrifying speed.

CHAPTER 28

Briar hit the ground with a bone-jarring thud, the impact knocking the breath out of her lungs. Pain radiated through her body, and she lay there, groaning, trying to collect herself. Every inch of her screamed in agony, but she forced herself to breathe deeply, willing the pain to subside. After a few agonizing moments, she slowly moved her limbs, checking for any broken bones or injuries. Miraculously, nothing seemed broken. It was a wonder she wasn't dead after falling from such a height.

As she finally managed to scramble to her feet, she took in her surroundings. She was in an unfamiliar field, dotted with ancient-looking trees and large boulders scattered here and there. The landscape was eerily still, with no signs of human or animal life for miles around. The air was thick with the scent of earth and moss. The silence was broken only by the occasional rustle of leaves.

Briar squinted into the distance and spotted twinkling lights, like tiny stars, on the horizon. There was a city far away. As her eyes adjusted, she could make out the outline of a distant castle perched on a hill. It seemed like they had fallen on the outskirts of the city.

She quickly turned her attention to finding her companions. Scanning the area, her eyes landed on Knight first. The horse's gleaming white coat was impossible to miss. He lay on the ground, unmoving. Briar's heart skipped a beat. "Knight!" she called out, but there was no response.

Next, she spotted Theodore. He was lying beneath Knight, his arms wrapped protectively around the horse's neck, as if he had tried to shield him from the fall. Theodore's satchel lay a few feet away, its contents spilled across the ground. But there was no sign of Prince Leon.

A horrible feeling clawed at Briar's stomach. What if Leon had fallen somewhere else? What if he was hurt, or worse? Shaking off the dreadful thoughts, she looked around more carefully. He was with them when they were falling. He must be nearby. "Leon!" Briar shouted, her voice echoing through the quiet field. "Where are you?"

"Up here," came a small, slightly irritated voice from above her.

Briar looked up and there, dangling from the branch of a giant tree like a hapless bat, was the prince. His royal attire was disheveled, and his face was flushed with a mixture of frustration and embarrassment. Relief washed over her at the sight of him.

"What are you doing up there?" Briar called out, half-laughing in disbelief.

"Just enjoying the view!" Leon yelled back. "Can't you see I'm stuck?"

One of his legs was caught between two branches, and no matter how hard he tugged, he couldn't free it. He grunted, twisting his body in a desperate attempt to extricate himself. With a grunt of effort, he heaved his body upward, grasping the branch with his hands and giving a mighty tug on his leg. Finally, with a groan of triumph, he managed to free his leg but lost his grip on the branch. He tumbled to the ground, landing face down with a pained yelp.

Briar ran to him. "Are you okay?"

Leon winced as he removed his boot and clutched his ankle, which was bleeding. "My ankle," he said through gritted teeth.

"It's okay. Theodore will heal you," Briar reassured him.

"The healer," Leon snapped, his eyes blazing with anger. "We could have died! All because of him and his stupid horse."

"It's not their fault," Briar said.

Leon narrowed his eyes. "You're still on their side, even after all this?" he spat.

Briar knew Leon had always disliked Knight. She had hoped that as they spent more time together and faced danger, he would come to appreciate the bond they shared. But after this incident, it seemed that hope was in vain. "I'm not taking sides," Briar said. "I just don't think it's fair to blame them without knowing what really happened."

Leon sighed. "So, what happened then?" he asked, slipping his boot back on and struggling to stand.

"Let's ask Theodore what happened," Briar said, glancing over at the unconscious horse. "We need to get him up first. Can you help me?"

Leon muttered something under his breath but reluctantly moved to help Briar untangle Theodore's arms from around the horse's neck. Together, they managed to push Knight off of Theodore, who groaned softly as he was freed. The horse and the healer both appeared uninjured, though Knight remained unconscious.

Briar kneeled beside Theodore and gently shook his shoulder. "Theodore, can you hear me?"

Theodore's eyes slowly fluttered open. He blinked several times, his expression one of confusion. Suddenly, he grasped Briar's arms, his eyes wide with terror. "BABA YAGA!" he screamed.

Briar jumped back, startled by his outburst.

Theodore looked around wildly, his face pale with fear. "Did the witch capture us again?" he asked, his voice trembling.

"No," Briar said, trying to calm him. "We fell from the sky."

"Thanks to your horse," Leon added. "We could have been killed."

Theodore blinked several times, his fear gradually giving way to relief. "Oh, thank goodness," he muttered. "I thought it was the witch. Knight has never fallen before. I felt something...magical pull us down."

"Maybe it was gravity," Leon taunted.

"Gravity doesn't work on a magical horse," Theodore replied, not understanding the jibe.

Leon rolled his eyes and hiked up his pants, revealing his bloody ankle. "Look what he did to my leg," he said. "I might never walk right again."

Briar rolled her eyes at Leon.

"I'm sorry," Theodore said, his voice full of genuine concern. "But where is Knight?"

"Behind you," Briar said, pointing to the horse's motionless form.

"Knight?" Theodore called out, rushing to his horse's side. He shook the horse gently, but Knight remained unresponsive. With a look of desperation, Theodore grabbed his satchel and pulled out a small bundle of blue grapes. He pried open Knight's mouth and squeezed the juice inside, his hands shaking with urgency.

But the horse still didn't wake. Theodore's face crumpled with fear. "It should have worked," he said, his voice breaking. "It should have woken him up."

"Try something else," Briar suggested, her panic rising.

Leon threw up his hands. "Why are you acting like he's dead?" he snapped. "He's just knocked out. Do your healing thing already!"

Theodore nodded, his hands shaking as he fumbled with his mortar and pestle, grinding up roots and fruits in a desperate attempt to wake Knight. Briar watched anxiously, her heart pounding in her chest.

As Theodore worked, Briar's eyes were drawn to a movement in the distance. At first, it seemed like a large, gray and pink boulder was rolling towards them. But as it came closer, she realized it wasn't a boulder at all. It had hands, feet, and a head. Her breath caught in her throat as recognition dawned on her. It was an ogre, just like the ones she had seen in her storybooks, but much larger and more terrifying in real life.

"Look!" she cried, pointing towards the approaching figure. "An ogre!"

The ogre looked like it was sculpted from rough stone, with skin that had the texture of cracked granite. Its large, muscular hands seemed capable of crushing boulders. A round head covered in a tangled mane of blond hair sat atop a thick neck, and two short, curved horns jutted out from either side of its head. Its face was dominated by a bulbous nose and far-set round eyes that gleamed with malice. A wide mouth stretched into a grin, revealing two prominent teeth poking out from its lips.

What was particularly striking, however, was the ogre's attire. It wore an expensive silk gown, shimmering with a delicate sheen, and trimmed in gold that accentuated its bulk. Around its thick neck hung layers of diamond and sapphire necklaces. A small, elaborate crown nestled awkwardly between its horns, giving it an air of absurdity rather than majesty. The ogre's face was caked with makeup. Its cheeks were painted a bright, unnatural red, and its lips were smeared with a garish crimson.

The ogre stopped near Theodore, who was engrossed in preparing a potion for Knight. The ogre folded its enormous arms across its chest and smirked at the healer. "Hello, Theodore," the ogre said, its voice a grating rasp, like rocks scraping against each other.

Theodore looked up, startled. His eyes widened in terror, and he let out a yelp, dropping a bundle of herbs. "Marigold," he stammered, his voice barely above a whisper, his hands trembling.

"Aren't you happy to see me?" the ogre grinned, baring her gleaming white teeth in a parody of a smile.

"I—Marigold—" Theodore's face turned ashen, and he looked like he might faint from sheer fright.

"WHAT DID YOU THINK?" Marigold's voice boomed, causing the ground to vibrate slightly. "YOU COULD LIE TO ME, TO THE OGRE PRINCESS, AND GET AWAY WITH IT?"

"No—I didn't lie—" Theodore's voice quivered, and he took a step back, almost tripping over his own feet.

"Oh, really!" Marigold took a step forward, her heavy footsteps echoing threateningly. "But it's fine. I know how to make you fall into my trap."

"You?" Theodore asked, his eyes darting nervously around for an escape route.

The ogre laughed, a sound that resembled the rumbling of distant thunder. "Me, yes. You may be wondering how I caught you. So, listen, when I realized you would never come to me willingly again, considering what an ungrateful creature you are, I enlisted the help of a witch. Together, we set up a little trap for your horse. I knew you would fly over my land one day."

Theodore's expression turned from fear to anger. "You realize this could have killed us," he said.

"Don't overreact," the ogre said dismissively, rolling her eyes. "I made sure you wouldn't fall to your death."

Briar pieced together why they had survived the fall from the sky. Her attention sharpened as Marigold suddenly reached out with one massive hand, grabbed Theodore by his shoulder, and shook him like a rag doll. "You ungrateful human! Why didn't you bring me my potion?"

Theodore whimpered, his face contorted with fear. "I was very busy."

"What is more important than my potion?" the ogre roared.

"Hey, ogre, leave him alone!" Briar shouted, stepping forward with her hand on the hilt of her sword.

Marigold's head snapped towards Briar. Noticing her for the first time, the ogre's eyes narrowed. With a snarl, she dropped Theodore to the ground and strode towards Briar in two long, purposeful steps.

"How dare you raise your voice at me?" Marigold shouted, towering over Briar. "Do you know who I am? I am Marigold, the fourth ogre princess. And I'm not an ogre. I'm an ogress."

"I don't care who you are," Briar said firmly, standing her ground and staring up at the ogress with defiance. "But you can't treat my friend like that."

"Yes, I can," said the ogress smugly, a cruel smile playing on her lips. "But you must treat me with respect and stay out of my way, or else..."

"Or else what?" Briar challenged, her grip tightening on her sword.

"Do not tempt me," Marigold growled, her massive chest puffing out in anger, making her look even more intimidating.

"Hey, ogress," Leon yelled. "Just because you can scare a weak man like Theodore doesn't mean you are powerful." He stepped forward, drawing his sword and aiming it at the ogress. "If you want to fight, consider a hero like me."

"Guys, please stop," Theodore pleaded, his voice tinged with desperation. "Don't mess with Marigold. You don't want the ogre army after you. And I'm not a weak man."

"Theodore, will you tell us what is going on?" Briar demanded. "How do you know this..." she glanced at Marigold and then back at Theodore, "...ogre princess?"

The ogress grabbed Theodore again. "Tell them!" she shouted, her face inches from his, and he flinched away from her.

"The world needs to know what a liar you are," she added, her eyes blazing with fury.

"Liar," Leon whispered to Briar, a hint of satisfaction in his voice. "I told you we shouldn't trust him."

"I'm not a liar," Theodore said, struggling against the ogress's powerful grip.

"Yes, you are. The dirtiest liar in the world," Marigold sneered, her lips curling back to reveal her teeth. "You lied to an innocent girl like me."

"Wait, is she his girlfriend or something?" Leon said, his eyes lighting up with amusement. "A match made in heaven. Don't you think so?"

Briar shot a withering glare at Leon before rushing to Theodore's side. She grabbed him by the arm and tried to pull him away from the ogress. "You can't hurt my friend."

Marigold yanked Theodore back towards her with such force that she also pulled Briar closer. "I can," she said with a cruel smile.

"You can't," Briar said, her grip on Theodore tightening as she pulled him towards her again.

"I can," Marigold insisted, pulling back with equal force. The two princesses engaged in a fierce tug-of-war with Theodore caught in the middle.

"STOP!" Theodore shouted, wrenching his hands free from both princesses. "Are you planning to rip my arms off?"

"If you don't give me my potion," Marigold threatened, her eyes narrowing dangerously, "I'll rip every part of you apart."

"Marigold, we are on an urgent mission," Theodore pleaded. "I will give you the potion later."

"Nothing is more important than what I want," Marigold growled, her eyes boring into Theodore's.

Theodore looked troubled, his face pale. "What you want... well... it will take time."

"No, healer. You have taken enough time already. I can't wait anymore. Do it now," Marigold demanded, stomping her foot on the ground with such force that it caused a small tremor.

"What does she want?" Briar asked.

Theodore looked at Briar, his eyes filled with despair. "She wants to—"

"I want him to heal me," Marigold said.

"Then heal her, Theodore," Briar said.

"It's not that easy," Theodore replied.

"You are a great healer. Aren't you?" Leon asked, his tone skeptical.

Briar knew Theodore was a skilled healer. He didn't seem like a liar, and he had risked his life to help her. Perhaps Marigold was suffering from a disease that was beyond cure.

"Heal me now," Marigold demanded, her voice echoing through the trees, "or tell me if you can't. And if you can't heal me, then I'll take the price. Do you know what the price is?"

Theodore shivered visibly. "Marigold, try to understand. Some potions take time."

"BUT I WANT IT NOW!" she screamed, her voice reverberating through the forest. Leaves fell from the trees, shaken loose by the sheer force of her scream.

"Hey," Briar said, her ears still ringing from the Marigold's outburst. "If he's telling you the potion will take time, then listen to him. You can't rush it."

"Yes, Marigold," Theodore said, his voice steadying. "Give me a few more days."

"Fine," the ogress said reluctantly. "Take as much time as you want."

"Really?" Theodore asked with disbelief etched on his face.

Marigold nodded, a sly smile playing on her lips.

"Thank you, Marigold. Thank you so much," Theodore said, relief flooding his features. "I'll return this time, I promise."

"I know you will," Marigold said, her voice low and menacing. Suddenly, she lunged at Briar, her hand wrapping around Briar's neck in a vice-like grip. "Because I'll keep your friend hostage in my dungeon until you return."

CHAPTER 29

Clutching Briar by the neck, the ogress hoisted her off the ground effortlessly. Briar's feet dangled in the air, her breath coming in shallow gasps. One wrong move and Briar felt certain that Marigold could snap her neck like a twig.

"Marigold, please," Theodore pleaded, stepping forward with his hands raised. "Let Briar go. She has nothing to do with this."

"No, healer!" Marigold bellowed. "Make me beautiful. And then I'll release her."

"Wait, what?" Briar sputtered, her voice strained as she stopped struggling for a moment. "You want him to make you beautiful?"

Briar had initially thought the ogress must be suffering from some kind of illness. Now she understood why Theodore had faced such difficulties in treating Marigold. The ogress's request was far more complex than a simple healing.

"Yes," Marigold growled, her grip tightening around Briar's throat. "Healer, I give you two days. Make my potion, or the girl stays with me."

"But why do you want to be beautiful?" Briar asked, her voice barely a whisper as the pressure on her neck increased.

"Who doesn't want to be beautiful?" Marigold snapped back. "Everyone desires beauty."

The ogress had a point, Briar realized, albeit a bitter one. She had always believed that the obsession with beauty was a distinctly human trait. It seemed, however, that this desire transcended species and boundaries.

"Besides," Marigold continued, "if I am beautiful, I will marry the prince and become the queen. And I don't have much time. The prince is hosting a ball to find a wife, and I can't go like this. He will not choose me. So, healer, make my potion, and I will release her."

"You can't take Briar!" Leon shouted.

Marigold turned her menacing gaze on Leon. "Do you wish to join the girl in my dungeon? We give our prisoners stones to crush, and every day, they receive a rat and a cup of water for their lunch."

"I'd rather die than eat rats!" Briar yelled, her stomach churning at the thought. The image of gnawing on a filthy rat flashed in her mind, making her feel nauseous.

"You will have to if the healer does not make my potion," the ogress said, a sinister smile creeping across her face. She then turned to Theodore, her voice taking on a deceptively sweet tone. "See you in two days." With Briar still in her grasp, Marigold began to turn away.

"Wait!" Leon shouted, leaping forward to block Marigold's path.

Marigold growled, her patience thinning. "You are beginning to irritate me, boy. Move, or I will take you both."

"You can't take Briar," Leon insisted. "If you want the potion."

"What do you mean?" Marigold asked, squinting at Leon with suspicion.

"Theodore can't make the potion without Briar," Leon said quickly. He turned to Theodore, who looked confused. "Isn't that right, Theodore?"

"Yes, yes!" Theodore nodded frantically, catching on to Leon's plan. "Briar's involvement is crucial. Without her, I cannot make the potion you need."

Briar, still suspended in Marigold's iron grip, felt a surge of panic. The boys were likely to get her killed faster with their plan.

Marigold looked between Briar and Theodore, her eyes narrowing. "Why is she so important?"

"Because... because," Theodore stammered, clearly struggling to fabricate a believable story. He looked at Leon for support.

"Because Briar is the head beauty healer!" Leon shouted, his voice rising in an attempt to sound authoritative. "She's incredibly talented and knows more about beauty than anyone else."

Everyone turned to Leon, their expressions a mix of surprise and skepticism.

"Is she?" Marigold asked, her grip on Briar loosening slightly.

"Am I?" Briar asked.

"Yes," Leon said, nodding vigorously. He shot Briar a look that said, 'Just go along with it.'

Briar's eyes met Leon's, silently pleading for him to stop. She had no idea where he was going with this, and it seemed like they were only digging her deeper into trouble.

"Why should I believe you?" Marigold demanded, her eyes narrowing further as she scrutinized Leon.

"Do you know about Sleeping Beauty?" Leon asked. "She is renowned as the most beautiful princess in all the lands. After sleeping for a hundred years, she awoke to find that the years had taken their toll on her beauty. She turned to her knowledge of magic and, with the help of fairies, developed her potions, beauty tips, and tricks. Now, she is the foremost expert in beauty magic."

"The best beautician." Marigold's eyes widened with a mixture of awe and hope.

"And Briar is Sleeping Beauty," Leon declared.

Marigold's gaze turned to Briar, scanning her from head to toe with renewed interest. "You do look beautiful," she mused. "Is what the boy says true?"

"Yes," Briar said, swallowing her fear. "I'm Sleeping Beauty." At least that part of the story was true.

"You know the consequences of lying to me," Marigold threatened, her eyes narrowing further into slits as she glared at them, her grip tightening once more around Briar's neck.

"It's true!" Theodore exclaimed, stepping forward earnestly. "I was sent to escort Briar to Fairyland. Marigold, I was going to tell her about you after we finished our business with the fairies."

Marigold stared at him, her eyes filled with suspicion but also a glimmer of hope. She loosened her grip on Briar, allowing her to take a shaky breath.

"Trust me, Marigold. I'm not lying," Theodore insisted. "I truly want to help you. But I can't do it alone." He glanced at Briar, seeking her support. "If you give me a second, I'll explain your problem to Briar. Together, we might find a solution for you."

Marigold's enormous eyes shifted from Theodore to Briar, weighing their sincerity. "Very well," Marigold said, her voice a low growl. "But if you are lying, you will all pay dearly." She released Briar, who stumbled but quickly regained her footing, massaging her sore neck.

"Thank you, Marigold. We won't let you down," Leon said.

"Can I be as beautiful as you?" Marigold's voice trembled with a mix of hope and desperation as she gazed at Briar with an almost childlike admiration.

Briar managed a warm smile. "More beautiful than me, Marigold. I promise you that."

Marigold's face lit up with glee, and she began to hop up and down, her massive frame shaking the ground. "Tell me how to be beautiful!" she demanded eagerly.

"We will," Leon interjected, stepping forward.

"Don't interrupt me!" Marigold snapped, her voice booming. "And who are you?"

"Prince Leon," he responded, his posture regal despite the fear in his eyes.

"A prince?" Marigold said. Her eyes narrowed as she appraised him with newfound curiosity. "Do you have a big, rich kingdom? When will you get the throne?"

Leon's face paled, and he darted behind Briar. "Never," he blurted out. "I have twenty-five siblings. I'm the least favorite child and last in line for the throne. My parents despise me. I'm poor and to support myself, I work for princess Sleeping Beauty."

Marigold wrinkled her nose in disdain. "I don't like poor princes," she declared dismissively.

"Marigold, please give us a few moments to discuss your problem," Theodore said gently. "Can we have a bit of privacy?"

"Talk in front of me," Marigold demanded.

"Well... we can't discuss a patient's needs in front of them," Theodore explained.

"Fine," Marigold huffed. "But only a few minutes."

The trio walked a short distance away.

"Why did you lie?" Briar hissed, punching Leon's arm.

"If I hadn't, you'd be locked in a dungeon eating rats by now," Leon whispered back, rubbing his arm.

Briar turned to Theodore, her eyes wide with worry. "Can you really make her beautiful?"

"I can't change her appearance," Theodore admitted. "Ogres are naturally ugly, and it's not something a simple potion can fix. It's just the way they are, how nature made them."

"Then why promise her that?" Briar asked.

"The ogres had some medicinal stones that I needed," Theodore explained. "Marigold gave me some, and in return, she asked to be made beautiful. I thought she wanted minor changes, not to look like a fairy."

"You get caught every time you go for medicine?" Leon questioned, raising an eyebrow.

"Is my potion ready?" Marigold's voice thundered from behind them.

"Have patience!" Briar snapped, turning to face the ogress.

"I can't!" Marigold roared. "My prince is dancing with other girls. What if he chooses one of them as his wife?"

"You could always eat the wife," Briar suggested dryly.

"Not a bad idea," Marigold said, a smug smile spreading across her face.

Briar shot her a disgusted look and turned back to Theodore. "She wants an instant solution."

Theodore looked troubled. "Briar, we need to convince her that beauty can't be instant. It takes time and effort."

Briar's mind raced for a solution as she felt Marigold's massive hand settle on her shoulder, perilously close to her neck. Goosebumps prickled her skin.

"Where is my potion?" Marigold asked, her voice filled with impatience. "I've waited long enough."

Briar took a deep breath. "Marigold, I see you have a rare problem," she began slowly. "You want to become something you're not, but we have a solution for that, too. Have you ever heard of inner beauty?"

"Is that a potion?" Marigold asked, her eyes widening. "Will it transform me?"

"In a way, yes," Briar answered, trying to sound convincing.

"Tell me about it!" Marigold urged excitedly.

"Well," Briar began, "you need to feel beautiful on the inside. Outer beauty is just a reflection of your inner beauty. And remember, beauty is in the eye of the beholder."

"I don't want to hear this!" Marigold interrupted, her voice rising in frustration. "I just want a potion!"

"Marigold," Briar said, trying to keep calm, "not everyone cares about appearance."

The ogress scoffed. "If you think that, you haven't seen much of the world. Now, make me beautiful so I can marry the prince."

"Marigold," Briar tried again, "if the prince truly loves you, he'll marry you regardless of how you look. You have a unique beauty."

Briar looked to Leon and Theodore for support. Both nodded in agreement.

"True love," Leon added earnestly.

"Yes, exactly," Theodore echoed. "He'll love you for who you are, not how you look."

Marigold growled in frustration. "I don't want to hear that nonsense! I want to be beautiful!"

"Yes, we're getting to that part," Briar said quickly. "First, Marigold, promise to listen without interrupting."

Marigold nodded grudgingly. "I promise."

"So, in my quest for beauty, I learned something very important. Real beauty takes time and patience. If you want lasting beauty, not a quick magic fix that fades, you need to avoid hasty magical solutions. Magic can backfire, you know. Do you want everlasting beauty?"

Marigold's eyes sparkled with anticipation. "Yes."

Briar sighed in relief. But the ogress's admiration could quickly turn to anger or, worse, hunger if she wasn't satisfied.

"So..." Briar continued, "you need a diet plan."

"A fight plan?" Marigold asked, confused.

"Not a fight plan," Briar corrected, shaking her head. "A diet plan—a way to change your eating habits and lifestyle. You see, we are what we eat. So, you need to start eating healthy foods."

"Healthy foods?" Marigold echoed. "What's that?"

"Good, green vegetables and fruits," Briar explained. "And no meat."

"No meat?" Marigold bellowed. "I'll die without meat!"

"For beauty, you must make sacrifices," Briar said firmly.

"If you want to marry a rich prince," Leon added.

"Yes, Marigold," Theodore said encouragingly.

Briar grabbed a parchment and quill from Theodore and quickly jotted down a list of healthy foods—mostly fruits and vegetables, with a few particularly bitter ones thrown in for good measure. She handed the parchment to Marigold.

"Follow this diet, and you'll be beautiful soon," Briar said.

Marigold's eyes sparkled as she clutched the parchment. "But where's the beauty potion?" she asked, still bouncing with joy.

Briar stifled a groan of frustration. They were back to square one.

Theodore stepped forward, trying to reason with the ogress. "But we—"

"We have the potion," Briar interjected, grabbing Theodore by the arm and pulling him aside.

"What are you doing?" Theodore whispered.

"Give her the beauty potion," Briar hissed back.

"But we don't have one!" he protested.

"Just give her any potion. We need to leave!" Briar demanded.

"What if it harms her?" Leon asked.

"Then you marry her and make her queen," Briar snapped.

"Leon is right," Theodore said, shaking his head. "I don't want to hurt anyone."

"Oh, Theodore," Briar sighed, "just give her a potion for good skin or health. We should have done that from the start instead of arguing with her."

Theodore rummaged through his satchel and pulled out a bottle filled with green liquid.

"Don't you have anything red?" Briar asked.

"I think so," Theodore replied, producing a red potion in a plain bottle.

"And put it in a fancy bottle," Briar instructed.

Theodore found a more decorative bottle, and Briar transferred the red potion into it. She then walked back to Marigold, holding up the bottle triumphantly.

"Here it is, the glow-up potion," Briar declared. "Take a sip each day after your special meals."

Marigold's eyes gleamed with excitement as she took the bottle. "Will I be beautiful by the last ball?"

"Think bigger, Marigold," Briar said. "Once you're beautiful, you can find any prince. A prince richer than the one hosting the ball. You won't have to worry about him choosing someone else."

Marigold's eyes widened as she considered this. "I never thought about that," she murmured. Then, with a sudden leap, she enveloped Briar in a crushing hug. The princes squealed in surprise. "Thank you! Not only for the potion but for easing my worries. Now I can marry any prince!"

"You're welcome," Briar wheezed, wriggling free from the hug. "Invite me to your wedding, okay?"

Marigold blushed and nodded. "I will."

"And please, release Knight," Briar said.

Marigold handed them a carrot. "Feed this to the horse, and he'll fly again."

Theodore quickly fed the carrot to Knight, who blinked open his eyes and stood up, shaking his mane.

"I'm in a terrible phase of my life," the horse groaned. "First a witch, now a deadly fall."

"Goodbye, Marigold," Theodore said.

The three of them quickly climbed onto Knight's back and took off before Marigold could demand them to make a prince fall in love with her.

CHAPTER 30

"It was so stupid," Leon muttered, as they soared through the sky. "How can you promise a beauty potion to an ogre?"

"I know," Theodore replied calmly, though his patience was wearing thin. "But at that moment, I didn't think of the consequences. I had to save someone's life."

"Still," Leon pressed on. "A beauty potion for an ogre? It's absurd."

"I told you," Theodore said, his tone edged with frustration. "I didn't think about it."

"You should have thought it through," Leon insisted.

"Enough!" Briar's voice cut through their argument. "We all make mistakes. It's not just Theodore's fault." She sighed, feeling the weight of exhaustion pressing down on her shoulders. They had been flying all night without rest, and the relentless bickering was fraying her nerves.

"I'm sorry, Prince Leon," Theodore said, though the apology was more to diffuse the situation than out of guilt. "If that will make you feel any better."

"I'm not blaming you," Leon said defensively. "I'm just warning you to be more careful in the future."

"I will be," Theodore responded, his tone strained but sincere. "Thank you for the reminder."

"You don't get my point," Leon began again, but Briar cut him off.

"If you don't stop arguing right now," she warned, her voice low and dangerous, "I swear I will throw you both off this horse."

"Gladly, princess," Knight exclaimed. The horse was so angry that he had barely spoken a word since they escaped Marigold.

"Knight," Briar said, trying to soften her tone as she addressed the disgruntled steed. "When will we reach the fairy godmother's place?"

"We are in Fairyland now," Knight replied.

Surprised, Briar looked around, her eyes widening as she took in the scenery. She had been so lost in her thoughts that she hadn't noticed the transformation around them. The dreary landscape had given way to a vibrant, magical world. The rugged mountains and dense forests had vanished, replaced by sprawling green fields dotted with trees and colorful flowers.

"That's the godmother's house," Knight said, his voice softening slightly as he pointed out a beautiful cottage nestled in the middle of a green field. After a few seconds, Knight landed in front of the house.

The house was a picturesque sight, straight out of a fairy tale. It was surrounded by a riot of colors from a garden filled with hundreds of varieties of roses on one side and a vegetable garden on the other. The vegetable garden was a wonder in itself, with tomatoes the size of pumpkins and pumpkins the size of carriages. Cabbages, bell peppers, and carrots, all impossibly large and vibrant, grew in neat rows. A cheerful scarecrow stood watch over the garden, waving its arms at the birds pecking at the giant tomatoes.

Fruit trees, heavy with ripe oranges, peaches, apples, and mangoes, encircled the house like a protective barrier. Each tree seemed to overflow with abundance, their branches drooping under the weight of the fruit. A clear pond lay in front of the house, its waters sparkling in the sunlight, and elegant swans gilded gracefully across its surface in perfect pairs.

Chickens roamed freely in the front yard, clucking contentedly as they pecked at the ground for bugs. They occasionally stopped to preen, wiping their beaks against their feathers. Briar couldn't help but fall in love with the place. It was more beautiful than any story she had ever heard. It was the kind of place where one could easily imagine spending a lifetime surrounded by magic.

"Unicorns!" Briar gasped, her eyes widening in awe as a herd of unicorns galloped past them, their hooves barely touching the ground. They were even more magnificent than the stories described, their smooth white coats shimmering in the sunlight. Each unicorn sported a majestic spiral horn, and their glossy manes flowed like silk in the breeze.

"Fairy godmother is quite fond of unicorns," Knight said, his voice tinged with a hint of jealousy. "I don't see what's so special about them. Just a horn, really."

"Hey, Knight!" A voice called from above, drawing their attention skyward.

Five stunning horses hovered above them. One had a distinctive red stripe running from his mouth to his forehead, giving him a striking appearance.

"Hello, brothers!" Knight exclaimed, his mood brightening instantly. "Long time no see!"

"We've missed you," said the horse with the red stripe.

"I've been busy," Knight said, puffing out with pride. "Serving humankind, you know."

"Want to join us?" asked a sleek brown horse, his mane so thick it nearly covered his face. "We're taking a tour of Fairyland. A lot has changed since your last visit."

Knight sighed wistfully. "I'd love to, but I have duties to attend to right now."

"Alright, see you next time!" the horses called in unison, their voices echoing as they soared away into the sky.

Leon watched the horses disappear with a longing gaze, his expression wistful as he murmured, "They're incredible."

A lanky fairy with short curly hair approached them, his steps quick and eager. His eyes sparkled with curiosity and a welcoming smile spread across his face as he reached them. "Knight, Sleeping Beauty, Prince Charming, Theodore the healer," he said, nodding to each in turn. "It's an honor to finally meet you all."

Briar blinked in surprise. "You know us?" she asked.

The fairy laughed, a sound as musical and warm as the ringing of tiny bells. "Of course! I know all about you. I'm Indigo, the fairy godmother's assistant."

"Can we speak to the fairy godmother?" Briar asked. "We need her help."

"Absolutely!" Indigo replied with a cheerful nod. "We're always happy to help."

He led them towards the garden of roses, the vibrant flowers creating a fragrant path. As they walked, Briar marveled at the sheer beauty of the place. The air was filled with the sweet scent of roses and the chirping of birds, creating a sense of serenity that was almost surreal.

Indigo chatted amiably as they walked, his laughter infectious and his demeanor warm and welcoming.

As they reached the entrance to the house, Indigo turned to them with a broad smile. "The fairy godmother," he said.

A middle-aged woman stood in front of several withered rose bushes, her blue gown twinkling under the soft sunlight. Her attire was completed with pristine white gloves, and her black hair was elegantly pulled into a bun. In her hand, she held a crystal wand topped with a shimmering star. She waved the wand gracefully, and the dead rose bushes sprang to life. Green leaves unfurled from the branches, and vibrant red roses blossomed in an instant, their petals radiating a rich, intoxicating fragrance.

"Godmother," Indigo called out. "We have special guests."

The fairy godmother turned towards them, her rosy cheeks dimpling as she smiled warmly. "Children!" she exclaimed happily, but then her expression shifted to one of concern as she took in their disheveled appearances. "What happened to you all? You look like you've come from a battlefield!"

"Nothing much," Briar replied, trying to sound nonchalant. "Just had to deal with a witch, a dragon, a three-headed snake, and an ogre princess who wants to be beautiful."

The fairy godmother gasped, her eyes wide with shock. "Oh, dear!"

"We're fine now," Briar said quickly, eager to move on. "But we need your help. We need your blood."

The fairy godmother's face darkened with a hint of unease, but she quickly replaced it with a reassuring smile. "I'll give you my blood," she said, her tone gentle but firm. "But first, let me fix you up."

"We don't have much time," Briar urged, glancing anxiously at the sky. "I need it now to complete the ritual."

The fairy godmother's expression turned serious. "Princess, I don't understand what you're saying. What ritual? Please, tell me everything."

"I'm cursed," Briar said, her voice trembling slightly.

"I know," the fairy godmother replied, her eyes filled with sympathy.

"No, I mean, I've been cursed again," Briar clarified.

"I know," the godmother repeated. "The Curse of Thorns."

"You know about it?" Briar asked, surprised.

The fairy godmother nodded sadly. "All fairies know about it. We've been searching for a cure, but sadly, we haven't found one yet."

"I have the cure," Briar said.

"What?" the godmother asked, her eyes widening in astonishment.

Briar began to recount her journey, detailing her treacherous trek to the Midnight Forest, her plea to Viatrix for the ritual, and the hard quest to gather the necessary magical objects.

The fairy godmother listened with rapt attention. "I knew you were brave," she said. "But I never imagined you would undertake something that even fairies could not accomplish."

"I was terrified that Viatrix wouldn't give me the ritual," Briar confessed, recalling the fear that had gripped her heart. "But her three daughters helped me."

"I can't blame Viatrix for her bitterness," the fairy godmother said softly. "She's endured so much loss. But she put aside her anger to help you. She's shown that she's a fairy at heart."

"Godmother, can you tell the fairy queen that the forest fairies helped me?" Briar asked. "They deserve to live in Fairyland. They're innocent."

"I'll speak to the fairy queen and the elder fairies," the fairy godmother promised. "This time, I'll make a stronger case for them." She then turned to Leon and Theodore, her eyes filled with gratitude. "And you two gentlemen, thank you for helping Briar so selflessly."

Leon puffed out his chest with pride. "It's a hero's duty."

"What about me?" Knight interjected, sounding a bit miffed. "Did you forget me?"

The fairy godmother laughed and patted the horse lovingly. "How could I forget you, Knight? If it weren't for you, Briar wouldn't have been able to gather all the magical objects in time. You're my favorite." She turned to her Indigo. "Fetch the juiciest apple for Knight."

"I'll be right back," Indigo said with a smile, picking up a wooden basket as he hurried away.

Knight looked pleased, nuzzling the fairy godmother's hand with affection.

The fairy godmother walked over to Briar, her expression turning serious. "So, my blood is the last thing you need for the ritual?"

Briar nodded. "Yes. Will you give me your blood?"

"What made you think I would refuse to help you?" the fairy godmother said. "I would do anything to help you, Briar. If it helps, I'd give all my blood."

"Oh, thank you," Briar cried, tears of relief welling in her eyes. She threw her arms around the fairy godmother, hugging her tightly. After facing so many dangers, it was hard to believe that help could come so willingly.

"Take the blood," the fairy godmother said gently. "Don't waste any more time."

Briar pulled out an empty vial and a small dagger from her satchel, her hands trembling slightly. "This is going to hurt," she warned the fairy godmother, her voice quivering.

The godmother laughed softly and extended her hand. "I'll be fine, dear."

Briar took a deep breath and carefully lowered the blade to the fairy's delicate skin. She made a slight cut, her heart pounding as the blood began to flow. The fairy godmother didn't flinch or show any sign of pain. Briar quickly collected the blood into the vial, her hands shaking with a mix of nerves and relief.

The fairy godmother tapped her wand on the wound, and it healed instantly, leaving no trace of the cut.

"Thank you," Briar said, as she closed the vial.

The fairy godmother placed a gentle kiss on Briar's forehead. "Go break the curse, dear. You've come so far, and you're almost there."

Briar nodded. Now she had all the magical items and the blessing of the fairy godmother. Nothing could stop her from breaking the curse.

CHAPTER 31

The fairy shrine was perched on top of a hill, surrounded by towering marble walls that gleamed. As Knight landed softly outside the gate, Briar's heart raced. She had finally made it to the shrine. She had collected all the magical objects necessary to break the curse. Excitement, nervousness, and fear flooded her all at once, making her chest tight and her hands tremble.

"You three are probably the first humans to ever set foot in the shrine," said Knight, his voice filled with awe. With a slight bow, he opened the gate, leading them inside. "This is Mirella," he said, stopping near an ornate fountain. "She is the luck granter."

In the center of the fountain stood a fairy statue, her smile as serene as a gentle stream. Her hair cascaded like liquid silver, blending seamlessly into her gown, which seemed to flow endlessly, made entirely of water. Her delicate hand held a wand raised high, as if ready to grant any wish with a single wave.

A large, intricately carved bowl filled with gold coins sat at the base of the fountain.

"Mirella is known to bring great fortune to magic rituals," Knight explained. "We should ask for her blessing for your ritual, Princess. Let's toss a coin together. It will bring us much luck."

Knight dipped his muzzle into the bowl, grabbing a mouthful of coins and motioning for the others to follow his lead.

Briar carefully picked a coin from the bowl, her eyes locking with the fairy's gentle gaze. The statue seemed almost alive, its smile radiating warmth and hope.

One by one, they tossed their coins into the fountain. The coins made soft plinks as they hit the water and sank to the bottom.

"Princess, now you have luck on your side. Nothing can stop you from breaking the curse," said Knight, his voice brimming with confidence.

Briar felt a surge of hope and smiled. She desperately needed luck.

"We should hurry," Leon said, glancing up at the sky where the first stars had begun to twinkle. "The moon will rise soon."

"Prince Leon, there is nothing to worry about," Knight reassured him. "We will reach the sacred circle before the moon comes out."

Knight took the lead, his hooves clicking softly on the cobblestone path, and they followed him. The fairy shrine might have looked like an ordinary garden if not for the white marble statues that adorned it and the tangible magic that hung in the air. They passed a mermaid statue, elegantly perched on a rock with her tail coiled around her. Her eyes sparkled with life as if she might leap into the fountain at any moment. A few steps away stood a centaur, frozen in a moment of triumph, his front hooves raised high and a bow and arrow aimed at some unseen target.

Further on, they came upon a majestic unicorn statue. Nearby, a phoenix was captured in the act of rising from a bed of ash, its wings outstretched and ready to soar into the sky.

As they ventured deeper into the shrine, the statues of magical creatures became more numerous and varied—winged horses, ethereal fairies, mischievous goblins, stout dwarfs, fearsome dragons, imposing werewolves, towering giants, and countless others.

"This place honors all magical creatures," Knight said, nodding respectfully at the statues. He lifted his head and took a deep breath. "The air here is thick with magic. It is said that the spirits of our ancestors bless this shrine."

"I always thought fairies never died," Leon mused, his brow furrowed in thought. "Aren't they immortal?"

"Every living being must face death eventually," Theodore said softly. "It's nature's law."

Knight halted before a grand statue of a fairy dressed in an amethyst-colored gown, her head crowned with an ornate diadem. "This is our fairy queen," he said, bowing deeply. The fairy's hair, a cascade of midnight black, framed a face that radiated wisdom and strength. Even though it was only a statue, Briar could sense the powerful aura that surrounded it, understanding why she had been chosen as the queen.

"And here are the Elder Fairies," Knight continued, nodding toward a group of eight statues. Each fairy wore a flowing white gown, their expressions serene and wise, almost indistinguishable from one another. "And there," Knight gestured toward a white circular pedestal facing a shimmering waterfall, "is the sacred circle."

Briar took a deep breath, her heart pounding in her chest. Her palms were sweaty, and she nervously fidgeted with the strap of her satchel as they approached the pedestal.

Just a few feet from the marble pedestal, Knight came to an abrupt stop. "One more thing," he said, his tone serious. "Only the person who performed the ritual may enter the sacred circle. The prince and the healer must remain here."

"We will stay here then," Theodore said.

Leon looked visibly disappointed but nodded in agreement. "Fine. As long as the curse gets broken."

Briar gave her friends a reassuring nod and, with her heart racing, stepped toward the pedestal alone.

At the center of the pedestal, outlined in gold, lay the sacred circle. It was a complex and intricate design, filled with an array of magical symbols and sigils, each one meticulously carved.

As if waiting for her, the clouds parted, revealing the full moon. Its silvery rays bathed the sacred circle in a soft, ethereal light. The symbols on the pedestal seemed to come alive, absorbing the moon's glow and beginning to rotate and pulse with energy.

Briar stood in the center, her breath shallow and her heart pounding. She could feel the magic thrumming in the air, a palpable force that filled her with both awe and trepidation. This was the moment she had been preparing for, the culmination of her quest. She took a deep breath and prepared to begin the ritual, her eyes fixed on the glowing symbols that seemed to beckon her to unlock their ancient secrets.

Briar lowered herself onto the cool, smooth edge of the sacred circle. She took a deep breath, her mind racing with the words the forest fairies had whispered to her. She repeated them silently, over and over, like a protective charm warding off her fears.

With trembling hands, she opened her satchel, her fingers brushing against the ancient leather cover of the Book of Spells. She withdrew it carefully, the weight of its ancient magic almost tangible. Unsheathing her sword, she carefully sliced through the rope binding the book. Briar braced herself, half expecting the book to leap from her hands and escape into the night. But it lay still, as if it, too, knew the significance of this moment.

Carefully, she placed the Ancient Book of Spells in the very heart of the sacred circle, ensuring it did not touch any of the shifting, glowing symbols that danced around the perimeter. Each symbol pulsed with a mysterious energy, their luminescence casting eerie shadows across Briar's face.

Next, she retrieved the other magical objects from her satchel. She placed the chunk of gold atop the book, followed by the mermaid flower, its petals shimmering like tiny stars caught in a delicate bloom. Lastly, she took out the vial of fairy godmother's blood and placed it carefully beside the other items.

Her heart pounded in her chest like a drum, each beat echoing the magnitude of the moment. Briar's hands shook as she placed them over the magical objects, her fingers barely touching the cool surface of the vial and the petals of the flower. She closed her eyes, summoning the magic from deep within her heart, feeling it rise like a warm, comforting tide.

Slowly, the warmth spread from the magical objects into her hand, a gentle heat that soon intensified, growing hotter and hotter until it felt as though her hand was aflame. The air around her began to buzz with a soft hum, the first whisperings of the ancient magic she was calling forth.

The hum grew louder, swelling into a thunderous roar that vibrated through the air, shaking the very ground beneath her. The sacred circle itself seemed to resonate with the power, the glowing symbols flickering and shifting in response. Briar bit her lip, her teeth digging into the soft flesh as she pressed her hand harder against the objects.

Suddenly, a brilliant light flared up before her eyes. Hovering above the circle was an orb of light, a perfect sphere radiating an intense, almost blinding energy. It crackled with power, each sparked a tiny bolt of lightning dancing across its surface. The orb grew, expanding rapidly, its glow enveloping the entire circle.

Just then, the orb exploded in a blinding flash of white light. The force of the blast knocked Briar off the pedestal, sending her tumbling onto the ground. Her vision swam with spots, the world around her a blur of brightness.

Though she couldn't see anything, Briar felt the cold marble beneath her cheek and the ringing in her ears. As she struggled to sit up, she heard a sound that sent a chill down her spine—a woman's laugh, soft and mocking, echoing through the air.

CHAPTER 32

After the blinding light faded, Briar scrambled to her feet, her heart pounding in her chest like a wild drum. The shrine, which had been alive with the roar of the waterfall and the hum of magic, now lay in an eerie silence. She spun around, her eyes wide with confusion and fear, searching for any sign of her friends. Her breath caught in her throat as she spotted them sprawled far from the sacred circle, their bodies motionless, looking as if they had been tossed aside like rag dolls.

"Leon! Theodore! Knight!" she cried out, her voice echoing in the unnaturally quiet space. But there was no response. They were all unconscious, their chests rising and falling shallowly in the cold air.

She turned back to the sacred circle, her eyes locking onto the orb of light that still hovered in mid-air, crackling with tendrils of electricity. Its glow was both mesmerizing and terrifying, like a beacon of untamed power.

Suddenly, a chilling laugh pierced the silence, making Briar's skin prickle with dread. She whipped around, her eyes scanning the shadows near the statue of the Fairy Queen. From behind the stone figure, a figure emerged, moving with a predatory grace that set Briar's pulse racing.

Briar squinted through the dim light, her heart sinking as the figure came into focus. Her breath hitched. She would recognize that face anywhere—it haunted her nightmares with a relentless persistence.

The Wicked Fairy.

The woman strode towards Briar with a cruel smirk playing on her lips. She wore a long gown of red and black, shimmering as if woven from the very fabric of the night sky, studded with countless stars. Her eyes, glowing embers set against the pale skin, burned with a malevolent glee. Dark, wild hair cascaded around her shoulders, framing a face that was twisted in a sneer. Her lips were as red as freshly spilled blood.

"Hello, Sleeping Beauty," the Wicked Fairy purred in a voice dripping with false sweetness. "It's been a long time, hasn't it?"

Briar's mind reeled. Was she dreaming? The shrine felt too real, the magical energy buzzing in the air around her too palpable. "You... you...?" she stammered, her voice barely a whisper. "Wicked Fairy."

The fairy's smile widened. "I'm flattered you remember me," she said with an unpleasant chuckle. "You were just a baby when we last met."

"But you were gone," Briar breathed, her voice shaking with disbelief. "Everyone said you were gone."

"Gone?" the Wicked Fairy repeated, arching an eyebrow in mock surprise. "Did they truly believe that in my absence, I ceased to exist?"

Briar's gaze flicked to her friends, lying still and silent. Panic surged through her veins. "What have you done to them?" she demanded.

The fairy glanced nonchalantly at the unconscious figures. "They're not dead," she said, examining her long, polished nails with feigned disinterest. "Just asleep. I didn't want any interruptions."

"What are you doing here?" Briar asked.

The fairy's smirk widened. "Ah, the burning question."

Briar's heart raced as a horrible thought took root in her mind. What if the Wicked Fairy was here to stop her from breaking the curse? But no, she had already broken it, hadn't she? "You're too late," she said with a burst of confidence. "I've broken the curse. You can't stop me."

The Wicked Fairy threw her head back and laughed, a cold, harsh sound that sent shivers down Briar's spine. "Oh, sweet child, you think it's over?" She gestured towards the glowing orb in the sacred circle. "I assure you, I'm right on time."

Fear coiled around Briar's heart, but she steeled herself, forcing it away. She had to be brave. She couldn't let the fairy see her fear.

"I think you need an explanation," the fairy said, as she began to circle Briar, much like a predator stalking its prey. "I won't hide anything from you, Sleeping Beauty, unlike your dear parents and friends."

Briar's stomach twisted in dread. How did she know so much about her? The knowledge made Briar feel naked and vulnerable under the fairy's piercing gaze.

"Sleeping Beauty," the fairy continued, her voice mocking, "you are not here to break any curse. You are here because I summoned you."

Briar's head spun the words a confusing whirl in her mind. What was she talking about? What game was she playing? She took a deep breath, determined not to let the fairy's words shake her.

"I know you're confused," the fairy said, leaning in closer, her face contorted into a parody of sympathy. "But once I'm done, you'll understand everything." She straightened up, her eyes gleaming with a fanatical light. "I was born to be the queen of Fairyland, born to wield power. But can you believe I lost the trial to become the fairy queen? That foolish Tara won!" The fairy's face twisted with rage, her voice rising with every word. "The elder fairies cheated! They were jealous of me, afraid I would become more powerful than they could ever imagine. Afraid I would shatter their precious rules."

The Wicked Fairy moved towards the statues of the elder fairies, her eyes burning with hatred as she looked at them. "But I didn't give up. I learned dark magic. I gained power. I fought for my rightful place. But Tara, with her legendary wand and the backing of the elders, defeated me again. They declared me a criminal for seeking what is rightfully mine. I was forced to flee, vowing to return stronger than ever. I sought greater power, a power beyond the fairy queen and the elders. And I found it." Her face lit up with a malevolent glee. "The Wand of Elements. The ultimate source of power, controlling the very forces of nature—earth, sky, water, fire, and air. But there was a catch." She turned to Briar, her expression darkening with loathing. "I can't summon it. Only the summoner can, and do you know who that is?" She spat the words, her voice dripping with venom. "You, Princess Briar Rose, are the summoner."

Briar's heart raced, thudding painfully against her ribcage. The Wicked Fairy's words echoed in her mind. She, a simple human girl, had the power to summon a wand capable of controlling all the elements of nature. It was beyond comprehension, a reality that seemed more like a cruel joke than a truth.

"Why?" the Wicked Fairy suddenly screamed, her voice filled with raw fury. "Why should a filthy human, who has no idea what the Wand of Elements can do, be granted the power? Why not me, a powerful fairy, destined for greatness?" Her eyes burned with an intense hatred, her fists clenched tightly at her sides. "It enraged me so much that I crashed your christening and cursed you to die," she continued, her voice trembling with barely contained rage. "But once my anger subsided, I realized it was fine if you were the summoner. You would summon the wand. For me." She leaned in closer, her lips curling into a twisted, malevolent smile. "I devised the perfect plan and waited a hundred years for you to awaken. And when you did, I took the first step by cursing your kingdom."

Briar's blood boiled at the casual way the fairy spoke about cursing her kingdom as if it were nothing more than a minor inconvenience.

The Wicked Fairy's eyes locked onto Briar's, a cold, unyielding gaze that seemed to pierce her very soul. "I had to make sure no one knew about my plan," she said, her voice low and menacing. "I couldn't risk the fairy queen ruining everything. So, I killed the soldiers your kingdom sent to meet my mother. I wanted you to come instead. And you did. Your presence forced my mother to open the library and give you the ritual to summon the wand."

"Don't forget I helped you," a familiar voice chimed in.

Briar spun towards the voice, her heart shattering at the sight. A fairy was walking towards the sacred circle, her face illuminated by the eerie glow of the orb. It was Evalina.

"Evalina?" Briar's voice trembled with a mixture of disbelief and betrayal.

Evalina approached with a smirk, her eyes cold and unfeeling. "Our stupid brother almost ruined everything," she said dismissively. "But I saved the day and convinced our mother to give you the ritual."

"You're with her?" Briar's voice wavered, still hoping it was some kind of twisted illusion created by the Wicked Fairy to break her spirit.

"I'm with my sister," Evalina replied coolly.

Briar's mind reeled. Why was Evalina calling the Wicked Fairy her sister? She had always spoken of her with such contempt, blaming her for their banishment from Fairyland. "You can't be with her," Briar insisted, her voice cracking. "You said you hated her."

Evalina's face twisted with disdain. "I never hated my sister," she spat. "Why would I? I hate the fairy queen and the elder fairies. They were too self-righteous, always shoving their rules of kindness and goodwill down our throats. It was suffocating."

Briar's breath caught in her throat. She needed to know the truth. "Are Viviana and Lilliana with you?" she asked.

"The fools," Evalina scoffed, rolling her eyes. "They would have ruined everything. I did it all myself. After mother gave me the key, I went to the library, found the ritual to summon the Wand of Elements, and handed it to you, claiming it was to break the curse. I gave you all the help you needed to collect the magical objects, playing my part perfectly."

Briar's mind raced, recalling how easily Evalina had offered her assistance, how she had played the role of a helpful ally to perfection. She had been nothing more than a pawn in Evalina's twisted game.

The Wicked Fairy let out a harsh, triumphant laugh. "The ritual required you, the summoner, to gather all the magical objects yourself," she said. She lunged forward, grabbing Briar's shoulder with a vice-like grip. "And you did, princess. You did it all on your own. You have the potential. You will bring me so much power in the future. You will be a great servant."

Briar's eyes flicked to the sacred circle. Within the giant orb of light, a long wand hovered, encased in a dazzling display of blue, green, and golden tendrils of energy. It pulsed with a raw, untamed power that sent shivers down her spine.

A crushing sense of defeat washed over Briar. Despite all her efforts, and all her struggles, she had failed to save her kingdom. The Wicked Fairy's plan had succeeded, and Briar had unwittingly played right into her hands.

Briar's mind raced, searching for a way out, a way to turn the tables. But deep down, she knew the truth. She was out of time, out of options. The Wicked Fairy's plan was about to come to fruition, and there was nothing she could do to stop it.

CHAPTER 33

Briar's breath came in ragged, heavy gasps. Her mind whirled with the realization that she had been nothing more than a puppet, dancing on strings controlled by the Wicked Fairy. The magical objects she had risked her life to collect—the ones that had brought her and her friends to the brink of death—had all been for nothing. They had nearly been devoured by the witch. Leon had narrowly escaped the deadly poison of the monstrous snake, and countless other perils had beset them. All for nothing. She felt like such a fool.

Her shock quickly transformed into a seething anger. She turned her furious gaze to Evalina, who had not only betrayed her but also her father, her kingdom, and everything she had fought to protect. "You!" Briar's voice trembled with fury as she lunged at Evalina, her hands closing around the fairy's neck. "Why did you do this?"

Evalina barely flinched. With a dismissive flick of her wrist, she tossed Briar aside effortlessly, as if the princess weighed no more than a feather. "To reclaim what is rightfully ours," she said coldly.

Before Briar could scramble to her feet and launch herself at the fairy again, an invisible force slammed into her, pinning her to the ground with a crushing weight. It felt as though a giant was standing on her back, pressing her deeper into the earth.

"Your place is in the dirt," the Wicked Fairy spat, her voice a venomous hiss. "You are born to serve us."

The more Briar struggled, the more the pressure increased. Her muscles screamed in protest, and she could barely breathe under the weight.

The Wicked Fairy, with a cold, satisfied smile, sauntered over to the fairy queen's statue. She gazed up at it with eyes full of contempt. "Tara failed to be the rightful ruler," she said. "She failed to teach the world to bow to our power. We are superior beings."

Evalina nodded in agreement, her expression mirroring the Wicked Fairy's hatred. "She was never the right one, Mowena. She seized your place. It should have been you all along."

A wicked smile spread across the Wicked Fairy's face. "I can fix that, sister," she said, raising her wand. A bolt of lightning shot from the wand's tip, striking the statue of the fairy queen. Cracks began to spiderweb across the stone surface, starting at the head and rapidly spreading down the body. With a final, ear-splitting crack, the statue shattered, the pieces tumbling to the ground in a cloud of dust and debris.

Briar watched helplessly from the ground, despair flooding her heart. This destruction, was all because of her. She had unwittingly enabled these monsters to wreak havoc.

"It won't be her statue standing here next time," the Wicked Fairy said, her voice filled with cruel satisfaction. She pointed her wand at the spot where the statue had stood moments before. With a rumbling sound, the earth split apart, and a new statue began to rise from the ground. It was taller and grander than the fairy queen's statue. It depicted the Wicked Fairy herself. The fairy queen's crown sat atop her head, and the Wand of Elements was clutched in her hand.

Evalina clapped her hands in glee. "Much better."

The Wicked Fairy turned her attention to the statues of the elder fairies, her eyes blazing with hatred. "They always criticized me, always sided with Tara," she snarled. "When I am queen, I will banish them from Fairyland. I will create my own rules."

"The elder fairies could be useful, sister," Evalina suggested. "They could serve as your advisors. You're going to rule the world. You'll need many servants."

"There is no place for servants in my shrine," the Wicked Fairy hissed. Her eyes flashed an ominous red, and with another lightning bolt from her wand, the statues of the elder fairies exploded into countless fragments.

Having demolished the symbols of her enemies, the Wicked Fairy turned her attention back to Briar. "Do you see what I have done to the fairy queen and the elder fairies?" she sneered.

"It was just some statues," Briar yelled. "The fairy queen has defeated you twice already. You are nothing compared to her!"

A powerful force yanked Briar from the ground, sending her hurtling into the air. She soared hundreds of feet above the earth, her body flailing helplessly, before the force released her, letting her plummet to the ground. She hit the earth with a bone-crunching impact, every nerve in her body screaming in agony.

The Wicked Fairy strode over and grabbed Briar by the hair, jerking her head up to face her. "Where is your fairy queen now?" she taunted. "She hasn't come to save you, has she?"

Briar tried to speak, but the pain was too overwhelming. She could only gasp, her vision blurring from the pain.

The Wicked Fairy laughed cruelly and let Briar's head drop back to the ground. "Don't worry, princess," she said mockingly. "I'll teach you to obey me. After all, you will be serving me for the rest of your life."

Briar mustered her strength and managed to croak out, "Never."

The words had barely left her lips when a searing bolt of lightning struck her, the pain like a million needles piercing her skin. She writhed on the ground, unable to scream, the agony too intense.

"No matter how much you resist, girl, it is your fate," the Wicked Fairy shouted, her voice echoing through the shrine. "You are my slave now. Get used to it. The sooner you accept it, the easier it will be for you."

"She will learn, sister," Evalina said. "Briar, you will follow Mowena's orders. She is the fairy queen now."

Briar shook her head weakly, refusing to give in, refusing to surrender to these monsters.

Suddenly, thick cords of lightning materialized out of thin air, coiling around Briar's neck like serpents. The cords tightened, cutting off her air supply. Her lungs burned, her vision darkening as she struggled to breathe.

"Now you will learn to never disobey me," the Wicked Fairy yelled, pulling the cord tighter. Her eyes gleamed with a sadistic satisfaction as Briar's struggles grew weaker.

The cords choked the life out of her, and the world darkened around the edges of her vision. Briar's thoughts became hazy, and she felt herself teetering on the brink of unconsciousness. Was this how it would end? Would she die here, a helpless pawn, in the grasp of the Wicked Fairy?

"Mowena!" Evalina's voice cut through the darkness. "You want her alive, remember?"

The cords loosened abruptly, and Briar collapsed to the ground, gasping for air. She sucked in huge gulps, her lungs burning as they filled with air. Her vision gradually cleared, and she found herself staring up at the two evil sisters.

"We will deal with her later," Evalina said dismissively. "Go take your wand, sister." She pointed toward the glowing Wand of Elements, floating within the sacred circle.

The Wicked Fairy's eyes lit up with a malevolent gleam. "My wand," she purred.

"Yes, your wand," Evalina echoed. "I can't wait to see it in your hand, sister."

The two sisters turned their backs on Briar and began walking toward the sacred circle.

Panic surged through Briar's heart. She knew that the moment the Wicked Fairy laid her hands on that wand, it would spell disaster for Fairyland—and then the world. And it was all because of her. She had been the one to bring together the magical objects, to summon the wand. She had handed the

Wicked Fairy the very power she needed to bring about untold destruction.

Briar's mind raced. She had to stop the Wicked fairy. But how? The Wicked Fairy was one of the most powerful fairies in existence, and Briar was just a human, powerless against such overwhelming magic. Despair clawed at her heart.

But no, she thought, shaking her head vehemently. She wasn't just a powerless human. She had summoned the wand. She had magic within her, even if she didn't fully understand it yet. She couldn't give up. She wouldn't.

But what could she do? She had no weapons, no magic spells at her disposal. Her hands clenched into fists, her nails digging into her palms. Please help me, she screamed silently, her plea echoing in the depths of her mind.

A gentle breeze stirred, ruffling her hair. And then, as if in answer to her desperate prayer, something rolled toward her and stopped just within her reach. Briar squinted at the small object, her eyes widening in recognition. It was a tiny glass vial, filled with a shimmering liquid.

Briar's heart leaped as a memory flashed before her eyes. Lavonna had given her this vial. "Use this against your enemy when the time comes," she had said. Briar had almost forgotten about it in the chaos of their quest. But now, hope surged within her like a beacon of light piercing through the darkness.

Maybe, just maybe, she still had a chance.

With trembling fingers, Briar grasped the vial and pulled herself to her feet. Her body screamed in protest, every muscle aching, but she forced herself to stand. She had to try. She couldn't afford to mess up this time.

CHAPTER 34

"Your reign has started," said Evalina, her voice brimming with excitement as both sisters reached the sacred circle. "Mowena, I can't tell you how happy I am. Years of waiting, of planning, are finally over."

The Wicked Fairy's eyes gleamed with a dark light as she advanced toward the wand.

"You will never be the fairy queen!" Briar yelled. She clutched the vial tightly, feeling its cool glass against her palm. The sisters turned to her.

The Wicked Fairy rolled her eyes. "Don't waste my time, girl," she spat.

Briar's heart pounded in her chest as she slowly made her way toward the sacred circle. "And I'm not your servant," she declared, her voice growing stronger with each step.

Without warning, Briar leaped at the fairies, her body propelled by a surge of determination. Time seemed to slow as she flung the vial's contents at the evil sisters. The liquid arced through the air, catching the light as it splashed over the Wicked Fairy and Evalina.

The moment the liquid touched them, the fairies froze. Their eyes widened in horror, their mouths open in a silent scream of agony. For a brief, surreal moment, they stood like statues, their bodies rigid and unmoving. Then, as if in slow motion, they toppled to the ground, their limbs sprawled awkwardly.

Briar sprang forward, her heart racing, and grabbed the Wand of Elements. As soon as her fingers closed around it, a torrent of power surged through her, making her gasp. It was as if she had been struck by lightning, her veins buzzing with golden energy that crackled and sizzled under her skin. She felt her muscles tighten, and her senses sharpen. She felt invincible.

She felt dangerous. She felt fearless. She felt supreme.

The wand's energy coursed through her, filling her with a sense of purpose and strength she had never known. And now Briar understood why the Wicked Fairy wanted this power so desperately.

"Sleeping Beauty," the Wicked Fairy's voice thundered. Briar turned to see the fairy pushing herself to her feet, her eyes blazing with fury. The liquid's effect had worn off. "Give me the wand!" she demanded.

Briar faced the fairy who had destroyed her kingdom and cursed her twice, her heart hardened by the memory of her father's monstrous transformation. Hate filled her veins, mingling with the wand's power. "The wand is mine," Briar said, her voice steady and unwavering. For the first time, she stood before the Wicket Fairy without trembling, without fear.

A flicker of fear flashed in the Wicked Fairy's eyes, but it was quickly replaced by anger. "It's not yours!" she yelled. "It belongs to me! I've waited years, centuries, to get it."

"And you will never get it," Briar said confidently, her grip on the wand tightening.

Evalina staggered to her feet. She advanced a step toward Briar, but when she saw the Wand of Elements in Briar's hand, she hesitated.

The Wicked Fairy's face turned a deep shade of red, her nostrils flaring with anger. Briar wouldn't have been surprised if flames had burst from her nose. "I'm asking you one last time," she bellowed, her voice echoing through the shrine. "GIVE ME THE WAND!"

"Never," Briar replied, her eyes locking with the fairy's blazing gaze. "The sooner you accept it, the easier it will be for you."

The Wicked Fairy's face twisted with rage, and she screamed, "Then I have no choice but to kill you!" She raised her wand and sent a lightning bolt streaking toward Briar, its electric tendrils snapping through the air.

But somehow, Briar knew what to do. It was as if the wand guided her. She lifted the Wand of Elements, and it sent out a jet of golden light that met the Wicked Fairy's lightning bolt in mid-air. The two forces collided with a deafening boom like thunder clapping in the sky. The shockwave rippled through the shrine, sending dust and debris flying.

The Wicked Fairy staggered back, her face a mask of disbelief.

"Let's make a deal," the Wicked Fairy said. "I won't make you my servant if you give me the wand."

Briar chuckled, a dry, mirthless sound. "Oh, yes, I trust you with all my heart," she said sarcastically.

"I'll break the curse," the Wicked Fairy offered, her tone suddenly pleading. "Your kingdom won't be filled with monsters. We still have time."

"I know how to break the curse," Briar said. In her heart, she knew the truth. "When you die, the curse will be broken."

The Wicked Fairy's eyes widened with shock and fear. She backed away, her wings unfurling in a desperate attempt to escape. "No!" she screamed, her voice filled with panic. She took to the sky, her wings beating frantically.

Briar raised the wand and sent a large fireball hurtling toward the fairy. It struck her left wing, engulfing it in flames. She shrieked in agony as she tumbled from the sky, crashing to the ground in a heap.

"Evalina!" the Wicked Fairy screamed. "Don't just stand there. Help me!"

Evalina raised her wand. But Briar was ready. She lifted the wand and summoned a giant tornado from the earth. The swirling vortex of wind and debris engulfed Evalina, trapping her within its whirling fury. Evalina's screams were lost in the roar of the tornado as it lifted her off her feet, spinning her helplessly.

The Wicked Fairy stood alone in the ruins of the shrine. She looked around, her eyes wide with desperation. She was helpless, just as Briar had once felt, just as her father felt, just as every single human in her kingdom had felt under the fairy's cruel reign.

The Wicked Fairy staggered to her feet, her movements slow and labored. Her once proud wings hung limply at her sides, their delicate membranes tattered and torn. "You think this is over?" she snarled, her voice a low, menacing growl. "You've only delayed the inevitable."

Briar stepped forward, her eyes blazing with determination. "This is over, Mowena," she said. "Now."

Briar's mind was flooded with images of her kingdom's suffering. She saw the thorn monsters. She saw her father, his eyes wild with the curse, throwing the table and roaring like a beast. She saw her mother, her face streaked with tears, crying in despair. She saw the pain and anguish that the Wicked Fairy had inflicted on her loved ones and countless innocent lives.

A wave of hatred surged through Briar's heart, spreading through her veins like wildfire. The pain and suffering of her people fueled her anger, turning it into a fierce, burning rage. All she could feel was hate, a pure and all-consuming hatred that blotted out any remnants of compassion or mercy.

The Wand of Elements seemed to resonate with her emotions, vibrating with a powerful energy. It lifted itself in her hand, glowing with a fierce, multicolored light. Lightning bolts of blue, green, and gold shot out from the wand, their energy crackling through the air with a deafening roar. The bolts struck the Wicked Fairy in the heart, their impact sending ripples of power through her frail body.

The Wicked Fairy screamed a high-pitched, agonized wail that echoed through the shrine. She clutched her heart, her fingers clawing at her chest as if trying to tear the pain away. Her body convulsed, her wings fluttering weakly in a desperate attempt to escape the torment. Then, with a final, shuddering breath, she crumpled to the ground, her body falling limp and lifeless.

Silence fell over the shrine, a heavy, oppressive silence that pressed down on Briar like a weight. She stood there for a few seconds, her breath coming in ragged gasps, her heart pounding in her chest. The air around her was still as if the world itself was holding its breath, waiting for what would happen next.

"She's gone," Briar whispered. The words hung in the air, a final, irrevocable truth that seemed to echo in the space around her.

A sudden weakness washed over her, the adrenaline that had fueled her rage draining away, leaving her feeling hollow and exhausted. Her legs gave out, and she fell to her knees, the wand slipping from her grasp and clattering to the ground.

"Briar!" a voice called out, urgent and filled with concern. Through her blurred vision, Briar saw the fairy godmother rushing toward her. Behind her, a group of fairies followed.

Briar heard their muffled voices, their words a jumbled, indistinct murmur that she could barely make out. She felt their hands on her shoulders, their touch gentle and comforting, but it seemed distant as if she were drifting away from them, sinking into a dark, endless void.

"Stay with us, Briar," the fairy godmother's voice cut through the haze. "You're safe now. We're here. You're safe."

But the darkness was relentless, pulling her under, wrapping her in its cold, inescapable embrace. Her vision dimmed, the world around her fading into shadow until all that remained was a black, impenetrable silence. And then, finally, even that was gone.

EPILOGUE

Briar opened her eyes to find herself in a room bathed in the warm glow of morning light. The familiar scent of roses filled the air, evoking memories of safety and happiness. She blinked, disoriented, and found herself surrounded by someone she thought she would never see again.

Her mother sat beside the bed. The queen looked frail and pale, her once-regal demeanour reduced to a shadow of weariness. Her hair was dishevelled, and her eyes were red and puffy from crying. She stared at the wall, her gaze vacant and unblinking.

"Mother," Briar said softly, her voice a mere whisper as she scrambled to sit up. Her limbs felt heavy as if they hadn't moved in days.

The queen jerked at the sound of Briar's voice, her eyes widening in shock. "Briar!" she squealed. In an instant, she lunged forward, enveloping Briar in a bone-crushing hug, her sobs wracking her body. "You're awake. You're awake," she repeated.

"Yes," Briar replied, her voice muffled against her mother's shoulder. She inhaled deeply, savouring the familiar scent of roses that clung to her mother's clothes. It felt so good to be in her mother's warm embrace, to feel her strength and love wrapping around her like a comforting blanket. It was a reminder of home, of everything good and happy that she had fought to protect.

Minutes passed before the queen finally pulled away, her hands trembling as she cupped Briar's cheeks. Her eyes, though still glistening with tears, were filled with fierce love and relief. "I will never forgive you for what you did," she said. "How dare you run away from home?" she added in a tone that was both scolding and affectionate. "You're never allowed to leave the castle again. This time, I will lock you in your chamber if I have to."

Briar smiled. "You don't need to lock me in my chamber," she said softly. "Because there is no curse and no wicked fairy anymore. It's over."

Tears streamed down the queen's pale cheeks, her body shaking with silent sobs. "She's gone!" she whispered, as if she hardly dared to believe it. Briar could hardly believe it herself.

"Briar," said another familiar voice, rich with emotion.

Briar turned to see her father rushing into the chamber, his steps unsteady but filled with urgency. The curse had been lifted, and he was once again a man, no longer the hideous monster he had been transformed into. Though he looked gaunt and exhausted, the light in his eyes shone with a brilliance that could illuminate the darkest of rooms.

Holding the Wand of Elements had given Briar the answer to breaking the curse. However, a tiny part of her had been unsure, afraid that perhaps it hadn't worked. But seeing her father standing there, whole and human, banished those fears entirely.

"Father!" Briar cried. She threw off the covers and leaped out of bed, running into her father's open arms.

The king enveloped her in a tight embrace, holding her as if afraid she would disappear. "Thank heavens you are all right," he murmured.

"I missed you," Briar sobbed, burying her face in his chest.

"I missed you more," he said, pulling back to look at her face, his eyes shining with tears. "But it's all right now. Everything is alright. We are here, together."

Briar nodded. As she gazed at her father's face, the love and pride in his eyes made her forget the trials and horrors she had faced. It was all worth it.

"Father, are you all right?" she asked.

The king smiled a weary but genuine smile that lit up his tired features. "Yes," he said. "I'm all right. I feel like myself again."

"Were you hurt?" Briar asked. "The transformation and the magic."

"How can I explain how I felt?" The king's face darkened. "It was agony. Torture. My mind was blurry, and I couldn't think clearly. There was this immense desire for violence. I wanted to kill. I wanted blood." He shook his head as if trying to dispel the dark memories. "That night, like every other night, we were locked in the fortress. The monsters were rattling the cage bars and howling. Then, suddenly, it all stopped. The pain, and the suffering, all vanished in a blink of an eye. Our bodies were transformed back into human form. It was as if I was waking up from a nightmare." The pain faded from his face, replaced by a small, hopeful smile. "After we understood that the curse was broken, we cried with joy and embraced each other. The cursed fortress was filled with happiness."

Briar's heart swelled with joy at the thought of her people being reunited with their loved ones. It was like a rebirth, a second chance for them all.

"I didn't know my little girl was so brave," the king said, looking at Briar with eyes full of pride. "You saved us, Briar. You did something that even the fairies couldn't do. I can't tell you how proud I am of you."

"What?" Briar's mother interjected, her voice filled with exasperation. "Now don't encourage her like that. No one is proud that she put herself in danger."

"Yes," the king agreed, making a mock angry face. "Yes, I'm proud and grateful, but you're grounded as well, young lady."

"Briar, you're awake!" a familiar voice chimed in.

Briar turned to see Leon, Theodore and Henry entering the chamber. Leon's eyes sparkled as he walked in, a wide grin on his face. "I thought I might have to kiss you again to wake you up."

Everyone laughed at Leon's words, the tension in the room melting away. Briar felt her cheeks flush a deep red, embarrassed by Leon's boldness. The prince, as always, didn't seem to have a filter between his thoughts and his words.

Briar's heart leaped with joy when she saw her friends standing there, alive and unharmed. Overcome with relief, she dashed across the room and threw her arms around them, pulling them into a tight embrace. "Thank the stars. You're all right!" she exclaimed. "I was so terrified when I saw you all lying there, motionless. I thought the Wicked Fairy..."

"Killed us," Leon gently finished her sentence. "I don't remember much after you walked towards the sacred circle. I'm sorry we weren't there when you needed us the most."

Before Briar could respond, the queen's voice, stern yet gentle, cut through the air. "We shall speak no more of the Wicked Fairy," she declared with a regal authority that brooked no argument. "This is an order from your queen."

Briar nodded solemnly. "Yes, Your Majesty," she replied.

Briar nodded solemnly. "Yes, Your Majesty," she replied, her voice steady but her eyes reflecting the gravity of the situation.

Henry pulled Briar into a tight hug. "You really scared me, Briar," he said, his voice thick with relief. "You should have at least told me before you left. You have no idea how helpless I felt."

"Sorry," Briar said softly, her heart aching for her brother. She knew the difficult position he had been in, unable to leave the kingdom and their mother to search for her. "But if I had told you, you would have never allowed me to go." She grasped her brother's hand, squeezing it reassuringly. "But now everything is all right."

Henry pulled back slightly. "But I'm still angry, and you have to make it up to me for the rest of your life," he said, a teasing smile breaking through his stern expression.

The king placed a firm yet gentle hand on Henry's shoulder. "I'm so proud of my children," he said, his voice filled with pride and affection. "Both of you have handled the situation so well in my absence."

Briar's heart felt light, surrounded by the warmth and love of her family and friends. For the first time in a long while, she felt truly safe and at peace. She looked around the room, her eyes lingering on each familiar face, and smiled. It was all worth it, she thought. Every hardship, every danger, had led to this moment of joy and reunion.

"By the way, Theodore, where is Knight? Is he angry with me?" Briar asked.

Theodore's lips curved into a reassuring smile. "No, Princess," he said softly. "Knight went to visit his family. He deserves a break after everything that's happened. But don't worry, he'll be back today to celebrate your birthday."

"My birthday?" Briar repeated, her eyes widening in surprise.

Leon chuckled. "Well, technically, your birthday was two days ago," he explained.

"Two days?" Briar echoed, blinking in astonishment. "So, I've been asleep for two whole days?"

The queen nodded. "Yes, and we were very worried," she said. "The fairies told us that using the Wand of Elements had drained your energy. We tried every medicine we knew, but nothing worked. Even the fairy magic failed to wake you."

"We were starting to fear the worst, but thankfully, you woke up," Henry added.

At that moment, the fairy godmother and Lavonna entered the chamber, their faces lighting up with relief as they saw Briar. Lavonna rushed to Briar's side and enveloped her in a tight, almost desperate hug. "I'm so sorry, Briar. I almost killed you. I didn't know the Wicked Fairy was behind all this. I just told you what I saw in my vision."

Briar returned the hug. "And your prediction came true," she smiled. "I went on the quest and broke the curse."

"That's what I'm trying to tell her," the fairy godmother interjected. "It's not your fault, Lavonna. It was fate."

Lavonna nodded, wiping away her tears with the back of her hand.

The fairy godmother turned to Briar. "How are you feeling now, my dear?"

"I'm feeling much better," she replied. "But, godmother, how did you find out about the Wicked Fairy and reach the shrine?"

The fairy godmother sighed, her eyes reflecting a deep sadness. "The elder fairies and I always knew you were a summoner, but we kept it a secret," she began. "When you left, I suddenly remembered the ritual. It was then that I realized the mistake I had made by not stopping you. I hurried to the fairy queen, and together, we rushed to the shrine. We were terrified of what we might find." She paused, then gave Briar a gentle smile. "But you, my brave child, you stopped a great disaster from happening."

Briar's face darkened as she thought of Evalina. "Evalina betrayed us," she said. Every time she thought of the blue-haired fairy, a wave of unpleasant emotions washed over her.

Leon shook his head. "They seemed so friendly," he said. "Except for the evil brother."

The fairy godmother placed a comforting hand on his shoulder. "Mowena must have manipulated Evalina into following her," she explained softly. "It's a great shame. Evalina was a wonderful fairy before all this."

Briar wanted to feel pity for Evalina, but the betrayal was too fresh, too painful. "But, godmother, remember I told you about the other forest fairies? They are good. Did you speak with the fairy queen about bringing them back to Fairyland?"

The fairy godmother nodded. "Yes, I did. The fairy queen has promised to look into it. I hope that soon, everyone will see that Viatrix and her family are innocent."

"And the Wand of Elements, is it safe?" she asked.

"The fairy queen and the elder fairies are building a secure place to keep it," the fairy godmother assured her. "There are many more dangers out there, like Mowena."

"Is she truly gone?" Briar asked. "Will she ever come back?" Even though she knew the Wicked Fairy was gone, the terror she had endured was hard to shake off.

The fairy godmother cupped Briar's face in her hands, her eyes filled with warmth and reassurance. "Yes, my dear," she said gently. "Mowena is gone, and so is her curse."

The queen, her face lined with concern, spoke up. "But Briar being a summoner..." she hesitated. "Will it create more problems for her in the future? Problems like the Wicked Fairy?"

Briar's heart skipped a beat. She hadn't considered the long-term implications of being a summoner. The thought of the immense responsibility that came with her power weighed heavily on her.

The fairy godmother sighed. "There are always advantages and disadvantages to everything," she said thoughtfully. "Yes, we will have to be cautious. But this time, Briar will not be alone. The fairy queen and other fairies will train her, help her learn to protect herself and her powers." She turned to Briar, her face breaking into a warm smile. "For now, you should worry about nothing and enjoy your birthday."

With a flourish of her wand, the fairy godmother conjured an oval-shaped amulet with a stunning scarlet stone that gleamed like a drop of blood. "The fairy queen sent this for you," she said. "She also asked me to convey her apologies for not being able to attend your birthday celebration." She gently placed the amulet around Briar's neck. "It's a protection charm, my dear."

Briar looked down at the amulet, feeling the comforting warmth against her chest. It was as if a protective halo enveloped her, easing her fears. The king and queen, their faces showing a measure of relief, exchanged hopeful glances.

"Oh, and there's one more thing," the fairy godmother said with a twinkle in her eye. She waved her wand once more, and a magnificent gown materialized out of thin air. The dress was a soft, shimmering pink, dusted with gold, and adorned with tiny crystals that sparkled like stars.

Briar gasped in awe, her eyes widening as she took in the breath-taking sight. The fairy godmother's smile widened with satisfaction. "A little gift for you," she said, her eyes dancing with delight. "And don't worry, it won't disappear even after midnight," she added with a playful wink.

The queen's eyes sparkled as she gaped at the gown. "It's absolutely gorgeous," she breathed.

"Do you like it, Briar?" the fairy godmother asked.

"I love it!" Briar exclaimed. She felt a surge of joy, so intense she could have danced around the room.

The fairy godmother leaned in and kissed her forehead tenderly. "I wish you a very happy birthday, my dear Sleeping Beauty."

The entire kingdom had gathered in the castle's courtyard, a sea of faces brimming with joy. As Briar, flanked by her mother and father, stepped into the courtyard, the crowd erupted in a chorus of cheers, chanting her name. The air was filled with the thunderous sound of clapping and the joyful shouts of her people.

Children, their faces alight with joy, rushed forward to greet her, each bearing gifts—flowers of every hue, hand-drawn cards, and handmade toys crafted with love. Each person in the kingdom had brought something, a token of their affection and gratitude for their beloved princess.

Briar's heart swelled with happiness as she looked around, seeing the love and respect shining in the eyes of her people. It was a sight she had longed for, the acceptance and adoration she had always dreamed of. And now that she had it, she vowed to protect it fiercely. She would do everything in her power to keep her kingdom happy, even if it meant breaking a thousand curses.

The fairies had prepared a magnificent cake, towering nearly twice Briar's height, adorned with intricate designs and her favourite flavours. As she blew out the candles, they soared into the sky, bursting into a dazzling display of fireworks that painted the night in vibrant colours. Laughter and music filled the air as everyone danced and feasted on the sumptuous food, the courtyard alive with the sounds of celebration.

After cutting the cake, Briar slipped away to a quieter corner of the garden with Leon and Theodore. She had something important to share with her friends, something she had been waiting to give them.

Leon was the first to approach her, his cape flowing dramatically behind him as he walked, a playful grin on his face. He had already changed into his third outfit of the evening, each more elaborate than the last. It seemed he was determined to showcase his entire wardrobe today. "Briar!" he called, his eyes twinkling with curiosity. "What is it you wanted to talk about?"

Briar smiled mysteriously and held up a large red pouch. "I have something for you," she said.

"What's this?" he asked. His eyes widened as he watched Briar pull a golden crown from the pouch, a perfect replica of the one he had lost. "It's... it's for me?"

Briar nodded, her smile widening. "Yes, it's yours. I asked the fairy godmother to make it for you."

Tears welled up in Leon's eyes as he gazed at the crown. "This is amazing," he said, his voice cracking as he wiped away the tears.

Briar gently placed the crown on his head, adjusting it so it sat perfectly.

Leon touched the crown. "Thank you," he said, grinning widely.

Briar turned to Theodore. "And I can't thank you enough for everything you've done to help me."

Theodore shook his head, a warm smile spreading across his face. "No need to thank me, Briar," he replied. "Seeing the people happy and healthy is all the reward I need. It's like curing the most dangerous disease."

Briar laughed and pulled out a gold, charmed bracelet from her pouch. "This is for you," she said, tying it around his wrist. "It's a token of our friendship. The charms will protect you from ghosts and evil energies."

"And possibly ogress," Leon added with a chuckle.

Theodore laughed, looking at the bracelet with appreciation. "Thank you, Briar," he said. "This means a lot to me."

Just then, Knight came galloping towards them, his white coat smeared with chocolate handprints. He looked exasperated, his mane ruffled and out of place. "Help me, Princess!" he called. "The children... they've covered me with chocolate and won't leave me alone! They're treating me like a toy!"

Briar couldn't help but laugh at the sight of him. "Oh, Knight, they're just children," she teased, patting his neck affectionately.

"They're a headache," Knight grumbled, glancing back at a group of children who were now licking their chocolate and giggling.

Theodore was already by his side, gently wiping the chocolate off with a silk cloth. "Don't worry, I'll give you a nice bath," he said soothingly.

Briar smiled and leaned closer to Knight. "I've asked father to build a special garden just for you," she said, her eyes twinkling with excitement. "It'll have a big pond and an apple orchard, and the fairy godmother gave me a magical apple seed to plant there."

Knight's eyes lit up with delight. "An entire garden of apples just for me!"

Briar nodded. "Yes, it's all yours."

Knight nuzzled her affectionately. "Thank you, Princess. No one has ever done something so kind for me."

Before Briar could respond, a group of children spotted Knight and came running towards them, their faces lit up with excitement. "Knight!" they called. "It's our turn to ride him!"

Knight, eyes wide with alarm, took off into the air before they could reach him. "I'm not a toy!" he shouted, disappearing into the sky.

A little boy with curly blond hair, his chocolate melting down his hands, tugged on Briar's dress. "Princess, it's my turn to ride Knight," he said.

Briar smiled down at him and nodded. "Don't worry, you'll get your turn."

The other children, not wanting to be left out, began to clamour around her.

Leon stepped in, grinning at the kids. "Hey, everyone, I have a surprise for you!" he said, his eyes sparkling with mischief. "Come with me. I promise it'll be amazing!"

With that, he led them towards a small house at the edge of the garden. As they rounded the corner, Briar gasped in surprise. The children squealed with joy.

Standing before them was a candy house. It was a dazzling spectacle, made entirely of sweets—walls of gingerbread, windows of sugar glass, and a roof tiled with chocolate. Inside, there were cakes, candies, cupcakes, and sweets of every variety, more than any child could ever dream of.

Briar turned to Leon. "When did you make this?" she asked.

Leon grinned proudly. "I've always wanted to make one since I saw the witch's house," he explained. "I told the fairy godmother, and she helped me."

The fairy godmother appeared at the door of the candy house, a tray of cakes in her hands. "And the best part is," she said, handing each child a piece of cake, "the sweets and candies are unlimited! No matter how much you eat, there will always be more!"

The children's eyes lit up with joy as they took the cakes. The fairy godmother went back inside to fetch more treats, leaving the children to marvel at the wonder before them.

Theodore chuckled as he watched the scene. "Too many sweets are bad for you, but I'd love to eat this entire house," he said.

Briar turned to Leon. "So, is this the surprise you were talking about?" she asked.

Leon shook his head, a mischievous grin spreading across his face. "No, this is just the beginning," he said, pointing to the sky.

Briar looked up and saw a white horse descending from the clouds. For a moment, she thought it was Knight, but as the horse landed, she realized it was someone new. This horse had a long, flowing mane and sparkling blue eyes that shone like jewels. He was too beautiful to be real, a creature straight out of a dream.

Leon beamed with pride. "Meet Marcus," he said, his voice filled with excitement.

The horse bowed gracefully, flashing a perfect smile. "It's an honour to meet you all," he said in a deep, melodic voice. "I am here to assist Prince Leon in his heroic duties."

The children went wild, clapping and cheering at the sight of Marcus. Theodore looked at the horse in awe. "He's so well-mannered," he said.

Leon puffed out his chest, clearly proud of his new companion. "Marcus, would you like to take Briar for a ride and show her how the kingdom is celebrating her birthday?" he asked.

Marcus bowed again. "It would be my pleasure, Princess," he said. He knelt, allowing Briar and Leon to climb onto his back.

As they soared into the sky, the fireworks exploded around them in a dazzling display of light and colour. Marcus flew with grace and elegance that made the experience even more magical, occasionally dipping close to the fireworks for a thrilling ride.

Leon turned to Briar, a playful smile on his face. "So, is this your happily ever after?" he asked.

Briar looked down at her kingdom, seeing the joy on the faces of her people. Everyone was smiling, dancing, and celebrating. She felt a warmth spread through her, a sense of fulfilment and contentment that she had never known before.

"Yes," Briar said, her voice soft and full of wonder. "This is my happily ever after."